MURDER WITH MAJESTY

Auguste Didier is enjoying the tranquillity of Farthing Court in Kent, where he is employed as chef for the wedding of Arthur, Lord Montfoy and his bride, which will be graced by the (unpublicised) attendance of King Edward VII. Meanwhile the villagers are busy preparing for their elaborate May Day celebrations.

However, all is not as it seems. Arthur is not the true lord of the manor, having sold his birthright, and the villagers have their own reasons for dressing up as characters from folklore.

Then the true lord is revealed as Pyotre Gregorin, employee of the Tsar, and sworn enemy of Didier...

MURDER WITH MAJESTY

by

Amy Myers

Magna Large Print Books
Long Preston, North Yorkshire,
BD23 4ND, England.

British Library Cataloguing in Publication Data.

Myers, Amy
    Murder with majesty.

    A catalogue record of this book is
    available from the British Library

    ISBN   0-7505-1571-6

First published in Great Britain by
Severn House Publishers Ltd., 1999

Copyright © 1999 by Amy Myers

Cover illustration by arrangement with
Severn House Publishers Ltd.

The moral right of the author has been asserted

Published in Large Print 2000 by arrangement with
Severn House Publishers Ltd.

Any situations in this publication are fictitious and
any resemblance to living persons is purely coincidental.

Magna Large Print is an imprint of Library Magna Books Ltd.

Printed and bound in Great Britain by
T.J. (International) Ltd., Cornwall, PL28 8RW

Author's Note

The press reported that on Saturday, 29th April 1905, His Majesty King Edward VII began a few days' private visit to Paris, and later, unusually, recorded his displeasure at Press curiosity about his movements during this visit. This novel reveals the reason why. However, a few minor adjustments have had to be made to His Majesty's official time-table later in the month.

Apart from tendering apologies to his late Majesty, I would also like to record my debt to Adrian Turner, who suggested one of the main storylines of this novel, and to my agent Dorothy Lumley of the Dorian Literary Agency for her usual helpful and knowledgeable hand on the tiller.

A.M.

Prologue

'Cursed are the Montfoys; the dragon will have his day.'

'Be shut of such talk, Aggie, there's work to do.'

Bert Wickman, mastering his own misgivings, took vigorous command of the Committee for the Preservation of the White Dragon Inn. It was in his interests to do so, for he was the landlord, even though he heavily endorsed Aggie's opinion of the Montfoys who had owned most of Frimhurst since the time of the Conqueror; this included his pub, whose emblem stemmed from the Montfoy armorial bearings. Three years earlier the present Lord Montfoy, all but bankrupt, had retreated to the former Dower House and sold Farthing Court together with the entire estate. Mr Thomas Entwhistle, away much of the time, had proved a surprisingly beneficent lord of the manor, but at times the long dark shadow of the Montfoys came home to roost with a vengeance. This was one of them.

Aggie Potter, cast in a role she had no difficulty in playing, that of ancient crone

7

and wise woman, glared morosely into her mild and bitter.

'Beware the fires of Beltane,' she muttered. At her side the small, cosy fire in the taproom spluttered in friendly sympathy at Aggie's cracked black boots and wool stockings which were revealed under the serge skirt she had hitched up 'to feel the benefit'.

Frimhurst, as it had for the last fourteen hundred years at least, was preparing to greet the rebirth of the land. Once it called it Beltane and lit bonfires, now it was May Day and was usually paid scant attention, save for a fifteen-foot pole in the grounds of the village school, round which garlanded tots endeavoured to strangle themselves with paper flowers and string.

In this year of 1905, however, a crisis had dramatically altered the situation. The Kentish writer Charles Igglesden on his saunters would – had he chanced upon Frimhurst – have observed that the village, which had evolved over the centuries by the river Crane in the Weald of Kent, earned itself a living through growing hops and fruit. Even though it retained its semi-feudal structure of subservience to the Farthing estate, it appeared to have been a comfortable living in the last few years since the coming of Mr Entwhistle and the just deserts (as the village worthies termed it) of the Montfoys. Its mellow red-brick houses with their peg-tiled roofs jostled side by side with oak-beamed mediaeval cottages; the grey-stone church, on the opposite side of the green to the White Dragon, smiled peacefully down on its flock. But now all this was under threat. The heart of the village, if not its soul, was at stake: the pub.

The committee of seven huddled round the fire on an early March evening: Bert and Bessie Wickman, Alf Spade (the aptly named builder), his wife Adelaide, Harry Thatcher, the young postman (to represent the younger generation), and the two ancients, Aggie Potter and Jacob Meadows (to represent the elders of the village).

'Dancing with bells,' snarled Bert, marching to the bar to dispatch his profit recklessly for once.

'Maypoles,' echoed his wife in disgust, conscious that her own days of playing May Queen were long past.

'We'll have to do it.' Bert looked round his team. 'But we must organise it proper. Give them a show, shall we?' He grinned. 'Americans,' he added disgustedly, spitting on the taproom floor. 'Let's show 'em what old England can do, eh? Squire Entwhistle means what he said all right. He'll close us down if we don't knuckle under, and what's the village going to do without the White Dragon?'

Much beer flowed in search of avoidance of this catastrophe and several hours later, tentative plans had been laid and agreed.

Only Mrs Aggie Potter entered a caveat, muttering into her medicinal pint, 'The fairy folk will not be mocked.'

But most of her fellow conspirators, to whom fairies were merely a matter of fluttering innocuous creatures in picture books and who had long forgotten their grandmothers' warnings of darker forces, unfortunately paid no attention.

One

It was only a wedding!

Auguste Didier, master chef (when he was permitted to cook), had feared the worst when His Majesty King Edward VII had demanded his presence that morning churning over in his mind what trespasses he could possibly have committed, as if he were back in the small school in Mont Chevalier in his native Cannes. Now he almost skipped away from Buckingham Palace and along Bird Cage Walk with relief. It had been *good* news.

'Ah, Did – Auguste, good morning.' His Majesty had remembered in time that Auguste was a member of the family, albeit second class. 'How do you fancy May Day in Kent?'

Auguste rose from his deep bow apprehensively. Was His Majesty suggesting a cousinly jaunt in his Daimler? His hopes grew. Cooking for Bertie was not the easiest task in the world. Auguste's marriage to Tatiana had brought problems, not least of which was that he, formerly apprenticed to Escoffier himself, was forbidden to cook, save privately – or for His Majesty.

11

'Cooking for a wedding,' the king amplified.

'Not for Your Majesty?' Hopes shot up even higher.

'Of course for me.' A certain testiness came into the royal voice. 'And a couple of thousand other people, too, if I know Horace Pennyfather.'

'Pennyfather?' Auguste knew that name. He had met the American soft drinks millionaire some years ago and liked him. He was an amiable man for all his steely determination to push Pennyfather non-alcoholic products down every throat in the world.

'Decent sort of fellow. His daughter's getting married to a friend of mine, Lord Montfoy.'

Auguste racked his brains. That name rang a bell too.

'The wedding's to be held on May Day.'

'Where will it be, Your Majesty?'

The King stared at him in amazement, then realised the fellow was a foreigner and his usual courtesy returned. 'Farthing Court in Kent. There have been Montfoys at Farthings since the Conquest. Ah,' he broke off, 'now there is one difficulty, two in fact.'

He should have guessed it. Auguste's heart sank. There always were difficulties with Bertie.

'They're both strictly secret.' His Majesty eyed his remote cousin by marriage warningly, as though half-French chefs were notorious for rushing round London society with their monarch's most private revelations. 'Farthing Court doesn't belong to Arthur Montfoy any longer. He's moved into the Dower House.'

'That is sad indeed. Farthing Court is one of your favourite weekend house-party venues, is it not?' Now the name of Montfoy came into focus in Auguste's mind.

The king frowned as though it were bad form to mention this. 'Couldn't afford to keep it. He's sold it to a splendid fellow. Thomas Entwhistle.' This name meant nothing to Auguste. 'He lives abroad most of the time. He's been very helpful, and allowed Arthur to move back in for the wedding.'

'I understand, Sir.' Auguste relaxed. Nothing too ominous.

'Now here's the important part. Entwhistle is to be best man, but so far as the bride, her family and guests know Lord Montfoy still owns Farthing Court – *and* lives in it. Got that?'

'I – yes.' That seemed the simplest answer, though several tantalising questions sprang to mind. However, as Tatiana had so often reminded him, 'Don't put Bertie in a bother.'

'Good. Now there's something else. I shall be there, but I'm not.'

'Je m'excuse?'

His Majesty looked irritated. 'I'm shortly leaving on a state visit to the Mediterranean. Algiers and so forth. I'll be away some weeks, but I'll arrive at Farthing Court the day before the wedding. The press are going to be under the impression I'm on a private visit to Paris, but I won't be there until it becomes official on the Wednesday, two days after the wedding. Clear?'

If only the question 'Why?' was one that could be asked of kings. For Bertie to give up the chance of a visit to the Folies Bergère and a very private dinner at Voisin afterwards, meant this wedding promised to be a most spectacular event.

Auguste bowed and retreated, his curiosity unsatisfied. However, as difficulties went with Bertie, these were very light. Or so he fondly imagined.

What could be more fortuitous? Tatiana was to be away in Paris in early May to see her Russian relations, and to while away the time (and to avoid his publisher's pressing demands for the manuscript of *Dining with Didier*, to which he was putting the last perfecting details) he had the bliss of cooking for a wedding. True, it would be a

14

little awkward maintaining the pretence that Farthing Court still belonged to Lord Montfoy for his conscience pricked him at the need for deceiving Horace Pennyfather.

However, Auguste reminded himself, he was merely the cook. Then a terrible thought struck him. Would the guests be expected to drink Pilgrim's Cherry Shrub, Pennyfather's famous non-alcoholic potion? He would not dignify such a beverage with the word *drink*. No. He recalled Pennyfather as a *sensible* gentleman.

He was conducted up to a suite in the Ritz Hotel where Horace Pennyfather, looking very little changed from their first meeting, save for greying hair, rose to greet him. A man of medium, sturdy build, his face still bore that pleasant but somewhat lost look that, together with the carefully waxed moustache, hid his shrewdness so well. Auguste was already planning in his mind the sumptuous banquet he would produce. Before his eyes floated images of turbot with truffles in champagne sauce, *caneton aux olives, pêches aiglon,* and others of the infinite wonders of the world of cuisine.

Horace Pennyfather greeted him warmly, though even as he talked of their earlier meeting it occurred to Auguste he was not quite the man he was. He appeared nervous, not the self-composed gentleman Auguste recalled.

'Before my daughter arrives,' he almost stuttered, 'perhaps I should show you what she has in mind for the menu.'

What *she* has in mind ... that sounded distinctly ominous.

Horace produced from the writing desk a long sheet of paper almost entirely covered in firm black copperplate writing, and handed it to Auguste in silence. And no wonder. Auguste had dim memories of having seen such words in books, but they bore *no* relation to a self-respecting chef's life.

'Succotash?' he asked grimly.

'Old settler dish,' Horace mumbled. 'Corn and lima beans. Very tasty.'

'Hominy grits?' Auguste had a vision of His Majesty supping on a dish of such a name.

'Southern food.'

'Shoofly Pie?'

'Pennsylvanian Dutch.'

'Jambalaya?'

'New Orleans.'

Auguste put the list down. 'Mr Pennyfather, I regret there is only one dish on this menu I feel qualified to undertake and that is Thomas Jefferson's vanilla ice cream. Perhaps a different chef—'

'No, no. *You*,' Horace pleaded unhappily. 'Gertrude is kind of patriotic, I guess. Why, she even takes chicken hash at breakfast,

16

and that was good enough for President Andrew Jackson.'

Faced not with a dead American president, but a very present British king and emperor, Auguste battled with his dilemma: to disobey His Majesty was treason, but after cooking such a meal any chef with honour should commit suicide. He decided he would rather lose his head than his integrity.

'*Non,*' he replied, as politely as he could make the word sound. *'Je regrette que cela n'est pas possible.'*

'There are no such words as *pas possible,* Mr Didier.'

Auguste leapt to his feet as the cool feminine voice from behind startled him. The lady who had just sailed through the door could only be Gertrude Pennyfather, and the reason for her father's nervousness promptly became apparent. This was a lady of even more decided views than Horace's own. She was a tall young woman, as tall as he himself, Auguste judged, at 5 feet 9 inches; her face immediately demanded attention, handsome rather than pretty, with large intense grey eyes, and something that may have been a gleam of humour behind them. The oval face, however, obviously preferred to remain formidably straight.

'You are correct, madame.' Auguste bowed on being introduced. 'In general impossibility might not exist, but in the particular, it does. Even when related to such a charming bride as yourself.'

'Why?' She seemed interested rather than angry.

Auguste, hesitating, decided on honesty. 'There are two reasons, madame. The first is my integrity as a chef; the second is His Majesty King Edward VII, your honoured guest, of whose palate I have a vast experience.'

'Your integrity, Mr Didier, does not concern me. I admit I am less certain of His Majesty.'

'Gertrude, honey,' Horace intervened feebly – so feebly now that Auguste wondered how the errand boy had ever risen to millionaire – 'I think you should listen to Mr Didier.'

'I *listen* to everyone, Father,' Gertrude replied equably. 'If what they tell me is rational, I then consider it.'

'Gertrude is an admirer of your Mrs Pankhurst,' Horace announced with a fine disregard of Auguste's nationality.

Auguste did not even notice, for he had lived in England so long that he was conditioned into accepting Mrs Pankhurst as one of his own. In any case, Tatiana introduced her suffragist movement and name so frequently at breakfast that he often felt as though Mrs Pankhurst lived next door.

'His Majesty's palate appreciates,' he explained, 'both the best and the simplest: a mutton chop well presented, or the most exquisite creations that French cuisine can produce.'

True to her word, Gertrude gave this earnest consideration. 'Pray be seated, Mr Didier.' She strode to the writing desk, turned her rejected menu over and began again. After a mere ten minutes, she rose and presented the fruits of her endeavours to Auguste.

In trepidation he read it, 'Salmagundi. Hindle Wakes. Whim-wham. Lancashire Hot Pot. Dressed mock turtle. Pickled Kent pippins. Tansy fritters. Spotted Dick. Green codling pudding...' Once again he lay the list down, searching for tactful words to explain that he could not present the monarch with an old boiling fowl disguised with lemon sauce and stuffed with prunes, not if he wished to remain married to Tatiana and the House of Lords was not to be summoned to issue, an instant divorce, on grounds of insanity.

Gertrude's eyes were on him. 'Well?' she demanded hopefully. 'Simple old-fashioned, English dishes. What more do you want?'

Horace fidgeted. 'I guess I should explain, Mr Didier. My daughter has long been interested in our own magnificent heritage, and is now planning to study your English folklore.'

'I aim to get into the English parliament, Mr Didier, with a message shouted loud and clear: "Preserve your heritage".'

Auguste was inclined to think that even if Mr Balfour, the Conservative prime minister, were miraculously to persuade parliament and the British public instantly that all women should have the vote, her marriage to a peer of the realm would prove a stumbling block to such a role. All he said was, 'You would, I am sure, be an asset to Mr Balfour's party.'

'Oh no, I'm aiming to join Mr Keir Hardie's new Labour Party. Pa agrees with me that's the way to the future. I intend to look after the rights of the downtrodden workers; I've already spoken to Arthur about my reforms for his estate.'

Auguste opened his mouth, and decided to close it again. He was even more glad he was returning to London the day after the wedding. After that, it seemed to him, there could be stormy waters at Farthing Court. However, his job was the preservation of the king's palate in the interests of the *entente cordiale* between England and France. Diplomacy was the solution.

'There is an excellent French phrase, madame, *le chef propose*... It is not essential for diners to follow such advice, but the true connoisseurs of cuisine know it is very wise to do so.'

'Why?'

'The chef's heart is in it. Moreover, the ingredients are frequently the fresher.'

Gertrude's eyes gleamed, and he could have sworn she was about to smile. She did not. 'The second would seem to follow from the first. So, Monsieur Didier, kindly *propose.*'

'For the wedding feast itself, an old-fashioned traditional English dinner in two courses–'

'In the States that wouldn't feed a flea,' Horace declared, outraged. 'Let me tell you, Mr Didier–'

'Each course,' Auguste continued hastily, 'would consist of twenty or so *plats*, presented simultaneously, of which guests may make their own choice according to taste. I suggest a mixture of your excellent English traditional dishes and French cuisine, such as roast duck and cucumbers, and *faisan au façon Didier* ... fruit, cheese, *entremets* and savouries would follow of course.'

He held his breath, mindful of his head being at stake if he had to bow out from this now appalling prospect.

'Good,' Gertrude agreed promptly.

Horace Pennyfather visibly relaxed. Indeed, he beamed. The late Mrs Pennyfather must have been very like her daughter, Auguste decided, for Horace seemed to be adept at playing second fiddle to his womenfolk.

'And I want the tables dressed in gold and nothing green upon the table.'

'I beg your pardon?'

'It is the fairies' colour and therefore dangerous for humans.'

Auguste gazed at her. This was after all the twentieth century. Could she be serious?

'But *la salade* ... and parsley. And...'

Gertrude considered this. 'Apart from the food.' Then she did smile. 'I'm not crazy, Mr Didier. Lord Montfoy has promised me a real traditional English wedding, like all the village brides have. He tells me Frimhurst is still steeped in old English customs and superstitions. I intend they shall never be forgotten. I am to write another *Golden Bough.*'

Auguste remembered Mr Frazer's excellent work was planned to run for twelve volumes, and they had so far been spread over fifteen years. (He hoped his own publisher would be so far-sighted.) However, Gertrude's plans boded ill for the estate workers.

'Are you planning to live at Farthing Court permanently?' Auguste could not resist this casual question.

Her face fell. 'No, Arthur prefers town

22

now, and anyway, I need to be near parliament and the British Museum. And I shall be going round the country campaigning for Mrs Pankhurst, of course.'

'Of course.'

'Arthur tells me,' Gertrude continued, 'they have a maypole and even a bonfire in celebration of some festival way back before Christianity. And the village girls dabble in the dew every May Day at dawn. That's why we chose to have the wedding on the first of May; the village will be celebrating May Day as they always do, in the lord of the manor's park, and we shall celebrate it with them.'

Auguste did not comment. Gertrude and His Majesty King Edward VII seemed to be talking about two different weddings. A discreet word in Horace Pennyfather's ear might not be a bad idea in the interests of the king's temper. He had never seen His Majesty cavorting around a maypole, and was quite certain he never would. Someone needed to work out a careful plan to avoid disaster, but it wasn't going to be him. An evil thought came to his mind. He would tell Egbert, Chief Inspector Egbert Rose of Scotland Yard, of his fears. After all, with His Majesty supposed to be in Paris, there was a political angle and, although this was strictly the concern of Special Branch, any threat to His Majesty's person was the concern of the whole of Scotland Yard.

Threat? Fears? Strange how quickly innocent excitement at the prospect of preparing a wedding banquet could change into something quite different. Later, as he was drifting into sleep, an old piece of English folklore culled from his years at Stockbery Towers drifted back to him. Wasn't May supposed to be an unlucky month for weddings?

Tension was rising in the White Dragon. On Monday evening, 24th April, one week before the wedding, the last meeting of the Committee for the Preservation of the White Dragon was in progress.

'Everyone set then?'

'Another pint of your best, Mus Wickman.'

'I didn't mean liquor.' All the same Bert refilled the glass – Jacob might be diddle-o, but he was useful as a figurehead, with his long white beard and boring tales of old railway days. Bert positioned himself by the blackboard fetched in from the public bar, ready for notes. 'Right then,' he said with heavy sarcasm, 'now everyone's drinks are all right, we'll begin the less interesting proceedings.'

Adelaide Spade and Bessie took no notice, intent on a whispered discussion of the questionable maiden state of the May

Queen. Adelaide took the view that young Mary Smith had long since ceded her innocence to young Harry (sitting only a yard or two from them) and gloomily predicted the worst. Bessie, envious of youthful love, nodded her head in hypocritical sympathy with Adelaide while comparing Mary's lot with her own as the recently spurned lover of Lord Montfoy.

Bert thumped the table. 'Silence,' he roared. 'We'll hear the reports one by one. All problems, foreseen and not foreseen, to be raised *now*. Bessie, you begin. You took on Special Ceremonies. All in order?'

Bessie pulled herself together. No good dreaming of what she'd like to do to Arthur Montfoy, even though it would ensure no little Montfoys would follow. Even now she couldn't get over it: after all she'd done for him over the years. Just, Goodbye, Bessie, I'm going to wed a Yankee. A mere slip of a girl, no doubt, when he'd had the privilege of Bessie Wickman, whose mature, dark beauty had been his to command. Or, at least, so she'd led him to believe. She donned an anxious expression. 'I'm still having trouble with the dabbling in the dew team. Too much fun and games by night to want to get up to see the dawn in, lazy lassies. And I've trouble with Jack in the Green. 'E won't wear his leaves.'

'Tell him,' Alfred Spade growled of his

25

apprentice, 'I'll thrash the living daylights out of him if he doesn't.'

'Dabbling in the dew's serious.' Bert frowned. 'Tell 'em no one who don't dabble in the dew can accompany the May Queen. It's an old tradition.'

'Who says?' Aggie shrieked. Old traditions were her domain.

'I do. I just thought of it. Don't dabble, don't dance, and that's that. Alfred, how you doing on Historical Heritage?'

Alf, a slow-talking, large-framed man, not known for genial companionship, did his best. 'One priesthole fitted at side of chimney breast, as requested. Panelling removed to construct apparent fallen-in secret tunnel, and replaced ajar. Round circle of prehistoric stones planted in Home Farm's Five Acre Field.' (Much to the fury of Farmer Beard who was about to sow his turnips, he might have added.)

Beer mugs were rattled as a sign of special commendation for effort.

'And the artificial thatch is coming on a treat.' Alf was gratified. 'I'll have it up by Friday.'

It was a time of magnanimity even if he were a bad-tempered nobbler in his drink. 'Well done, Alf. Adelaide?' Adelaide, anxious and nervy in her perpetual race to keep up with the rest of mankind, had been put in charge of the relatively safe division

26

of Dancing and Singing, also to include General Costuming.

'I can't find anyone to do the Sunday midnight shift at the Court.' She looked hopefully for help from their leader.

'I'll do it,' Jacob Meadows wheezed.

Once upon a time Jacob had had an excellent tenor voice. That time had long passed. 'No, you won't, you daft old ha'p'orth,' Harry Thatcher informed him cheerfully. 'Too late for you to be from your bed. I'll do it.'

'You can't. You're on maypole duty,' Bessie pointed out. She flattered herself she kept a motherly eye on young Harry; though motherly, she acknowledged, did not represent all her thoughts about him.

'What about the rector? He can sing.'

'Can't have the rector singing songs of lust at midnight. Wouldn't look good in church next day,' Alf pointed out.

Bert heaved a sigh. 'I'll do it.'

'You? In tights and doublet?' Bessie screamed with laughter.

Bert glared at her. 'Harry?' he said moving on quickly. 'How's Maypole and Village Sports Division?' (Sports except cricket which Bert had commandeered himself.) Harry had the easiest task of all, bat and trap and tug of war were simple, as was maypole-erecting and decoration. Even garland-making had been allotted to

27

Adelaide's division.

'Aggie and Jacob?' Bert asked. 'You all right for the Old Superstitions and Traditions? Need any suggestions for new ones?'

'We've done 'em,' Aggie boasted.

'What are they then?' Bessie asked.

'No point telling you. Just you wait.'

'What's rector going to say to all this?' Adelaide suddenly asked, spotting a new concern.

'He's been squared,' Bert said dismissively. 'Squire Entwhistle promised him new church bells if he kept mum. Now, you'll want to know about my bit. Ghosts and Cricket. I done the ghost of the Mighty Mynn, and just need one or two more smugglers.'

'What do you want smugglers for?' Aggie asked.

'*Ghosts*, Aggie. Not real ones. We're going to re-enact the battle of Frimhurst that's why.'

'Dere weren't one,' Jacob pointed out, as representative of time immemorial.

'There is now,' Bert replied shortly.

Aggie cackled. 'You're a one, Bert Wickman. Have you appeased the farisees yet? That's what I want to know. There's an old tradition that that's where the name Farthing Court come from. Farthing, see? I hope dey got an all-seeing eye outside the

28

house – a stone wid a hole bored in it. Come to that, you need one here, Bert. Keeps the bad 'uns away from the beer.'

'No, I don't. I've got more important things to do than worry about your blessed fairies.'

'Ain't nothing more important than getting on the right side of the farisees,' Aggie said belligerently. 'You'll find dat out, see if you don't.'

On Tuesday morning Auguste alighted at Cranbrook railway station on the Paddock Wood to Hawkhurst branch line and superintended the unloading and loading of many precious hampers for the second time that morning. They were carefully transferred to the wagon for Farthing Court and he climbed up to the seat beside the driver, which gave him a splendid view of the rolling, newly green Kentish countryside. Indeed, there was little to be seen but countryside, for there was no sign of Cranbrook village, only a public house and a few scattered cottages as the wagon clattered into the Cranbrook-Hawkhurst Road.

Today, he had decided, would be devoted to reconnaissance: he would survey the vegetable gardens and kitchens, meet the staff, and discuss the arrangement of the tables. It was a job he loved, made all the more precious now that Cousin Bertie's embargo had prevented his enjoying it save on rare occasions. Cranbrook, when the wagon reached it, was a busy bustling village, almost a town compared with Frimhurst. The latter lay a mile or two away from it, along lanes so narrow that the driver had to pull into a field opening to allow a carriage coming in the other direction to pass. He doffed his hat to the coachman in an extremely polite manner.

'Good day to you, sir,' he called.

Auguste was impressed. His memories of Kent workmen were of far earthier language and behaviour.

Frimhurst which they passed through to reach Farthing Court, seemed a peaceful slumbering village. Daffodils in their last brave trumpeting mingled with tulips; early bluebells were to be seen in the hedgerows. Woods bordering the road had that faint tinge of blue that stood between barren wood and carpet of colour. How Auguste remembered the bluebells of Kent. He admired the peg-tiled roofs of the cottages, and the comfortable-looking White Dragon. So comfortable, he decided that he would tell the driver to stop and go in to buy a drink. He had often found that by the local inn the whole village could be judged, a strange similarity growing between them like long-married husbands and wives.

The White Dragon did not provide a memorable experience. Auguste had the uncomfortable impression that everyone had stopped talking as he entered, and although he knew well that 'furriners', by which the Kentish meant anyone new to the village, often had this effect, he sensed he had interrupted some important discussion rather than casual conversation. He asked for a whisky and lemon but the landlady refused to serve it, and was insistent on his drinking a sweet concoction called mead. She leant her mature buxom figure almost menacingly over the bar towards him and watched his progress intently. Was it poisoned? he wondered anxiously. It certainly had an unusual taste. He left without finishing the drink.

Farthing Court was a huge, mellow, stone house, Elizabethan in façade, though its layout suggested an older ancestry. Auguste had discovered that His Majesty was so fond of it that his all too frequent visits had provided the reason for Lord Montfoy having to sell the house three years ago: they had almost bankrupted him. Auguste sincerely hoped that Mr Entwhistle was well-equipped to continue on the same grand lines. In three years, no doubt he had already had a taste of ordeal by Bertie. At the moment Mr Entwhistle was still away, which pleased Auguste greatly for it meant he could prowl round house and kitchen relatively undisturbed.

Having decided that whatever his 'downstairs' mission, his status as remote cousin by marriage to the king demanded his arrival by the 'upstairs' front entrance, he pulled at the old-fashioned bell rope. An extremely tall, thin butler opened the door speedily, closing his eyes briefly as though the sight of a Frenchman on *his* doorstep were too much for his English imperturbability.

'Good morning, sir. You are the chef, I presume.'

Good butlerdom enveloped Auguste to a degree he had not met with for many a long year. It even extended to waving a majestic hand towards the wagon with its precious load, thus despatching it into the jungle while he conducted his very own Dr Livingstone to the areas of the house normally invisible to those who entered by front doors.

Auguste looked round with interest as he followed in the butler's wake. Farthing Court was clearly already wearing its wedding face. Montfoy portraits, heraldic devices and odd pieces of armour leapt out aggressively from every wall and niche he passed. Any signs of Mr Entwhistle's ancestry must have been painstakingly obliterated. Auguste, had a sudden fear that the kitchens might be as mediaeval as these trappings.

'Ah, Mrs Honey. May I present Mr Pennyfather's chef? Mrs Honey is our housekeeper.'

The plump motherly lady had appeared from a passage-way as they entered the servants' domain, keys clanking on black bombazine. Almost Auguste expected to see an old-fashioned nutmeg tin hanging by the keys; in his early days in England this precious spice had still been under the close guard of the housekeeper. He bowed. 'My name is Auguste Didier, madame.'

Mrs Honey's round face glowed warmly like a Provençal peach. A picturebook housekeeper. 'Thank you, Mr Tudor.' She beamed at the gaunt giant, then turned to the newcomer. 'Welcome to Farthing Court, Monsieur Didier.'

Of course such an *English* butler would be called Tudor, Auguste thought, slightly dazed by such perfection. Only the kitchens now remained to be faced – and the resident chef. To his immense relief, when they eventually arrived he found that Mr Entwhistle, if not the Montfoys before him, had a good eye for the most modern equipment. No open fires and spitjacks here. Cake mixers, chopping machines, ice caves and dutch ovens met his relieved eye.

At their entrance he was amazed, and

33

flattered, to find the kitchen staff, from the humblest scullery maid to the deputy head chef (judging by his hat) springing to instant attention and even according him a small bob or bow. They are probably practising for His Majesty's arrival, he told his ego firmly, but it refused to be entirely deflated. Never had he visited – much less worked in – such a polite kitchen. Normally kitchen tempers were like cream simmering just under boiling-over point. Where, however, was the chef himself? This was the most delicate relationship of all to handle in his situation.

A flying figure carrying a bunch of asparagus before him like a bouquet hurtled through the garden door. His hat and apron declared his occupation but the spikes of red hair escaping from under the hat and his wiry thinness made him look like an over used pipe-cleaner. Could this mere youth with his freckled face and piercing brown eyes truly be the head cook at such a large establishment as Farthing Court? Apparently so, for he bowed deeply, declaring, 'Ethelred Perkins at your service, sir – don't *do* that, Percy,' he shrieked, to Auguste's alarm, at the pastry cook. 'Caress your dough, don't beat it.'

'Sorry, Mr Perkins.' The minion looked shamefaced.

How very extraordinary, Auguste thought;

most pastry chefs he came across retained a sullen indifference to the finer points of their trade. He began his usual apologia, for bursting in upon another's domain, but this was dismissed impatiently by Mr Perkins.

'What is more natural?' he pointed out with some surprise. 'His Majesty is to grace us with his presence, Mr Pennyfather is our guest here, and I am hoping to learn a great deal from his chef.'

Curiouser and curiouser, in Mr Lewis Carroll's famous words. In Auguste's experience, resident chefs were only too happy to spike the intruder's guns – or worse, their ingredients. Such professed wholehearted co-operation was something rare indeed. Auguste began to look forward to meeting a gentleman who could attract such jewels to his service. Nevertheless, he decided he would still walk with care during his time in the Farthing Court kitchen. A man, as Hamlet had discovered, could smile and smile and be a villain. Ethelred Perkins might still prove such a man.

In Paris, in an apartment in the Place Vendôme, the Squire of Farthing Court was preparing to return to England. It would all prove, he was sure, the most delightful and amusing experience. His Majesty, whom he was to meet at Calais on the return from his Mediterranean state visit, would once more be his guest, but on this occasion it would be the culmination of all his aspirations. The visit was spiced by the piquancy of marriage between Arthur Montfoy and Gertrude Pennyfather, and his own temporary abrogation of the role of lord of the manor in favour of Arthur. His friend Arthur, an amiable but not over-intelligent gentleman, appeared to him to be overlooking one fact. To marry a rich American heiress whose family as well as herself were under the impression that the Montfoy fortunes were unimpaired, was a splendid move. But all wedding days had a morrow, and in this case sooner or later the heiress was going to discover that her Kentish estates consisted merely of one small Dower House and a ninety by twenty foot garden. This, however, was not his concern. His part was done, the village was well primed, and Horace Pennyfather was even bringing his own chef.

Normally His Majesty insisted on despatching most of the palace cooks to cook for him, in addition to the usual retinue of household retainers, so Horace Pennyfather must be high in the popularity stakes for the king to trust his choice. He was glad. It meant that he, Thomas Entwhistle, could stand aside and let events take their course. As, thanks to his planning, they would.

Early on the morning of Saturday, 29th April, Arthur Montfoy was driving down from London for his wedding, to which he was greatly looking forward. Soon all his troubles would be over, the splendid Gertrude would be his, and in due course they might even be able to buy back Farthing Court. Thomas had intimated as much though for some reason he hadn't seemed at all confident that Arthur would be able to do so. Anyway, Thomas had organised everything in corking fashion, Arthur would enjoy being back in the old house, and Gertrude would get her heart's desire – an old-fashioned English wedding. It was all going to be perfectly idyllic.

He had rather fancied driving down with Gertrude, but she had pointed out how unlucky it was for the bride to be too much in the bridegroom's company, and he had reluctantly agreed to drive some woman Gertrude had been friendly with in Paris. He quickly brightened up when he arrived at the Carlton Hotel and found the Comtesse Eleonore de Balleville awaiting him in the Palm Court. She was a stunner with her black hair and dark eyes, even if she did look over thirty, and the bodice of her tightly fitting deep-blue walking dress suggested a figure to match. Arthur gathered that her husband was away a lot for diplomatic reasons, but whether the diplomacy was for his career or for marital convenience, was not clear. He took to her immediately. Gertrude was splendid but, on the whole, she didn't spend much time telling him what a fantastic fellow he was as the countess seemed only too willing to do as they rattled through the Kentish countryside.

'*Artur*–' the countess's husky voice imbued his name in French with a music it could have gained from no other direction – 'Gertrude tells me that your village always celebrates May Day in your park. How generous. It shows the strong link between manor and village. The peasants must be devoted to you, and no wonder.'

'Er, yes.' Arthur Montfoy had left all that sort of thing to Thomas, and had little notion what kind of preparations were in hand. He only hoped the countess's beauty would offset any awkwardness in her all-too-literal translation of her native *paysans* if she were to use it within the hearing of Alf Spade, for example.

'In France we present flowers, lilies of the valley, on the first of May.'

'Very nice too, I'm sure,' Arthur commented heartily. It sounded a lot cheaper than Thomas's methods.

'Gertrude has given me a list of the rules when His Majesty is to be a fellow guest,' Eleonore continued happily. 'My baggage was collected yesterday. Only four trunks and twenty smaller cases. Apart from hatboxes of course. I am afraid, being *de passage*, I could not make it more. If a misadventure occurs to *anything* I shall have to break one of the rules and appear in the same garment twice. Or,' she paused, and turned towards Arthur, 'would it be better to appear *en chemise* or naked, do you think?'

Arthur blushed bright red. This conjured up images that did not fit well with the need to keep an eye open as the Napier swung round corners. He almost wished there was a little more time between himself and marriage. He was quite certain as to which His Majesty would prefer – in private at any rate.

Fortunately Eleonore did not require an answer, as she continued, 'I have of course included deepest mourning, and so–'

'*Mourning?*' The steering wheel nearly shot out of his hand.

'Gertrude tells me it is essential when the king is present, in case news reaches him that one of his relations has been assassinated.'

Arthur wondered frantically whether his valet had thought to transfer deepest mourning along with his wedding clothes to the closets at Farthing Court. Then his solid English common sense came to his rescue.

This was a wedding, not a wake.

The Montfoy family, cursed or not, was not solely represented by Arthur. His older sister Belinda, unmarried at thirty-two at her own choosing, was a keen student of hieroglyphs and Egyptology at London's University College and intent on a career. She had reluctantly been prised away for the wedding, and was on her way by railway train, accompanied by her cousin 'Young Gerald'. Gerald Montfoy had been thus indulgently deemed ever since his first misadventure at the age of five, when he purloined a fine silver nef from one of the statelier homes of England. As his passion for disgracing the family name had not changed, neither had his soubriquet. He had been despatched to South Africa at the earliest age possible, where he had distinguished himself by being the only English gentleman not to make a fortune, and had returned to London still penniless only three weeks ago. He was of an age with Arthur at twenty-eight, and blessed with more good looks, though far less money than Arthur had prior to his acquaintance with His Majesty. He had decided that henceforth the world should be his oyster and save when there was an 'r' in the month, London his playground. A round of shooting parties followed by Cannes would take care of the rest. This morning, unusually, he was sunk in gloom, despite Belinda's best efforts to interest him in the Osireion at Abydos.

'Nice woman, Gertrude,' he finally remarked savagely as they waited at Paddock Wood for the Cranbrook train. 'Healthy type.'

Belinda, who if forced was observant in more directions than the Rosetta Stone, glanced at him. 'Indeed Gerald, I believe you may count on several little Montfoys to toddle between you and the title.'

He grinned reluctantly. 'And any money that goes with it, dear Belinda, pray do not forget that.'

'I don't forget it. You may not have observed, Gerald, that I am earning my own living.'

'No one could forget that.' Gerald Montfoy glanced at his cousin: the hair taken back in a bun that would be severe if it had succeeded in capturing all the stray ends of natural curls; the grey tweed costume; the grey felt hat. It was obviously going to be up to him to lighten the tone of the forthcoming proceedings on Gertrude's behalf he decided, since Gertrude was to join the family. Lucky dog, Arthur. He had everything, title, estate, money, and now he was walking off with an American heiress. He didn't *need* an heiress while Gerald did.

He pondered what to do. After all, Arthur was a nincompoop and Gertrude was a very attractive woman.

Jeanne Planchet was on the same railway train as Thomas and Belinda, together with the great majority of the Pennyfather and Montfoy wedding guests, but she was travelling third class, along with the other servants. They would all climb up into the charabancs and not into the carriages waiting at Cranbrook for the last part of the journey. Jeanne was merely Mademoiselle Pennyfather's maid. Already she was missing her native Paris, where she had applied for this position. She had heard of the English countryside, but so far was not impressed. Like London, it had no style. It was a higgledy-piggledy assortment of trees, houses, woods and streams. It had no grand concept like the French plains and rivers, or Paris's splendid boulevards. It was not planned, it merely happened. America must be an entirely different matter, and she would have looked forward to going there. She had heard that in Washington and New York there was indeed style. There was only one barrier to this dream. Mademoiselle Pennyfather was to marry this English lord and actually wanted to live *here*. For ever, and ever, and ever. Her youth and beauty would be wasted in this barbarous wasteland. Jeanne glared at the bluebell woods and regretted leaving the bridges of Paris, clochards and all, despite its problems and despite the reason she had fled from it so short a time ago.

'My dear Mr Waites, how very fortuitous. Do please join me.'

'Your Grace.' Richard Waites, rising diplomat of the Foreign Office with a particular speciality in European matters, bowed deeply to Louisa, Duchess of Wessex, for whom he had a cautious admiration – and sympathy. Of all roles, that of fading star in the firmament of the king's amorous life was the least enviable, and with Mrs Keppel's dominance, all stars shone less brightly even that of the 'Dizzy Duchess' as she was known. The dizziness had obviously been too much for the duke who had died while travelling across the Sahara wastes some years ago. How had she wangled her way onto the guest list? He supposed that even His Majesty could not exercise his usual vetoes over a wedding-party list.

'How nice to see you again, Mr Waites. Are you a friend of dear Arthur's?' Louisa unintentionally revealed her route to the list, as Richard followed her into the first-class carriage.

'Of his wife to be.'

'How very brave of him, don't you think,

43

to marry an American?'

'A charming lady,' he replied shortly. Too shortly for the duchess, whose career was devoted to such nuances. She was amused. 'Jealous, Mr Waites?'

Was he? Richard found to his dismay that he was. He had seen much of Gertrude in the past few weeks, having been detailed by the Foreign Secretary (with an eye on monitoring relations with the President of the USA) to explain the workings of the 'quaint' English parliament. When she had told him of her forthcoming marriage, he had realised with some surprise she was exactly the bride he would have chosen for himself, fortune or not. That surprise had turned to jealousy surprised him even more.

'His Majesty will have much on his mind,' Louisa observed innocently. 'I must do what I can to make his stay a pleasant one.'

'Will he?' The answer was meant to be off-putting.

'This new friendship between the Tsar and the Kaiser must be most worrying for you.'

He smiled. 'With your present company and a wedding before me, nothing could worry me, Your Grace.' Damned woman, he was thinking. The last thing he wanted was the Dizzy Duchess snooping around. The Foreign Office had had all its many channels working non-stop ever since the

Kaiser had decided, with that Machiavellian Von Holstein's help, to visit Tangier a month ago and assure the Sultan that not only was his independence guaranteed, but that Germany, for all the Kaiser's protestations to His Majesty last June to the contrary, had a great interest in Morocco's future and would protect it. France, with its own labyrinthine plans, was consequently on the point of war with Germany and that might split His Majesty's *entente cordiale* with France wide open, since Britain had no intention of joining in, if conflict broke out. Yet with the Tsar under German influence, would that leave Britain isolated? The Tsar needed to be gently wooed back to where his best interests lay, with France and Britain, but above all the alliance with France must be maintained.

'If there is anything I can do to help...' Louisa's still splendid blue eyes stared earnestly into his.

In Richard's view, King Edward VII was quite astute enough as a politician to manage very nicely without the help of anyone – including, unfortunately, his Foreign Office. (Provided, Richard conceded, he did not get sidetracked.)

'You are most kind, Your Grace.' Deftly Richard turned the talk to safe ground, such as who was, and even more excitingly, who was *not* on the guest list. The Dizzy

Duchess, for once, was disappointed.

Harvey Bolland was finding the company of Bluebell Pennyfather, Gertrude's younger sister, distinctly trying. Back in the States, he had cultivated the kid's friendship as a sure way to Gertrude's heart, since the sisters appeared to be devoted to each other. It had failed as a policy, and he was burdened with the consequences. His dogged pursuit of Gertrude from Colorado to New York, then to Paris and now London, had resulted only in a invitation to her wedding to someone else. He'd heard a lot about the general uselessness of the English aristocracy but Lord Montfoy beat everything. The fellow wasn't even good-looking. Harvey complacently thought of his own strapping, tall figure. Why, Buffalo Bill had even asked him to take part in his show. This Arthur wouldn't last ten minutes in Denver. And he, Harvey, was just as rich as Arthur; there was still money in the ground in Colorado. Horace had approved of him, too, until he had the wool pulled over his eyes by this old England stuff.

'I'm going to be the *only* bridesmaid.'

Harvey looked at the gawky twelve-year-old, in many respects a younger version of Gertrude, but not so far in looks and figure. She was much shorter, much sharper featured, much more sturdy, and her round, heavy spectacles did not help. Sure, the sisters shared a disconcerting stare and that he didn't care for.

'That's if there *is* a wedding,' Bluebell added matter-of-factly.

He was startled, and then cautiously interested. 'Why shouldn't there be, Bluebell?'

'She might change her mind.'

'I doubt it.' Harvey relapsed into depression. For a moment he thought Bluebell had a plan.

'I don't like Arthur and I don't want her to live in England.'

'Gertrude does, unfortunately.'

Bluebell ignored this. 'Nor does Father.'

Here Harvey disagreed, pointing out savagely, 'He's delighted about it. He's aiming to put "Purveyors to His Majesty" on his blessed Pilgrim's Cherry Shrub.'

Gertrude and Horace were passengers in a Rolls-Royce – new to the market, Horace had been told, but thought to have promise. He'd bought it, and now in the hands of their chauffeur it was taking them to Farthing Court. So far they had made seven stops in Horace's anxiety to close the top lest it rain, and Gertrude's determination to see as much as possible of the countryside she was shortly to make her own.

'It should be here, sir. Somewhere.' The chauffeur had stopped near the village of

Sissinghurst and was peering at a map on which roads were a matter of far less importance than railways and rivers. After asking directions of a postman, who seemed to have heard only vaguely of Frimhurst the chauffeur turned one corner, then another, and found what must surely be the road to Frimhurst. Farmers in smocks industriously tilled the fields, a shepherd raised a horn to his lips and blew loudly three times. 'Like Little Boy Blue calling his sheep,' murmured Gertrude entranced. Then the shepherd proceeded to let the flock of sheep out in front of the motor car, which provided an advance guard to the village.

'Oh, it's enchanting,' Gertrude said, and even Horace was impressed.

A milkmaid in bonnet and pale-blue dress and white stockings, a stool under one arm and bucket on the other, swept low in a curtsey. A chimney sweep trudging along the road, a small boy at his side covered in black from top to bottom (Bert had paid extra out of the budget), gave them a merry grin.

'It's lucky to see a chimney sweep on the way to one's wedding, so Arthur tells me,' Gertrude breathed in ecstasy.

The thatched roofs including that of the old pub looked cosy and inviting. Children bowled hoops and bobbed respectfully, one shyly presented a bouquet of wild primroses, old ladies at doorways, clad in black, energetically spun wool and lace. Voices, raised in merry song, issued from the public house, 'Ha, ha, ha, you and me/Little brown jug, don't I love thee...' The church bells began to ring in competition, and a group of village girls, skipping round the well, promptly joined hands to run to the church.

'I wish I could have heard what they were saying as they danced.' Gertrude sighed wistfully.

It was just as well she could not. Mary Smith, the supposedly virginal May Queen elect, was giving a graphic account of her previous night's rendezvous with Harry in what was called locally something rather more crude than Lovers' Lane.

'Father, *look!*' Gertrude cried, pointing to the green before the church, now adorned by a wooden contrivance for temporarily restraining malefactors and exposing them to the ridicule of their more virtuous friends and neighbours. 'Aren't they stocks?'

As if on cue, a screaming figure was escorted by three burly men out of the White Dragon in front of them.

'Dere you stay, George Higgins,' shouted the landlord. 'Into the stocks wid you till you do cool off. What de Montfoys going to think, eh?'

Gertrude watched as the man's head was

49

bowed in shame and his legs were duly fastened into his humiliating punishment.

'Let him go, good people, for my sake,' she called, and grudgingly one of the men said 'Half an hour, then, thanks to the kind lady, George.'

Spring flowers seemed to bloom everywhere, merry smiles and respectful nods accompanied the slow passage of the motor car through the village towards the Farthing Court gates.

An ancient crone tottered forth from her dwelling, tears in her eyes. 'Blessed be de Montfoys, miss, and blessed be the bride that comes among us.'

A rheumy-eyed old gentleman swept off his hat and brushed his eyes with his sleeve. 'Dat I should see dis day, I thank 'ee, Lord.'

Gertrude Pennyfather glanced at her father, who was entranced by his daughter's forthcoming domain. She smiled.

Two

It was highly inconvenient of oysters to plan their reproductive life to begin on the first of May, thus necessitating a closed season. His Majesty, as Auguste well knew, considered grilled oysters an indispensable forerunner to retiring for the night, and now that, owing to his age, ladies were not quite so indispensable, the dish had gained even more importance on the royal menu. Even lobsters chose this month to devote their best efforts to spawning, and were it not for the consignment of Norwegian lobsters (who saw their duty to the royal palate more clearly), fish would be but poorly represented. Even sole were out of season, ruling out his *soles au chablis Didier*. Fortunately turbot was much more obliging. But would the consignment of turbot arrive on Monday from Hythe? What if – Auguste firmly dismissed his fears. If Ethelred Perkins declared a fishmonger reliable, that was good enough for him. In the few days he had been here, his confidence in this strange chef had mushroomed into a *chanterelles à la crème*. Ethelred was a dish fit for a king.

He had tried to relax earlier that Saturday morning, as the wagon had trundled through Frimhurst village on its way to Cranbrook to pick up his supplies sent down from London. His time at Farthing Court had gone well, and his surroundings were pleasant – surprisingly so, he thought, as the surly innkeeper's wife of earlier in the week came out to give him a sudden bob. A lacemaker outside her cottage, bobbins busy flying, called out a friendly greeting, and a child, clad in pinafore and boots, handed him a posy of wild flowers – including, to his delight, wild garlic. This seemed a different village from the one he had passed through on Tuesday.

Indeed, Auguste had suddenly wondered if it *were* a different village. He could have sworn the White Dragon pub and the row of adjacent cottages had had ordinary tiled roofs, yet abundant thatch was everywhere. He must have had his mind on ortolans (much more eager to oblige His Majesty in May) and not his surroundings.

Oak, ash and thorn
Guard Montfoy morn.
Mother elder sacred be
Blessed be Montfoys in their fee.

A very old lady stood respectfully at the side of the road, having chanted her poetical offering. 'The blessings of Tir Nan Og be upon you, young man.' Yes, this was indeed a happy village. Or was it? Something made him glance back, the black-clad old lady was staring after him with an expressionless face; it occurred to him that in former times the word 'witch' would have fitted her perfectly. And wasn't Tir Nan Og some kind of Celtic pagan paradise?

He had dismissed witches from his mind by the time he had returned to the house and replaced them with the glories of the coming days, devoted to the wonders of preparing a wedding banquet, glories only slightly diluted by the fact that His Majesty was one of the guests. At least the wonderful kitchens of Farthing Court had not changed. As he had entered, the smell of roast guinea fowl met his nostrils, and the comforting figure of Ethelred Perkins could be seen whisking round his spotless and obedient kingdom, a kingdom over which Auguste would now reign for three glorious days.

Ethelred executed a neat bow, and beamed. 'In your absence, Mr Didier, there has been excellent news from the fishmonger – the halibut is of sufficiently high standard to serve, and the gardener assures me the hothouse strawberries will after all be available.'

Very wise of them, in Auguste's opinion. 'And the asparagus?'

'But of course.' Ethelred appeared shocked that Auguste could have presumed that in his constant battle with the gardener to relinquish his produce he would have been other than the victor.

'And the consommé?'

'Clarification now complete.'

Auguste's contented eyes fell on his allotted table awaiting him, well-scrubbed and with knives, ladles, spoons all laid in correct campaign style – and on the delightful young kitchen maid standing respectfully by it, ready for his next orders.

'Mr Didier, can I hazard a guess that from your deep knowledge of His Majesty's requirements, and from the fact he has chosen not to bring his own chef, that you have on occasion had the privilege of cooking for His Majesty?'

'I have, yes.' Privilege was not quite the word he would have chosen, however. 'In fact, I can now *only* cook for His Majesty.' Auguste explained his difficult position.

Ethelred's eyes grew round with horror. 'But my dear sir, every honour must be accorded to you. I will notify Mr Tudor immediately, and Mrs Honey must be informed at once. The bedroom allotted to you is not fitting for a relative of His Majesty.'

54

'It is absolutely fitting,' Auguste interrupted in some alarm, lest Ethelred prostrate himself before him. 'I am here as a chef, not as His Majesty's relation. I am employed by Mr Pennyfather.' It suddenly occurred to him that he might therefore receive a fee, but decided that since Cousin Bertie was involved this was unlikely in the extreme. He was merely a feudal retainer who owed services to his lord in return for – for what? In his case, happiness.

'At the very least,' Ethelred said earnestly, 'you must now have sole access to the servants' bathroom. We shall all be honoured to have cold hip baths in our rooms.'

'No, I beg of you.' How could he make this charming youth understand he *wanted* to be one of them again?

'I insist. The honour is ours.'

Reluctantly, he had given way, and the morning had hummed and glowed, as twenty kitchen staff slid efficiently about their work. Ducklings were salted, stocks were prepared, game lovingly checked in the larders, gardens routinely inspected, ices churned, with not a word of dissension. And all this wasted on a master away for much of the time. Did Mr Entwhistle keep Ethelred Perkins bottled up like a genie until such time as he rubbed his magic lamp?

The delightful chief kitchen maid allotted to Auguste was a village girl by name of

Jenny Potter, who seemed to think that raising her eyes from the task in front of her would secure instant dismissal, and displayed the same eager acceptance of whatever he demanded of her. Only one item had caused a problem. The Jersey vegetables imported for the dish of green beans cooked with shallots, chervil and cream.

Jenny's eyes grew round in horror. 'Green beans? Oh no, Mr Didier, I couldn't do that.'

'Do you think such a simple dish out of place on the menu, Jenny?' Auguste was perplexed. 'His Majesty, while an admirer of the most intricate recipes, likes simple food as well.'

'It's not His Majesty, sir. It's my grannie.'

'She is not dining here, is she?'

She shook her head miserably. 'No, but she do say beans are the food of the dead, and green is the colour of the fairies.'

'And you believe that?' He was incredulous, and suddenly recalled Gertrude's stipulation over the table arrangements. Even she had excluded his food from her ban, however.

'The fairies don't like it if they think humans do mock them, so Grannie Potter says.'

'Your grandmother is not responsible for the menu for His Majesty's supper,' Auguste said as gently as he could, 'and Jenny, fairies are kind creatures.' Memories of fairy godmothers in Charles Perrault's collected tales came hazily back to him.

Jenny's eyes dropped. 'Oh no, sir. You're wrong,' she said, but so quietly that he did not hear and he thought his argument won.

By the servants' dinnertime, the majority of the guests and the bridal party had arrived, and Auguste's schedule was working smoothly. This morning the ice cream for the *bombes*, this afternoon tammy cloths and spoons would come out for jellies... That moment of satisfaction had arrived when his brain said stop; the menu and its organisation could be seen as one glorious whole instead of a series of disjointed operations and apparently insurmountable obstacles. Never had he worked in such a peaceable kitchen. Indeed the whole household below stairs seem to reverberate with remarkable good nature.

At five to twelve the upper servants congregated in Pug's Parlour, the butler's room, in order to parade in ceremonial style to join the lower servants in the servants' hall for dinner. He now knew Mr Tudor (who, Auguste had discovered, rejoiced in the splendidly British forename of Stuart), Mrs Honey, beaming in bombazine, lace cap over her grey curls, Lord Montfoy's valet, the head housemaid, and the under butler and Ethelred, but from today their number would be greatly swelled by the personal servants of the guests. Auguste was asked to escort Mademoiselle Jeanne Planchet, lady's maid to Gertrude Pennyfather, in to dinner, presumably on the grounds that they were both French.

Auguste had found it oddly pleasing to be back in the world of the servants' hall, remembering his days at Stockbery Towers, and he relaxed in the familiar formality of advancing two by two to attend dinner with the lower servants. Hierarchy here counted for as much, if not more, than it did to the people whom they served, which he found both ridiculous and charming.

Jeanne was a handsome rather than a pretty girl, with a sullen expression, dark eyes, heavy jaw and magnolia white skin. Attractive to men, of that there was little doubt. She did not appeal to him, but many would find the earthy energy expressed in that face irresistible.

'Paris? You come from *Paris?*' Her eyes lit up at Mrs Honey's introduction.

'I have worked there, mademoiselle, in the rue Daru.' Auguste looked back with mixed feelings on that time in his life. It was there he had met Tatiana, there he had parted from her, and near there too that her uncle, Pyotr Gregorin, who had vowed to murder him, also lived.

'Ah. By the Russian church.'

'So you know it. Have you worked nearby?' Auguste was surprised, for it was a small community and a close one.

Caution entered her voice. 'I did not like my employer and left to work for Mademoiselle Pennyfather. Like you, monsieur, I wished to see the world. Especially America.'

'But your mistress prefers to live here.'

'She will change her mind,' Jeanne announced. 'She is a lady of good sense. Monsieur, do you remember the *petit restaurant* in the rue Pierre le Grand? Ah, the cooking. It is superb.'

'And I can promise you it will be superb here also.'

'For His Majesty perhaps,' she snorted.

'And for you, mademoiselle. Look.' He pointed to the huge roasts ready for Mr Tudor to carve on the tables before them.

'Rosbif...' Jeanne's nose wrinkled in disdain and Auguste sighed for those who could not appreciate the glories of the country they were in while they mourned the one they were parted from.

'And this,' Arthur waved a proud hand towards a small stone building resembling a ruined Gothic chapel; it nestled on the edge of the woodland, shrouded in carefully

59

planted ivy and bushes, 'is the folly where the seventh Earl killed his cook.'

Gertrude was entranced and demanded entrance. She was not disappointed. Inside the walls were adorned with the means of slaughtering any number of cooks, ranging from bows and arrows to South African War bayonets and Maxim guns. Swords hung menacingly over the fireplace, a deer's antlered head hung dusty and gloomy between them, a small cannon poked invitingly out from one corner, more antlers adorned the walls. Only an occasional table, one armchair, two decanters and a glass spoke of life not death.

'He *murdered* him here?'

'He was the cook. He strangled him, because the picnic arrived late for the shooting party. I suppose you'd call it murder.'

'I would,' Gertrude said decidedly.

'Things were done differently in those days.' Arthur's offhand words might have been meant as an explanation or even apology.

'I'm glad. I'm sure Father wouldn't want to risk Mr Didier's neck.'

'Of course not. Didn't your father tell me he was related to the king?'

Gertrude stared at him. 'I'm sure looking forward to getting into your parliament. It seems to me I'll be able to do some good.'

'Good? In parliament? You'd only be in the

Lower House,' Arthur pointed out, puzzled.

'Arthur dear, that's where democracy and justice dwell.'

He thought about this. 'You may be right, Gertrude. It was the House of Lords that condemned the seventh Earl – he was hung by a silken rope though,' he added in satisfaction.

Gertrude swallowed. There was work to be done in this country. Arthur was a darling, but totally blinded by the stultifying past. Once married, he would see her point of view; as a partnership, she working from the Lower House and Arthur in the Lords, they could change the course of history. When she was lady of the manor, she'd bring some fresh air here too. The best should be kept, the worst should go. Poverty banished, Merrie England remain. She thought fondly of Frimhurst village, and of the pleasures to come. It occurred to her as they walked back across the gardens that she had given little thought to one of the usual pleasures of marriage: the marital bed. She dismissed this momentary cloud, consoling herself that her dabbling in the dew might bring about a transformation in Arthur's lovemaking – sorely needed if the meagre and unexciting foretastes she had so far received were anything to judge by.

'And this,' Arthur was saying of a naked Venus spouting forth water from her mouth, as were eight little Cupids at her feet, 'is the fountain erected by the eighth Earl. His wife is said to have poisoned the water.'

'What happened?'

'He died.'

'And who else?' Gertrude asked.

'No one – oh, except a gamekeeper and his dog. They'd been forbidden to drink from it though.'

'Did the dog know that?'

'I say, Gertrude, you're not taking me seriously.' Arthur was hurt.

'Oh, but I am, darling. Very seriously.'

At a quarter to three the guests were beginning to make their way across the formal gardens and greensward beyond with its view down to the lake, and across to the Great Meadow which lay between it and the ancient woodland, where the grand ceremony of erecting the maypole was to take place. This meadow was so called from the attempt of an eighteenth-century Montfoy to imitate nature with art. The field had been firmly reclaimed from nature, then replanted with less stubborn grass and carefully selected wild flowers chosen to give ample opportunities for posy-gathering throughout the year, and kept confined to the outskirts of the field and selected places within in order that no change of footwear would be involved when picnics were taken in this country setting. Queen Marie-Antoinette was said to have gathered inspiration for her *Petit Hameau* at Versailles from hearing of this felicitous spot.

Beyond the Great Meadow lay Home Farm's Five Acre Field with its newly planted crop of prehistoric stones. On rising ground, the stones were perfectly silhouetted against the skyline, and Bert had argued long and hard with the farmer to have the maypole ceremony there. For once he had lost.

'Where's Arthur?' Richard Waites, in the vanguard of the guests, was a little surprised at Gertrude's having sought him out to escort her to the maypole ceremony. Not that he had any objection.

'The lord of the manor, Arthur told me, has to help lift the pole off the wagon. It's expected of him.'

Richard noted some vicarious pride in this reply, and his frustration grew.

'It's good luck,' Gertrude added defiantly, detecting disapproval.

It was Richard's private thought that it was Gertrude who would need the good luck, but he refrained (just) from comment on her choice of bridegroom. He attacked on safer ground.

'How do you reconcile your suffrage aspirations with this love of irrelevant tradition and folklore, Gertrude? This is the twentieth century, and here you are revelling in prehistoric rituals.'

'Even in the States we have traditions.' Gertrude skilfully avoided answering, which did not go unnoticed. 'Thanksgiving for example. Would you say that was irrelevant?'

'Not quite the same. I gather you don't have lords of the manor in America.'

'A country grows from its roots, Richard. The stronger the roots, the stronger the growth up above.'

'Very neat.'

'You can't not enjoy the English country traditions, just because you rarely step a foot outside London.'

'As Dr Johnson observed, he who is tired of London is tired of life. I am neither.'

'Which is why I'm marrying Arthur,' Gertrude retaliated, for once without thinking, and resting her arm in his. 'You have no need of me.'

'*I* have no need?' he rejoined.

She blushed. 'Someone *like* you would not need me.' She regained her composure. 'You're a diplomat, Richard, so don't say anything that might mean we could not be friends. I'd not like that.'

'Impossible, Gertrude. It would be easier to make an *entente cordiale* with Germany than for you and I to be friends, as you say. Even diplomats speak their minds at times;

how can a friend, much less a lover, stand by and see you rushing into disaster?'

The hand was withdrawn, and the voice became cool. 'I believe I see my father over there. I will sit by him. Do excuse me, Richard.'

Horace had accompanied Louisa, Duchess of Wessex to the meadow, and was sitting on one of the two hundred cushioned seats specially covered that morning to resemble meadowy banks and tuffets, but was finding conversation difficult owing to Louisa's hat. She was constantly twisting and turning in her endeavours to tell him exactly who each new arrival was; the turns were acceptable, the twists brought the sharp pheasant feather in her hat (for country wear) uncomfortably near his eye.

'What a dear girl Gertrude is,' Louisa cooed, having just discovered Gertrude's mother was dead, and aware that she was herself dressed by Worth; in addition, her complexion, coiffure and title were entirely captivating, even if they failed to captivate His Majesty nowadays. 'And dear little Bluebell too.' Would all Mr Pennyfather's delightful money make up for the disadvantages of being married again? She would have to forego her title and she supposed, change her way of life if she remarried, but on the other hand if her son married that horsy humourless lass he had his eye on, it would mean Louisa would become the dowager duchess, a title that had a very unpleasant ring to it. She slid a little closer, in order that her scent could do its share in the captivating of Horace.

Horace was devoted to his two daughters, but the words 'dear girl' and 'little' did not immediately spring to mind when he considered Gertrude's forthright strength and Bluebell's even more serious and determined chin.

'Why, thank you, Duchess.'

'Pray call me Louisa. This is a gathering of *friends*, is it not?'

Taken aback at this lowering of the drawbridge of what he well knew to be English social reserve, and overpowered by the scent of attar of roses, Horace warmed to her. 'I certainly hope so,' he replied heartily.

'And the country seems so friendly, does it not?'

'Don't you have a country estate, Louisa?' Horace was puzzled. He thought dukes had some kind of land attached to them.

Louisa did, but she saw little of it, being away much of the time. She had an excellent bailiff, a son who had inherited the estate and the title, and so her duty was done. 'Ah yes, and the villagers are devoted to me, as here they will be to your daughter. Gertrude is fortunate.' As friend both to His Majesty and to Arthur, she knew perfectly well that Gertrude was going to have a rude awakening, but as she had no desire to be eliminated from royal approval, she put the matter from her mind.

Horace wavered, unsure what he felt. There was something to be proud of, having Gertrude married to an English earl, and a rich one at that. After all, it wasn't up to him to question Gertrude's taste, and Arthur was a friend of His Majesty himself. They went shooting together, which Horace knew was as good as exchanging blood vows. He sought for an answer and found one. 'Yes, indeed, Louisa. I know where I am with someone like Arthur. Honest as the day.' It was true. No one pulled the wool over Horace Pennyfather's eyes. Pilgrim's Cherry Shrub hadn't made him the fortune it had without his being a shrewd judge of character.

Belinda hunted in vain for Gerald among the vast crowd of guests making their way to the maypole ceremony. She was not entirely surprised not to find him, since he had seemed to be making a determined bid to seduce Gertrude's lady's maid when she had last seen him. In the entrance hall, recognising Mr Harvey Bolland by whom she had been sitting at luncheon, she decided to join him. He had a young girl at his side who, from her likeness to Gertrude, could only be her younger sister Bluebell. Much as she disliked her own name, Belinda decided Bluebell was infinitely worse, particularly for a young girl so unlike that delicate flower.

Harvey promptly rose to his feet and swept off his extremely strange broad-brimmed American hat. Formality ended there. 'Afternoon, Belinda.'

Belinda, taken aback to be addressed by her Christian name on such short acquaintance, decided she rather liked it, but she could in no way let him know this. She therefore bowed, as a signal that she had given him permission for him to address her at all.

'Good afternoon, Miss Montfoy.' Bluebell, it seemed, had more sense of decorum.

Belinda tried hard to be easy and informal. 'Good afternoon, Miss Penny-father. Are you going to the maypole-raising ceremony?'

'We are that. Gertrude said we mustn't miss it.' Bluebell's eyes gleamed. She had a curious stare, but it occurred to Belinda this was less rudeness than short-sightedness.

'Do you like England, Bluebell?'

The girl considered the question. 'No.'

Belinda was surprised. 'Why ever not?'

'I don't want Gertrude to stay here. I think

this is a horrid place.'

Belinda took this affront to England personally. 'What's horrid about England?' she asked sharply.

'I guess we'd all like Gertrude to come back home,' Harvey answered wistfully.

'Perhaps not all England is horrid,' Bluebell conceded. 'Just this place.' She pointed to the woods, towards which they were walking, where magnificent English oaks had spread their leafy branches for hundreds of years. 'Don't you feel it?' she asked earnestly. 'You live here. When you walk in those woods, doesn't it seem kind of weird?'

Belinda thought of the glade by the folly, which as a child she'd called the faery glade. She loved it and she loved the woods. It had been their half-sensed link with the ancient world that had kindled her interest in times of long ago. That it should have resulted in Egyptian rather than British antiquity she had sometimes thought odd. But the more she learnt, the more she realised they were one and the same thing. But these were her private thoughts, and of the mind not her emotions.

'You wait until you see the maypole,' she replied heartily. Only afterwards did she recollect that Bluebell was at the age when she herself had been drawn to the woods. Didn't growing girls often have sensory powers that were denied to them in later years?

Auguste, guiltily remembering he was a happily married man, wondered whether he should be taking quite so much pleasure in the company of Eleonore, Comtesse de Balleville. His schedule allowed for this brief diversion from his kitchen duties, but he had hardly expected it to be as diverting as this.

'And, monsieur,' she said, as she took his arm, even without introduction, while they strolled round the gardens, 'are you a friend of dear Arthur's or of Gertrude's?'

A delicate matter. The position must be made clear at once. 'I am here as the chef, Comtesse.'

'The chef? But that is splendid.' To his amazement the arm stayed where it was. Most English ladies – and he had to admit most French ladies – would have fainted with shock. 'Much more *amusant* than stuffy courtiers and guests. And French too. Of course, how could the chef be other than French? Now you must tell me the secret of preparing *bergamottes de Nancy, tarte* à *l'oignon,* oh, and *pommes Normandes en Belle Vue.*'

Auguste was charmed. The countess's title sprang from Normandy, and so he would begin with the *pommes Normande*. Or was

70

that her husband's title?

'Your husband is here?' he asked cautiously.

'*Non*. He is a diplomat, and often away.' Eleonore's low husky voice managed to imbue this with great meaning. 'And you, Mr Chef, there is a Mrs Chef?'

'Oh yes. She too is away. Perhaps you have heard of her. She is the Princess Tatiana Maniovskaya.'

Eleonore stared at him. 'But indeed I have heard of her. I even met her when she lived in Paris. Then you must be Monsieur Auguste Didier, and by your marriage related to His Majesty.'

'I have that honour.' He tried to sound enthusiastic.

She laughed. 'My dear Monsieur Didier, I am delighted Gertrude invited me to her wedding celebrations. And would be even more if you would prepare a galantine of *cochon avec tarte de quetsches* for me.'

'They are out of season, Comtesse. *Un petit peu de l'eau de quetsches* perhaps.'

'Much better, Mr Didier. I see we shall be *close* friends.'

Bessie Wickman stood hand on hip, bosom well thrust out and leaning backwards to emphasise the fact. Artie, otherwise Arthur Lord Montfoy, should remember exactly what he had so lightly thrown away. She

71

watched the noble lord struggling in-
effectually with the maypole, having been
left alone to support it, while Bert and a
couple of young 'uns went off to dig the
hole. Once his lordship's physical ineptitude
had sent her wild with desire, now it
engendered contempt and great amusement
at the expense of that gullible American
wench. Not that she felt any the more
forgiving of Artie for her change of heart.
Indeed she was even more enraged that
such a nincompoop could ever have jilted
her. It was the way he did it, trying to brush
her off as though she were a fly on his
ermine collar. She might be a fly to him, but
she intended to be in his soup, not on his
collar. How dared he say he wouldn't insult
her by giving her money? Insult away, Artie,
she'd said. Even then he wouldn't cough up,
and for all he was supposed to be skint he
must have had a few bob left over from the
sale of the estate.

'You'll have to get more strength up than
that,' she jeered – softly in case Bert
overheard. She had a suspicion that he'd
guessed about her and Artie, but it didn't
concern her in the least. 'That's a fine
strapping lass you've to straddle Monday
night.'

Arthur Montfoy forgot his duty to the
maypole which overbalanced and crashed to
the ground. 'That lady, Mrs Wickman,' he

said, centuries of Montfoy haughtiness coming to his aid, 'is my future bride. The future lady of the manor.'

Bessie threw back her head and laughed. 'For a day only, Artie; she'll enjoy it no longer.'

Too late Arthur remembered that the title was no longer his to bestow. It had gone with the wind – or rather with the sale of the estate to old Thomas. Terrified, he also remembered belatedly what harm Bessie might do with the Pennyfathers still in blissful ignorance of this fact.

He grinned awkwardly. 'Bessie, in token of our former love, why don't I give you a little present?'

'Here, Artie?'' she cried in mock outrage.

He blushed. Bessie always was on the earthy side. He wondered how he could have been attracted to her, and decided that her more mature years meant he was the innocent party. He had been seduced, and was guiltless.

'Not *that*. A real gift,' he emphasised, racking his brains as to what this might be.

'When?'

'After I'm married.'

Bessie took the point immediately. 'Don't you trust me, Artie? You really don't know a lady when you meet one.' She thought rapidly. 'Very well, then. I'll meet you here by the maypole, after it's dark; eleven thirty

Monday night. I'm sure Gertrude can wait a little to receive your elfin charms. You might fancy a touch of your *droit de seigneur* first. Who knows, she might not let you near her.'

The maypole of fine English oak was swung into place by twelve good men and true, headed by the pending bridegroom. The latter was none too popular for dropping it in the mud, though as Alf Spade muttered, what else could you expect of a Montfoy? Its ropes and hoops for Monday's garland dance hung down from the top, and the pole was hauled upright with as much groaning as though Stonehenge were once more being erected. The seated chattering guests politely applauded, wondering why English village customs always seemed to take place in extremely chilly weather. The upper servants (standing), required to be present as this was a feudal ritual, applauded enthusiastically.

The landlord of the White Dragon bowed low before Lord Montfoy, sweeping off his humble cap. 'May it please your lordship to give your consent for the ceremonies of welcoming the spirit of the oak.'

'I give it freely, good fellow,' Arthur answered. Auguste hoped he could get more enthusiasm into his voice for his responses on Monday.

'Welcome, oak,' Bert bawled.

A small girl prodded by her mother advanced on the pole with a bunch of flowers, forgot what she was supposed to be doing and brought it back again. Bert hauled her to the pole once more, seized the bouquet and stuck it in the iron band provided. Everyone clapped, save the little girl who burst into tears.

A circle of twenty more little girls dressed in white joined hands and danced round the maypole to the accompaniment of a violin playing something which Auguste dimly recognised as 'Do y'ken John Peel', while an outer circle of men clad in smocks, corduroy trousers and straw hats, alternately waved their hats in the air at the maypole shouting 'Hail', and turned to club rounded bats against their neighbour's.

'Is this the English game of cricket?' Eleonore hissed at Auguste.

'Not dissimilar,' Auguste could not resist saying. He had never understood cricket.

'There's bat and trap later,' Bluebell informed them gloomily, overhearing. 'Gertrude told me about it. It's an old Kentish game. But there is a cricket match tomorrow afternoon, Comtesse.'

Cricket? No one had said anything to Auguste about cricket, and he had a shrewd suspicion this hadn't been mentioned to His Majesty either, or it would swiftly be off his agenda at least.

'Hail!' yelled the voices, crash went the bats, as the dance came to an end.

It was Aggie Potter's turn next, she who had so fervently blessed the Montfoys earlier that morning. Now she addressed the pole, raising her arms in the air, in a manner Macbeth's witches might have admired.

'Fairy folks are in old oaks,' she quavered, careful to make it loud enough to quaver to the back of her audience.

'Hail!' went the voices, crash went the bats, this time with the smocked gentlemen doing a tasteful twirl on the spot.

Oh mighty oak
Oh spirit green
We ask your welcome
For May Day's queen.

A pretty fair-haired girl whom Auguste had not seen before came forward and curtseyed to the pole.

Arthur smiled knowledgeably at his guests. 'One must observe these old customs. The oak was a sacred tree, of course, once upon a time; it possessed a living spirit, whose permission had to be sought before the oak is used in any way.'

'Then fairies do live in the oak?' Gertrude enquired.

'A fairy spirit. It has never emerged to my

76

knowledge.' Arthur laughed heartily.

Jacob Meadows then decided his moment had come. He hobbled to the centre, pushed Aggie out of the way, and doffed his hat to the maypole.

Farthings' lord be nobly crowned
When may doth pass the stone that's ground.

He turned round and performed the same courtesy to Arthur. 'You be coppicing in the old wood, I see, your lordship.'

'What of it?' Arthur asked cautiously, unaware of Entwhistle's current programme on the estate.

Jacob shook his head gravely. 'Bad spirits spring from the roots of the old oak, once 'tis coppiced.'

'I'll throw away the cheap whisky then,' his lordship jested.

''Tis no laughing matter, sir. He's listening.'

'Who?'

'Old Herne himself.'

'*Who?*' Arthur wondered vaguely which of his former ancient retainers this might be.

'Herne the Hunter, he who walks by night from the oak.'

'Another poacher, eh?' Gerald Montfoy shouted with laughter. Belinda pursed her lips, surprised to see him, but still register-

77

ing strong disapproval.

'Be quiet, Gerald. You see, darling,' Arthur turned warningly to Gertrude, 'they take these things very seriously.'

'Aye,' Jacob agreed. 'Old Herne don't like being stopped in his hunt. I heard his horn once. Never no more. I stop my ears. Beware the moonlight night, when old Herne comes forth from his oak, his stag's antlers on his head. The devil he is, so they do say, who do bring death to those who see 'im.'

'I thought Herne the Hunter only lived in the grounds of Windsor Castle,' observed Gertrude.

'Some do say,' agreed Jacob hastily. 'But others do say he abides in every oak. Even there.' He pointed to the maypole. 'There be a legend about old Herne and Frimhurst Old Herne, he be a lusty spirit, and he do walk in search of a bride from time to time. Jealous he is, so if there's to be a wedding at Farthing Court, the lord has to ask old Herne's permission on behalf of the bridegroom, whether it be he or one of his retainers, before–' Jacob paused delicately – 'the bridegroom can bed her.'

'O 'Ern,' must Farthings' lord cry, 'pray spare
'Your 'Orn to 'Ear my prayer.
'Let yon virgin and 'er groom
'Repair un'armed to their bedroom.'

78

'Bedroom? I thought in feudal times they were called–'

'You said Herne brought death to all who saw him just now.' Gertrude interrupted Louisa's puzzled comment, though not through annoyance on the part of the virgin concerned, but in the interests of accuracy. She liked her legends to be neat and tidy, and was less concerned about delicacy.

'That's when he's walking, miss,' Jacob informed her, annoyed at having his poetical pièce de résistance cut short. 'He'll be walking for sure now the old oak's coppiced.'

Seeing an opportunity, Aggie joined Jacob and pointed a quivering finger at the bridegroom.

Cut not the elder tree
Or Montfoy might shall turn to night.

'That's enough.' Arthur stood up angrily. 'You're frightening my bride.'

'No, they're not, Arthur,' Gertrude replied. 'I'm real interested.'

'You daft old besom,' hissed Bert in Aggie's ears. 'Put it right, or it's no more beer for you, see?'

Aggie lifted her arms in appeal to the pole, and twisted around to inform her audience of the results.

Neither oak nor elder care
When Montfoys wish their wood to share.

'That's better.' Arthur sat down, well pleased.

Late that night, his work finished for the evening, Auguste went for a stroll to get some air after the intensity of the kitchen heat. Heat from the ovens, of course, not from tempers. Everything was still gliding as smoothly as perfectly beaten cream. Fruit jellies had been laboriously pressed through tammy cloths, ices churned in freezing machines, roasts for the cold dishes sizzled in the ovens, and still no tempers lost. Surely it could not last? This was truly a chef's Tir Nan Og. Tomorrow it would all begin again. He was thoroughly enjoying being a servant again, while the rich folk danced the night away. Tomorrow His Majesty would arrive, in his motor car, together with his real host, Thomas Entwhistle. Perhaps that was the reason for the only slight cloud on the horizon; the pretence of having as apparent host, a man who had sold the estate three years earlier. Could it be that his Tir Nan Og, like this whole celebration, was a fairyland of make-believe?

Auguste shivered, and was suddenly aware that he was in the old wood, that the moon was out and that the night was indeed eerie. It was easy enough to imagine, in Shakespeare's words, each bush a bear; or rather the black dog; that was the fairies' demon animal, Jenny Potter had informed him. There was nothing to be heard but the faint scamper of some night animal, and the rustle of a leaf stirred by no human hand. If he listened harder would he hear faintly in the distance the sound of Herne's horn? Nonsense, he told himself. All he needed was a *petit cognac,* and to avoid stumbling on the uneven ground. He swung his lantern defiantly, and tried not to think that the twisted tree roots underneath his feet looked like the bones of the dead in the catacombs of Paris, stretching out towards the living who passed by. Fairies, he tried hard to remind himself, whether good or evil spirits, were mere superstition, twisted remnants of religions long forgotten. *Le Bon Seigneur* was his lantern, and He would guide him home.

His path led him past the main doors of the south front, and he was puzzled to see they had acquired a large flat stone with a hole in the centre propped up to one side. Once again, he felt, more might be going on in this house than he had been told, and uneasily he remembered His Majesty would be arriving tomorrow morning, and that Special Branch who supplied the King's detectives had refused to sanction Egbert Rose's attendance at the wedding in addition to themselves.

Outside the kitchen door he stumbled over a tray of grain, bread and cheese, and it took him a moment or two to think what this might be. Kindness to hedgehogs? They required milk, not bread. He picked up the dish and took it inside, in case it lay there by mistake. It was no mistake, for Jenny cried out in alarm when she saw the tray in his hand.

'Oh, Mr Didier, you haven't eaten any, have you?'

'I have not. Why?'

''Tis the fairies' food; they don't like humans stealing it.'

Nor do hedgehogs, he thought sleepily, as he tumbled into bed half an hour later. Or rats. If only Egbert were here! How he missed his pragmatic presence. No fairy would dare cause trouble with Egbert around. As it was...

By morning common sense was re-established. There was no more talk of fairies, and servants' breakfast was satisfyingly substantial. Being swung between the two kingdoms within this house, above and below stairs, had its compensations, he had to admit. Whether this would continue to be so with His Majesty about to arrive was a moot point, however. Much depended on Cousin Bertie's mood. Menus had hastily to be re-thought if His Majesty's face declared thunder in the air. On the other hand, a beaming serene countenance paved the way for a less 'safe' menu, which might win praise or condemnation. Auguste decided he would present himself with the welcoming group on the front steps in order to gain the earliest possible warning of danger. A crossing by Channel steamer which His Majesty would just have endured, did not bode well for the royal palate or temper.

'*Bonjour, Auguste.*' Eleonore, wrapped in furs against the spring chill, appeared at his side.

He bowed. '*Madame la comtesse, bonjour.*'

'Ah, Auguste. To you I am Eleonore.'

In the distance he could see the cavalcade of motor cars arriving, the second bearing the royal standard. The Daimler drew to a halt, the detectives sprang down from the car behind and in front, and came to stand by the king's car, the chauffeur opened the door, and His Majesty Edward VII, King and Emperor, stepped down.

He looked in a good mood, almost jovial, and Auguste began to relax. All was well, mutton chops could be relegated to 'standby' instead of 'pride of place'.

'Who is that with him?' Eleonore whispered.

He spoke, even as his eyes went to the slight man of medium height who had stepped down behind His Majesty, immaculate in striped trousers, morning coat and grey top hat... 'He must be Mr Thomas Entwhistle, lord of the manor.'

Eleonore noticed nothing wrong, but Auguste almost stumbled in horror at his own terrible mistake, a worse shock than he could ever have imagined. The true lord of the manor might be known by that name at Farthing Court. But to Auguste he was only too familiar under another.

It was Pyotr Gregorin, his would-be murderer.

Three

'My dear Auguste, are you quite well?' Eleonore looked concerned.

He was not. Somehow he had to escape, but how could he do so before His Majesty had passed them in the welcoming party? Even in his present state of dizziness it occurred to him one of the few advantages of his anomalous position as both guest and chef meant he could claim the excuse of returning to his kitchen. Nevertheless Auguste took a quick look to ensure His Majesty was well occupied with his usual task of assessing guests and their attire. Summoning as much suave courtesy as circumstances permitted, he murmured, 'If you will excuse me, Eleonore, I must attend to my whim-wham.' An eighteenth-century trifle was not the most tactful reason he had ever given for leaving a beautiful woman, but it could not be helped.

'Indeed?' Eleonore was amused. 'So, Auguste, when tonight your whim-wham is sufficiently prepared, we must ensure we meet again to enjoy it.'

Did she mean–? At any other time Auguste would have followed this distressingly interesting thought through, but not today. As Eleonore moved forward to be introduced by Lord Montfoy to His Majesty and then to Mr Entwhistle, he quietly melted away as imperceptibly and speedily as an ice block in summer.

Now the enormity of what he had just seen began to dawn on him. He longed for doubt to enter his head, but it did not come. It *was* Gregorin. A certain turn of the head, the sharp eyes, the lithe movement, the suppressed sense of energy. But what was Pyotr Gregorin, Tatiana's uncle, and a prominent member of the Tsar's secret service, the Okhrana, doing masquerading as one Thomas Entwhistle, English gentleman?

There was only one answer. It was a dark conspiracy to murder Auguste Didier, master chef. Gregorin had sworn to kill him, and had made several attempts already, but neither Auguste nor Egbert Rose at Scotland Yard had heard anything of him for three years – in England, at any rate. He was living quietly in Paris in the Russian quarter near the Parc Monceau, according to Tatiana, and his occupational (no doubt murderous) trips abroad all took him east, south and occasionally north. Never west. Now, Auguste was forced to realise that somehow for three years Gregorin had been building up an alias as Thomas Entwhistle in the green countryside of Kent. Why? The Okhrana, Auguste knew, was famed for its patience in waiting until the moment was ripe to strike. Panic gripped him. *He* was the overhung pheasant now ready for the plucking. He would never see Tatiana again, unless he left now, but if he did leave now His Majesty would no doubt join the conspiracy to murder him. He was caught, and the stew pot awaited him.

After a calming cup of vervain taken in the relative quiet of the servants' hall, his panic began to subside. He reasoned that it had been Horace Pennyfather who had asked him to provide the banquet, and he had understood that Mr Pennyfather had never met Thomas Entwhistle, since he was still under the happy delusion that his future son-in-law owned Farthing Court. Also Thomas Entwhistle's kitchen staff had not known Auguste's name until his arrival, which suggested that Entwhistle had not passed the name on to them, and might therefore – a tiny surge of hope – not have known of his presence.

The hope promptly vanished when Auguste remembered that there was a link between Horace Pennyfather and Thomas Entwhistle: His Majesty King Edward VII, Cousin Bertie. It could be a conspiracy between all three of them. Panic rose again, and then retreated a little. Auguste was well aware he was not popular with His Majesty for marrying Tatiana, but on reflection it seemed unlikely that his Britannic Majesty would stoop so far as murder to free Tatiana of the burden of her spouse.

Or would he? There was certainly precedent for it in English history.

'Will no one rid me of this turbulent cook?' Had Bertie in a royal passion, imitated his predecessor Henry II in demanding the removal of his archbishop Thomas à Becket, and had Messrs Pennyfather and Entwhistle proved only too happy to oblige in disposing of this unwanted chef?

Another cup of vervain tea dismissed this thesis but a second one, more stubborn than the last, replaced it. Had Gregorin planted the idea in His Majesty's mind that Auguste should cook the wedding banquet, and had His Majesty duly passed it on to Horace Pennyfather?

He had a third thought. Was this terrible picture all part of what he had thought of so recently as a paradise? Young Jenny, in the course of her unwanted instruction to him about fairyland, had referred to glamour, the enchantment the fairies cast over human eyes so that they should not see things as they really were. Perhaps he should get some four-leaf clover ointment which apparently was the only cure. A third cup of tea replaced the need for a hunt for four-leaf clover as yet another nightmare idea seized him. Surely His Majesty could not be aware that he was accepting the hospitality, not of the 'decent chap' he imagined Entwhistle to be, but a member of the Tsar's Okhrana? With the present inclination of the Tsar to fawn upon the Kaiser, rather than France and Britain, as a means of guaranteeing stability in Europe, which the present disastrous state of their war with Japan could not provide in Asia, Bertie would surely not be happy at this situation? The peaceable relations with France since the *entente cordiale,* so dear to Bertie's heart, would be seriously in danger. His Majesty, Auguste remembered, would now be at church, but when he returned Auguste decided he must see him immediately.

For once he found himself reluctant to resume work. The delights of flummery, of ortolans and galantines had receded (temporarily) at the terrible predicament he faced. He forced himself to concentrate on the glories before him, and slowly inched his way through the schedule of work. There was satisfaction in the pulping of cucumbers and peas through a colander; it took one's mind off less pleasant subjects like imminent death and moreover resulted in such delights as *Summer Soup Didier.*

Jenny had been commandeered by

Ethelred to prepare boiled macaroni with mustard and parmesan cheese for the servants' luncheon, a delicacy Auguste felt he could sacrifice in favour of the *fricandeau* of veal he had noticed Ethelred quietly removing from the entrees being set aside for the guests. When the time for the servants' dinner came, therefore, he was eager to join the upper servants in Pug's Parlour.

He was rapidly to change his mind. Against all unwritten tradition in the management of country houses, two minutes after he had arrived, Thomas Entwhistle came through the green baize door and actually entered Pug's Parlour.

Auguste froze. Mr Tudor was claiming his master's attention in order to introduce the hypnotised chef.

'Pray forgive this intrusion, Mr Didier.' Gregorin's courteous eyes looked into his. 'I could not, in the circumstances, speak to my staff anywhere but here, and indeed I must be gone rapidly for I understand that the visiting servants will be arriving at any moment.'

Auguste tried to reassure himself that even Gregorin could not murder him before approximately forty people – or could he? Gregorin was capable of anything; he was the cat that walked alone as in Mr Kipling's *Just So Stories*. Never had Auguste longed more for Egbert Rose's stalwart presence.

'I am honoured to meet such a distinguished chef,' Gregorin continued. 'Tudor tells me you are related to His Majesty. I had no idea or I would naturally have given special orders for your visit.'

Should he bow in grateful acknowledgement of such thoughtfulness, Auguste wondered? No, bowing would mean taking his eyes off Gregorin.

'I will explain to Lord Montfoy,' Entwhistle added the *coup de grâce*, 'and you will dine with us this evening.'

Of course! Gregorin was going to poison him!

'Alas,' Auguste managed to blurt out, 'in the interests of my work for tomorrow's banquet, that will not be possible. The spinach and almond blancmange–'

'I am quite sure His Majesty will expect precedence over a blancmange.'

Not by the slightest gesture was Gregorin displaying any sign of recognition. There was nothing to suggest he was other than a somewhat nondescript English country gentleman. But Gregorin's speciality was disguise, Auguste reminded himself. He could almost have believed that he'd been mistaken in thinking this Gregorin but for one thing: there was an invisible wall of cold around him that almost made Auguste physically step back. It was the cold of evil, and that he could not mistake. He sensed its smell like that of a bad rabbit stew.

He left, to Auguste's relief, just as the first of the visiting servants arrived, including some of His Majesty's whom Auguste recognised. 'Monsieur,' murmured Jeanne Planchet, promptly dropping Gregorin a deep curtsey. Even she, Auguste noticed, looked horrified to see such a break with tradition. Pug's Parlour, whether in England or France, was sacrosanct.

Auguste ate his way through several slices of *fricandeau* and a portion of bottled plum pie, as he mused over the best time to interrupt His Majesty. He glanced at the junior equerry deep in conversation with Ethelred, and wondered whether to consult him. No, he would choose his own time, and then go to the royal apartments and appeal to Gold Stick with whom he had always got on well. He would not go before His Majesty's luncheon, nor during coffee and brandy, but *before* the cricket match.

'Nonsense!'

Auguste's heart sank. His Majesty's usual Sunday luncheon of roast beef and Yorkshire pudding had been followed by cheese and a flummery of *Aphrodite's Paphos Temple*, but it seemed to have done little to mitigate His Majesty's testiness. This couldn't all be due to his presence, and Auguste could only ascribe it to news of the coming cricket match having just reached him.

'Look at him, Didier,' Bertie continued to bellow, 'he's *English*. Any idiot can see that.'

Auguste bravely held firm. Idiots could see Entwhistle's Jermyn Street shirts, they could see the Savile Row lounge suit, they could see the elegant monocle, but they were observing only the disguise Gregorin had adopted. It was the most clever disguise of all: his concentration on the playing of his part.

'I think you should mention it to your detectives, sir, just in case.'

'It's you he wants to murder, not me,' His Majesty pointed out, rather pleased with his wit. 'If you're right, Tom Entwhistle is a clever fellow. But you're not. I've just travelled from Calais with him, I've stayed with him in Paris, I shall do so again, his name is Thomas Entwhistle, and that's that.'

'But your detective Mr Sweeney will know that he's Gregorin. He's well known to Special Branch.'

'Have you been drinking, Didier? He *has* seen him. He's Thomas Entwhistle, not a paid assassin for blasted cousin Nicholas. Understand?'

Unconvinced, and leaving the preparation of the aspic in the sure hands of Ethelred Perkins, Auguste hurried to the village. He must telephone Egbert Rose immediately, but not from Farthing Court, since Gregorin might be listening, which would undoubtedly shorten Auguste's lifespan. His heart sank as he remembered it was Sunday and the post office would be closed. Where else would have a telephone? The rectory. Of course. Auguste flew up the drive of the sprawling red-brick rectory and rang the bell. The rector, he discovered, was an elderly gentleman who seemed extremely nervous at requests from strange gentlemen to use the new-fangled apparatus his bishop had insisted on his installing.

'All is going well, I trust?' the rector asked.

'Thank you,' Auguste answered automatically. 'All is nearly ready for tomorrow.'

'I don't like your coming to me.' The rector's voice grew querulous. 'I told them I'd have no official part in Mr Entwhistle's plans. They can do what they like, but I won't be involved.'

August retreated in horror. So the rector knew about the conspiracy to murder him too. He couldn't stay here, telephoning in front of one of Gregorin's confederates. He would have a dagger plunged into him at the very mention of Scotland Yard. Where else could he go? Nowhere in Frimhurst village, that was clear. They were all in Gregorin's pay. He was imprisoned at Farthing Court, and he must risk the house telephone while

Gregorin was at the cricket match.

Inspector Egbert Rose was not pleased to be interrupted in the course of his one Sunday off this month. He had indigestion, as he usually did after a luncheon that involved Mr Pinpole's meat, and a short sleep had seemed a fine idea. He listened grumpily while Auguste's voice waxed eloquent over the telephone.

'Gregorin in England? You've had an overdose of imagination.'

The line crackled. 'There is something wrong, Egbert. I know it, and His Majesty will take no notice.'

'Suppose Entwhistle is Gregorin, it's you he's after.' Although Rose believed in being practical, he regretted it when the torrent of words grew even faster.

'It can't be Gregorin, Auguste,' he finally managed to cut in. 'If he'd been coming into this country disguised as Thomas Ent--whistle or Alexander the Great for that matter, we'd have noticed.'

'He's a clever man, Egbert.'

'So am I.'

'Then listen to me. If Thomas Entwhistle is really Pyotr Gregorin of the Tsar's Okhrana, then not only I but His Majesty is in danger.'

'Gregorin won't assassinate him. The Tsar wouldn't sanction that.'

'There are other kinds of danger.'

A pause. Then, 'That's Special Branch territory, Auguste, and you've got them at Farthing Court already. What I will do is to get on to Chesnais at the Sûreté and ask him to check Gregorin's whereabouts this afternoon.'

'And if he is away, known to be in England?'

'I'll telegraph.'

'It's Sunday.'

'Farthing Court will have set up a telegraph office with the king there.'

Auguste hung the telephone apparatus up on its hook, only partly relieved. The Dizzy Duchess, listening through the slightly open door of the next room, was not at all relieved, but she was keenly interested.

His Majesty congratulated himself on showing forbearance towards his Cousin Tatiana's husband. It only went to show what happened when you let cooks into the family. He had a vague idea that this must be something to do with working in proximity to ovens – you flared up and boiled over from time to time. The day was bad enough as it was without being informed old Tom was some sort of Russian spy. He'd had enough rude shocks for one day. At luncheon he had broached the subject of this afternoon's recreation and Horace promptly began babbling about some cricket match. This, he was convinced, had not been on the agreed agenda. He'd never have come if so. Unfortunately a glance at the written agenda just before that cook insisted on seeing him revealed that he had misread cricket as croquet. That *was* a sport. He'd made more assignations during a game of croquet than W.G. Grace had scored in runs.

Unfortunately he now found himself sitting with Horace, Arthur and Gertrude in this so-called royal box – more like a blasted horse box in his opinion – watching not only a cricket match, but one which looked likely to score heavily over Lords in the boredom stakes, and that was saying something. Both sides, the Gentlemen of Frimhurst and the Players of Frimhurst were lined up for an opening ceremony in honour, not of him, but some fellow they called the Mighty Mynn. He was some cricketer or other who had been born locally, he gathered, and weighed eighteen stone. So much for sport keeping your weight down. He watched politely as both teams began to leap up and down to the sound of a fiddle, morris bells ringing madly and cricket bats clashing. This, he gathered, was a dance. Not to him. A dance involved holding a woman in your arms, even if it were only Alexandra. The performance ended with the players lined up and their bats making an arch. For one terrible moment, he thought he might be invited to run the gauntlet through it, but fortunately for their heads, which might otherwise have rolled, this did not seem part of the festivities.

Cricket, as played in Frimhurst was not an exciting event. Indeed even the players seemed to realise they were remarkably bad at the game and as anxious to get it over as His Majesty was himself. He had noticed a rather smart football pitch on the outskirts of the village, and wondered whether this had anything to do with the lack of enthusiasm shown by the players.

'I don't understand this game,' Horace declared, to the full sympathy of His Majesty. 'Why do these fellows keep moving about?'

'The field changes,' Arthur explained kindly.

'Looks the same to me.' Horace paused. 'Are you sure you're going to be happy here, Gertrude?'

'Of course, Father.' Gertrude laid her hand over her fiancé's. 'How could I not be happy as Arthur's wife and the Lady of Farthing Court?'

Arthur grinned self-consciously, for a moment forgetting that all too soon the clock would strike midnight on his masquerade, and Cinderella's rags would once again be revealed.

Not all the guests had obediently followed the bridal couple to the cricket field. Young Gerald had plans of his own, though he took some time to put them into operation since he could not find Jeanne Planchet anywhere. Surely she had not forgotten their assignation? He decided to take a risk, and visit the ladies' corridor at Farthing Court, since everyone should be safely at the match.

His daring was rewarded in finding Jeanne leaving Gertrude's room in somewhat abstracted mood. She did not even look surprised to see him, but merely said, 'Not today, monsieur.'

Gerald was indignant. 'Why not? Your mistress won't need you until it's time to change for tea.'

'I've had a shock.'

'What?' He was all concern, since usually this was the cause of immediate rapport.

She hesitated. 'I saw Lord Montfoy coming out of a lady's bedroom.'

Gerald laughed aloud. The old dog. Arthur must have more to him than he'd suspected. He wondered what use he could make of the information. 'Which room?'

'I don't know.'

Jeanne knew perfectly well but it didn't do to let too much information pass out of one's hands. Her memory would return

Gerald reasoned, and meanwhile he knew the surest remedy for girls' shock: the application of a strong dose of himself. His hand went round her waist. It was removed.

'*Non*, monsieur.'

'Maiden over.'

'Excuse me?' Harvey Bolland, miles away in a dream of making another fortune by industrialising the whole of Colorado with Gertrude at his side, jumped at this extraordinary statement. Was Bluebell making some youthful declaration?

'That's what it's called when no runs are scored.' Bluebell's face gleamed with satisfaction. She, at least, was enjoying this quaint archaic survival.

Harvey perceived that maidens had something to do with the extremely dull game in progress before them. In baseball the whole object was for something to happen, in cricket the object seemed to be that nothing should. Occasionally one of the fellows stirred himself to run up to the opposite wicket and then run back; or someone hanging around the field exerted himself to run after the ball, but much of the time they just strolled after it, or merely stood and watched it. He could make nothing of it, and decided that the rules stated that only if the king were in danger from a ball striking him on the head would someone make some effort to run to prevent his premature removal from the throne.

'I think there's something strange going on.'

'Sure is,' Harvey agreed gloomily. 'Beats me why the English get so excited about it.'

Bluebell cast him a scathing look, none too sure that Harvey was any advance on Arthur, save in his choice of domicile.

'At Farthing Court, I mean.'

'In what way?' Harvey's curiosity was at last aroused.

'Arthur doesn't seem to know his staff.'

Harvey was disappointed. 'That's England for you, honey.'

'And when do these village folks get any work done? They're always playing games.'

'It's a kind of holiday, I guess, when the lord of the manor gets married.'

'And what was Lord Montfoy doing coming out of another woman's bedroom?'

'*What?*'

'A maid told me.' Bluebell was greatly pleased at his reaction. 'I don't know which room, but she saw him come out and run down the ladies' stairs.'

'Say, Bluebell, find out, will you? And quickly. There's no time to lose.' Harvey's eyes lit up with the enthusiasm of a settler with his Newfoundland before him. His dream could well be on the way to fulfilment. He'd heard about the antics of the decadent English aristocracy, and now he knew his mission was to save Gertrude. Using any means at his disposal.

Jeanne Planchet had retreated to the bedroom she shared with two other ladies' maids, glad to find it empty. She needed time to think about the shocking discovery she had made. This house was not what it seemed, and it might hold dangerous problems for her. America loomed all the more enticingly. She had not been over-surprised to see Lord Montfoy coming out of a lady's bedroom, and it had not been that of his bride-to-be. These things happened. He had looked guilty too. Jeanne had seen too many men, startled in the midst of their misdeeds, to mistake it. She had no time for men now; she merely had to consider how to turn the menacing events of today to her advantage. Telling her lady's young sister and Mr Montfoy about Lord Montfoy's odd visit was a good start. But if America was to become a reality, she needed to take positive action in the field she most feared.

Auguste tried hard to devote himself to the finer points of cuisine, but for once his concentration flagged. One might feel passionately over the correctness of the precise proportions of foie gras to forcemeat in the stuffing for the specially imported snipe in *côtelettes de bécassines à la Souvaroff* but compared with the worry of whether one would still be in the world to hear His Majesty's appreciation of it, it was an irrelevant matter. Around him the kitchen rose to boiling point with excitement and subsided again, yet he found himself staring at the foundations of one of the *flancs*, to decorate one of the table corners, with unseeing eyes. He was a maypole in the midst of an unknown dance.

'The quails have not yet arrived!' Once, Ethelred Perkins' desperate shriek would have thrown him into panic. Now, it was one more minor hiccup.

'I'm sorry to hear that,' he heard himself saying.

Ethelred stared at him in amazement. 'His Majesty insists on them. You told me.'

Auguste forced himself to sound concerned. 'Of course, of course. But I will substitute ortolans and tell him they are a sign of good fortune.'

Ethelred, perplexed, cast him a look of deep suspicion.

His Majesty, in Auguste's view, needed good fortune. They both did, with Gregorin in the house.

'The jelly hasn't set, Mr Didier. It's the fairies.' Jenny pulled a long face.

'It is far more likely to be the temperature

103

in this kitchen,' Auguste pointed out. 'Or insufficient gelatine.'

Jenny's face remained doleful. 'The fairies tampered with the calf's foot. They're watching, you see.'

Jenny's future husband, Auguste sincerely hoped, would be a patient, long-suffering man. He had now discovered that the Potters came from a long line of witches. Most village wise women cried in the wilderness. Not the Potters. They intended to be heard at every opportunity. Whether the fairies were watching or not, they seemed unlikely to be powerful enough to avert the horror awaiting him this evening – dining at His Majesty's table with a man who had every intention of murdering him. Moreover, it meant that part of his schedule must be left to Ethelred and Jenny to carry out. What if the glorious Ethelred were in Gregorin's pay? What if the snipe were poisoned in his, Auguste's, absence? Was this part of Gregorin's plan for him or for His Majesty? Should he suggest a food taster for His Majesty?

The cuckoo in the kitchen clock flew out to mock him. Five o'clock. His Majesty would be returning crossly for his tea, normally provided an hour earlier. Hearing sounds outside, Auguste peered out of the window, unable to see anything because of the laurel hedge that divided the sordid working domain of the house from elegant view. He wondered whether it was beneath the dignity of a master chef to climb on a chair, decided it was, and ran through to the garden entrance on the far side of the green baize door.

He was relieved to see in the open Peugeot His Majesty, still alive, and moreover looking a much happier man than could be expected after enduring a cricket match. The reason was not far to seek. Sitting at his side was the Comtesse Eleonore. Her beauty and charm had the power of keeping the beam on His Majesty's face despite a bevy of village maidens running alongside the motor car. Each one of the latter was anxiously being assessed by the two Special Branch detectives lest she were an assassin in disguise. Fortunately none of them was, though their intent was not wholly innocent.

Bert Wickman had unwisely left this part of the arrangements to Bessie, Adelaide and Alf, being preoccupied with raising sufficient ghosts; he was fearful lest now squire was here, something might displease him, and the White Dragon would slip from his grasp.

'I'll do it,' Bessie had said complacently. 'After all, I do know the house.' And the summer house, she reflected, the folly, the

Dower House and on several occasions the old copse. She preferred a bed, but Artie had told her it was lucky in that copse. It hadn't proved so.

All Bert had approved was a few humble obeisances to His Majesty and heaps of flowers strewn before the house. Aggie Potter, sensing her opportunity for revenge upon the Montfoys, and aided and abetted by Bessie, had moved in on the ceremony. Six village maidens (officially) at Aggie's suggestion abandoned tiresome primroses, violets and anemones and instead cut armfuls of white may, which they happily waved gracefully at His Majesty as he beamed from the motor car.

Wisely, Bessie allowed His Majesty, against whom she had no quarrel, to enter his temporary domain in peace. As soon as he, his detectives, ushers, gentlemen ushers, Gold Stick and several equerries, had vanished to their allotted wing, Aggie pulled the bellrope on the main door, and looked approvingly at the holed flat stone which had now been moved to pride of place at the front entrance.

Mr Stuart Tudor gazed aghast at what he saw, and forgot his impeccable butler English. 'What the blazes are you doing here, Aggie Potter?' he hissed. 'You'll have the whole bloomin' Household Cavalry down here and us in the Tower.'

106

Aggie merely grinned at him, did a ritual totter, and beckoned to her team, who obediently chorused after her:

Rat tat, welcome we pray,
Cursed be him that bids us nay,
For we bring the happy may
To dress the bridal home hooray.

Mr Tudor, with three years' experience of Aggie, was highly doubtful of the provenance of this ancient rhyme, but since Mr Entwhistle's instructions were to let all village customs take their course, he reluctantly let them in. One old lady, one fine strapping woman and six comely wenches couldn't do much harm. He hoped not, anyway, for it was impossible to keep an eye on all of them as they gambolled around the entrance hall, poking branches of flowers on furniture, behind pictures of ancestral Montfoys and in the balustrade of the stairs. The hall looked pretty when they had done. Brightened it up a bit in Mr Tudor's opinion, and after all he was only doing his duty. He carefully counted them as he showed them out again. All eight obediently exited.

Opinions of their efforts varied greatly. Gertrude, descending for dinner in an unfashionably simply cut peach-coloured satin evening skirt and bodice which, without the flounces and frills so beloved of London Society, showed off her statuesque figure to best advantage, was delighted. Horace did not notice. Mrs Honey recoiled in horror, and promptly sought out Mr Tudor who, somewhat bewildered, explained the reason for its presence. Mrs Honey lost all her plump motherliness.

'What's Aggie Potter thinking of? She be fair crazed,' she shouted.

'Why's that, Mrs Honey?'

'Everyone knows white may in the house means bad luck. And what's that stone doing out in the porch?'

'It just arrived.' Mr Tudor grew uneasy. He had suddenly remembered old Jacob Meadows' rhyme: 'When may doth pass the stone that's ground...', and the mysterious stone that had appeared with a hole bored through its centre acquired an ominous significance. Mr Tudor did not believe in farisees (he had done too much stir for that) but he did believe in a sixth sense for trouble if it was heading for Stuart Tudor. And he had it now. Still, it was none of his business what happened. He was only the butler, following orders, and the rhyme had said nothing about butlers. Then he had a happy thought: the rhyme had surely begun, 'Farthings' lord be nobly crowned', and was intended for Lord Montfoy. Moreover, Jacob had implied it was good luck, not bad.

He voiced his happy thought.

'Cuckolded,' Mrs Honey declared succinctly in reply. 'That's what it means.'

Mr Tudor appeared shocked. 'Mrs Honey, it's his lordship's wedding day tomorrow. Surely the new Lady Montfoy would not be thinking of taking a lover? No, no, you have it wrong. It is a happy sign that the marriage will be crowned in triumph.'

'Cuckolded,' Mrs Honey repeated in gloomy satisfaction. 'You mark my words.'

There was one comforting thought for Auguste. He was to take Eleonore in to dinner and sit by her. She was looking particularly appealing this evening, shimmering in a dinner gown of pale-blue satin, diamonds gleaming at her throat and sparkling in her dark hair. His comfort did not last very long, as Mr Tudor came up to her with a murmured message. She turned to Auguste with a regretful, but delightful, moué of discontent.

'My dear Auguste, we are to be parted yet again. It seems His Majesty wishes to continue the conversation on Longchamp that we embarked upon this afternoon. I am to sit on one side of him, Gertrude on the other. I fear Mr Tudor is not pleased at this late change.'

Auguste was absolutely certain he would not be. All afternoon Mr Tudor had been busy in arranging the tables (suitably non-green to accommodate Gertrude's wishes), and a last minute change would greatly annoy him.

'Do be kind to Louisa, won't you, Auguste? She has been displaced, I fear.' A gurgle of laughter. 'And as for our *own* conversation, shall we say – *later?*'

He felt sorry for the duchess, relegated to sit by his side, when she was used to a far more exalted position, and was pleasantly flattered when, in between many swivels of the head, she displayed not only a deep knowledge of Paris, but a great interest in Tatiana and his connection with the Russian community. The rest of the time her head was turned to where His Majesty was engaging in spirited talk with Eleonore.

Auguste pitied Eleonore too. It was no easy matter to keep the king amused, let alone amusing him by encouraging him to do much of the talking. All the guests had reason to be grateful to her, for if the king did not talk, he finished each course the faster. When he had finished, everyone felt obliged to finish, and as he was a rapid eater, many were the times Auguste had seen the choicest morsels of sole, or soufflé, returned to the kitchen, followed by the anguished looks of diners, as their sad, desirous eyes followed the journey of the remains of the ambrosia still untasted on the plates.

He regretted the Dizzy Duchess's abstraction for, to his horror, Thomas Entwhistle was placed opposite him, and he, unlike the duchess, seemed disposed to chat.

'The comtesse is an attractive lady, is she not?'

'Yes, Mr Entwhistle. Have you met her in Paris?' This exchange of small talk with one's would-be murderer was quite ridiculous.

'We move in different circles, but I am acquainted with her and with her husband. I understand you too lived in Paris at one time.'

'Indeed, and my wife still maintains a home there.' As Gregorin knows full well, Auguste thought savagely.

'Might I enquire where?'

'In the rue Daru. And you, sir?' He knew all too well. By the Parc Monceau.

'Place Vendôme,' Entwhistle replied blandly. 'I trust I may have the pleasure of your calling upon me there?'

At last! Auguste rejoiced. There he had tripped him up. He would ask Egbert to check. There would be no home in the Place Vendome.

'Tell me, Mr Didier. What is your opinion of English versus French cheeses? These English cheeses are admirable. I have a particular...' Entwhistle stopped for a moment before continuing smoothly, but it was enough. Auguste shivered, as confirmation joined conviction. Gregorin unusually had made a mistake, and realised it, for English cheese had brought them face to face for the first time in Yorkshire. Just for an instant the disguise had slipped. It was Gregorin.

How he longed to be back in the comparative safety of the kitchen, yet later that evening, he was still a prisoner. The only good news was a whispered message from Mr Tudor that the quail had arrived. He made them sound like honoured guests. Auguste looked round the gathering, His Majesty was playing bridge with Eleonore as his enforced partner, and ladies and gentlemen conversed in small groups around this elegant drawing room. He was immensely bored and, unable to leave until His Majesty had retired, longed for something to break the monotony. His wish was dramatically granted.

The door was thrown open and Mr Tudor, bereft of words, ushered in Bert Wickman, who appeared to have taken up farming. His corduroy trousers were tied round with string, an old-fashioned smock and a cap adorned his upper half, the latter being swiftly removed. Small pieces of straw, sticking out wherever possible, completed his ensemble.

'Beg pardon, but it's happened, your lordship,' he groaned. 'I thought you ought to know.' There was a long pause.

'And what's that, my good man?' Lord Arthur belatedly remembered he was lord of the manor again today.

''Tis the battle, sir. Once every ten years they do come.' Bert raised his voice, determined no one should miss that. 'The smugglers.'

'Call the police,' Richard Waites suggested practically.

'No sir, 'tis ghosts. Can't arrest 'em.'

'*Ghosts*?' Belinda repeated, very interested.

'They won't do outsiders no harm,' Bert explained hastily. 'Anyone can watch,' he suggested. 'The old Preventive do catch up with them old smugglers, that's the Hawkhurst gang o' course. Villains down that way, they are.'

'And what happens in this battle?' Gertrude demanded.

'Well, madam,' Bert was only too eager to tell her. ''Tis said, the smugglers rolled all the barrels out of sight. Only one were forgotten and the Preventive found it. It were prize brandy and so it were fought over.'

'With guns?' shrieked Louisa, swaying dizzily on her feet as if to swoon, in the hope His Majesty would support her. He didn't.

'Oh no.' Guns, even ghostly ones, would not find favour with Special Branch, Bert

113

had realised. ''Tis a rare sight, though.'

'Do let's go, Arthur.' Gertrude issued it as a command, not a request.

Mindful of etiquette, Arthur consulted his principal guest.

'My partner's feet are scarcely shod for ghost watching,' His Majesty replied good-humouredly, seeing an excellent chance for a tête-à-tête. He knew all about Eleonore's footwear from explorations under the table with his own. 'I've no objections to you all going though,' he declared firmly. 'Better take my detectives with you too. You never know these days. Assassins disguise themselves as all sorts of things, eh, Didier? Even ghosts.'

Auguste managed to laugh, conscious of Gregorin nearby.

'Come, Arthur,' Gertrude cried in excitement. 'You never know, perhaps we'll find all those missing barrels.'

'Them old smugglers,' Bert put in hastily, 'rolled all them old barrels into the lake, and there, for all I know, they still do lie.'

Arthur saw an opportunity to play St George. 'I'll see you're in no danger, Gertrude. Tudor, organise some lanterns and candles, will you?'

'Do hurry,' Gertrude cried, 'or they may be gone!'

'I doubt that, madam,' Bert assured her.

Once outside, Gertrude, declaring it was

bad luck to hold her fiancé's arm the day before their wedding, elected Auguste as a substitute. He was glad, for it took his mind off the uncomfortable facts that Gregorin was behind him, and the night was very dark. Ghosts in front were preferable to Gregorin behind, and the statistics of murder by ghost were comfortingly non-existent.

The party included Louisa, who reluctantly abandoned His Majesty to Eleonore – since she had no choice – and clung in compensation to Horace's arm. Bert led them all to the edge of the copse from where, emanating out of the more thickly wooded area, oddly muffled and withdrawn sounds could be heard. Auguste's neck suddenly felt vulnerable not only from behind but with prickles of sudden fear lest he had underestimated what lay in front.

''Tis best not to go nearer,' Bert whispered hoarsely to his flock, 'or they do vanish.'

Gertrude's clutch on Auguste's arm suddenly intensified and she failed to restrain a yelp as ghastly glowing figures could indeed be seen flitting to and fro in the trees. Every so often a mournful remote, 'Avant ye knaves', could be heard, or 'have at thee, then, scurvy rascals'. Had it not been for the events of the last twenty-four hours, Auguste would not have believed any of it (he told himself). As it was, 'Do you

115

think they are real, Miss Pennyfather?' he asked cautiously.

'What is real, Mr Didier?'

This philosophical concept brought their conversation to an end. Auguste listened to the squeals of the rest of the party, praying for silence. In such a hullabaloo Gregorin could slip a dagger between his shoulder blades at any moment with impunity. His cries would not be heard. Finally, he could stand it no longer.

'At midnight,' Bert shouted, 'it do stop.'

No doubt, but Auguste was going *now*. He relinquished Gertrude to Richard Waites, and murmuring about seeing to the ices turned to slip thankfully away. He found himself face to face with Gregorin, who looked as shocked as he felt.

'My dear Didier, do forgive me. I mistook you for Arthur Montfoy.'

Auguste murmured something, slipped past him and broke into a run towards the security of the kitchens. Had he not from behind have resembled Lord Montfoy and been with Gertrude, he would now be dead. Of that, he was sure.

In the kitchens, surrounded by stalwart normality, he worked on, gradually calming down – until Mr Tudor came in, roused from his bed. 'A telephone call for you,' he snarled. His voice was having a hard job maintaining perfect butlerdom.

That it was Tatiana was Auguste's first thought, but it was not. It was Egbert Rose, and he was laughing. 'You can have a good night's sleep, Auguste. Entwhistle is away, but lives in the Place Vendôme. Gregorin is safely in Paris, tucked up in his home in the Avenue Vandyck. Chesnais has seen him.'

Glamour! Jenny had been right: the fairies could cast a spell over human eyes to make them blind to their mischievous activities. Auguste sank down on the silken white counterpane of his bed, hastily added by Mrs Honey after the revelation of his exalted status. He must indeed have been subjected to some kind of spell, if so much could deceive his normally sharp perceptions. If only Egbert were here ... someone to *talk* to. He remembered Eleonore and then her invitation. There was little doubt about its meaning, he was forced to admit. He was a married man, said horrified conscience. Yes, but just to *talk* could do no harm, snapped reason. But what if Eleonore had more in mind than a midnight chat, wailed conscience. The king's life and welfare must come first, decreed reason. And his own, it added. Reason immediately won, and pointed out that as tomorrow (or by now today) was the wedding day, Auguste should go *now*. He had no choice. His halo firmly wedged in place, he crept down the servants' staircase to the corridor leading to the lady guests' rooms.

Reason congratulated him on his decision as he saw the plate of sandwiches outside Eleonore's room, a signal familiar to him from his days at Stockbery Towers. His hand went to the door to knock very gently before entering. Something made him glance down. Surely not? Were his eyes deceiving him? A *bone* was coyly emerging from the quail filling of the sandwiches. A *bone?* From a kitchen that was temporarily under his control? The focus of attention in Auguste's body promptly shifted from his lower to his upper regions as he reeled in horror. This must be checked immediately. He picked up the plate, and hurried back the way he had come. It would take but five minutes. His conscience breathed a sigh of relief. It had been a narrow escape.

It had indeed. As Auguste turned left towards the servants' stairs, he was aware of a candle advancing from the right, towards the corridor he had just left. Quickly, he stepped into an alcove, occupied by half a Greek torso, until the coast was clear once more. The night's horrors were not yet over. Turning the corner was a familiar portly figure who had obviously escaped from his two detectives.

Auguste looked desolately at the plate of sandwiches in his hand. They had been for

Cousin Bertie and not for him. A mixture of emotions seized him, jealousy, relief, annoyance – and considerable trepidation as to what would happen when His Majesty failed to find his signal awaiting him. Just as he was about to make a rush for the servants' staircase, he realised someone was following His Majesty. A candle was zig-zagging along the corridor. He froze. A detective? If so, how could he explain his own presence? As the figure turned the corner, he relaxed, however. It was a woman, clad in a flowing house coat, hair down her back. It took him a moment or two to recognise the Dizzy Duchess in pursuit of her lost love.

The ramifications of this novel twist were too great to contemplate. Auguste ran for the stairs, sandwiches clutched safely to him. Losing all interest in bones, he found himself in the safety of his own room, still with the sandwiches. And there they stayed, as he dived for his bed. With the covers over his head, the horrors of the day and the fears for tomorrow might be forgotten in sleep.

But sleep was some time coming. Below his window, the haunting sound of 'Green-sleeves' being sung and played outside the bride's room beneath, drifted up to him. Bert Wickman, dressed in wrinkly green tights, doublet and Robin Hood hat, was doing his best.

Four

'Dabbling party this way, if you please.' A bleary-eyed Stuart Tudor, unaccustomed to having to adopt his perfect butler's manner at dawn on a May morning, sounded more like a lift attendant in Whiteley's store. The party obediently followed him to the bootroom, where the lampboy had laid out an assortment of wellington boots, galoshes and heavy mackintoshes to protect the ladies from the dire effects of dew.

'What are these for?' Gertrude, leader of the party, was as bright-eyed at four-fifteen in the morning as at midnight.

'The fields are wet at dawn, miss.'

'That is the purpose of dabbling,' she explained briskly. 'I can't dabble in wellington boots. One has to dance barefoot.'

Mr Tudor had never danced barefoot himself but if Americans wanted to do it, let them. He said no more.

The party in fact was very small, consisting merely of Gertrude, her maid (unwillingly) and Bluebell, the latter still in search of any last-minute inspiration that might prevent this marriage. The scorned galoshes were, however, reluctantly donned,

121

as even Gertrude did not relish the prospect of strolling barefoot in the dark over the Farthing Court gravel and gardens to the allotted dabbling ground in the Great Meadow. Just as they were leaving, escorted by Mr Tudor and the lampboy bearing lanterns, there was a last minute addition to the party. Richard arrived, clad in plus fours, long socks and Norfolk jacket.

'What are you doing here, Richard?' Gertrude was annoyed.

'I've come to dabble.'

'You know very well that won't do. You're a man.'

'Observer?'

'No, Richard.'

'Do let him come, Gertrude,' Bluebell pleaded, spotting an ally. 'I'm sure it's not bad luck if gentlemen come too.'

Gertrude hesitated. 'But Arthur–'

'Bad luck for the groom to see the bride before the wedding,' Richard cut in quickly.

She surrendered. 'Very well. But you are to take it *seriously*, Richard.'

'Of course.'

In the meadow, Bessie Wickman was shivering with her party of dabbling village maidens, who were painstakingly sprucing up the fairy rings they'd planted yesterday. Dew there was in plenty. Bert, who had never known Bessie get up before nine o'clock, in their long married life, promptly regretted having assigned the ceremony to his wife, and the morning had begun with an argument, in which Bessie had pointed out that she rarely presented her person to her many lovers in wet fields at dawn and that therefore Bert had no cause for concern.

Her black hair streamed down her back; a bright kerchief and shawl surrounded her neck, and a red petticoat peeped from under her black skirt. She flattered herself she looked an attractive village maiden, and summed up Richard Waites' potential with some enthusiasm. However, immediately sensing that Richard's interest was in Gertrude, and almost as quickly deciding that the sudden scowl on the girl's face was caused by it, she set herself out to charm madam's little sister. An idea occurred to her, and she was glad she had taken the trouble to acquaint herself with Jacob's full repertoire of new Frimhurst legends.

Although it was growing lighter, the sun was showing no signs at all of bursting forth as it should surely do on an English May Day, and it was decidedly chilly, Gertrude refused to regret the scorned mackintoshes, and bravely followed suit when the village maidens began to remove their footwear to reveal an assortment of rather unattractive knobbly feet. Glad she had had the sense not to wear stockings, she tried to ignore

Richard's presence. 'Hurry, Bluebell.'

Her sister gingerly began to roll down her stockings.

'You shouldn't be here, Richard. I'm sure it's bad luck, isn't it, Bessie?'

'Not that I've heard, ma'am.'

Bluebell decided to change allies. She had liked Richard when she first met him, but now he might prove a problem. Even if the wedding could miraculously still be called off, it appeared all too likely that Gertrude would remain in England, and probably with Mr Waites. Harvey Bolland, Bluebell concluded, was no competition. Bother these Englishmen. Perhaps the best thing would be for Gertrude to marry Lord Arthur, and then decide she preferred to live in America. But how was this to be achieved? With Farthing Court to live in in England, she'd never come back home.

'Go on,' urged Richard, as Gertrude hesitated to join the village maidens, now holding hands and dancing in a circle. 'Dabble.'

Gertrude cast him a scathing look and broke into the circle, hauling Bluebell after her.

'Drop hands and dabble, ladies,' Bessie trilled. 'Hold your skirts up, madam.'

Sneaking a look at her neighbours to see how high 'up' implied, Gertrude, doing her best to forget Richard's presence, lifted her skirts above her ankles, and found the experience rather enjoyable.

'Mind the worms,' Richard called.

Gertrude lifted her head higher and stamped even more energetically.

'Now, hold hands again, ladies,' came Bessie's dulcet tones. ''Tis time for our wishes.'

'For what?' Bluebell asked.

'For future husbands.'

Bluebell shut her eyes and imagined a gentleman called Percival who would gallop out of the mists like Sir Lancelot in her book of stories of King Arthur and wouldn't even notice that she wore spectacles and had one or two spots. Gertrude tried hard to think of Arthur.

Bessie ducked into the centre of the circle and proclaimed solemnly:

Blessed be the bride that treads underfoot
The buttercup and daisy root,
Cursed be he whom old Herne holds fast
The bride must weep till the night be past.

'What does that mean?' Gertrude asked sharply.

'Who knows, miss?' Bessie looked mysterious. 'The meaning's lost in the mists since time out of mind. But I reckon it has something to do with Jacob's story, don't you? If there be a wedding at Farthing

Court, the lord of the manor must go to ask Herne's permission before the two are bedded.'

Gertrude said nothing, but observing her suddenly white face, Richard came up to her, and took her arm. 'Does that mean I should tell Arthur to go to seek Herne's permission? He's both bridegroom *and* lord of the manor.'

The muscles in Richard's face struggled to retain his usual imperturbability and not the spasm of jealousy that forced itself on him so suddenly and ferociously.

Bessie shook her head gravely.

'It means *nothing*, Gertrude, it's just gibberish.' He sincerely hoped it was, but he didn't like that smirk on that woman's face as she recited her drivel.

'Perhaps I should go too?' Gertrude was still worried.

'Have you had breakfast?' was all he replied, as he walked with her back to the house.

'Of course not.'

'Then let us hammer on the green baize door and insist on sustenance; it is by far the best remedy to make fairies disappear and turn legends into mere stories.'

Ahead of them, Richard noticed Bluebell walking with Bessie, with whom she seemed to be in earnest discussion. He had the impression that Bluebell was as eager for this

126

wedding to be called off as he was. But what could one young girl and one village woman achieve? Nothing, unfortunately, despite all the spells and rhymes in the witches' calendar. Or could they? For all the practical common sense that kept his feet on the ground in London, here in the country, he was beginning to sense there were forces at work that might metaphorically be sending him flying through the air with the ease of a Peter Pan in Mr J.M. Barrie's new play.

Most of the ladies chose to breakfast in their rooms, in order to conserve their strength for the vast ordeal ahead of them: dressing in a suitable fashion to be viewed (if one were lucky) by His Majesty. This tended to be an energetic process, from being strung into one's corsets to having one's hair tweaked painfully into submission for reception of one's hat, and dabbling in the dew was not part of it. Two of the few ladies who decided otherwise, and chose to appear at breakfast were Eleonore and Louisa.

The duchess, Eleonore could not help noticing, looked extremely smug. Eleonore was mystified as to the reason her own plans for the preceding night had gone awry. The plate of sandwiches had most certainly been placed there, and had then disappeared. Why had it been taken away and by whom? Or had the plate languished there until a housemaid removed it early this morning because no one had accepted her invitation? No, Eleonore could not believe that. She was not a vain woman, but she knew her own strengths and powers of attraction. She looked at the duchess more carefully. Those flushed cheeks suggested guilt, and, what's more, a delightful night. Why guilt? There could only be one reason. Her Grace had acted most disgracefully, ignoring all the rules of polite behaviour, and removed the plate of sandwiches herself. Not from hunger, but from jealousy. She looked at the duchess's face, which boasted fifteen more years of life than Eleonore's, and tried to feel sorry for her. She failed. She was still furious, and something must be done.

She smiled sweetly as she helped herself to kedgeree. 'I am so looking forward to the ball this evening, aren't you, Your Grace?'

'Indeed I am. What more delightful than to circle in the arms of a gallant and noble gentleman.'

'I understood your husband died tragically some years ago.'

The duchess paused. 'You are right, Comtesse. You, too I understand, have no husband.'

'You are misinformed, I am glad to say. Alas, we are frequently parted when his work takes him from me.'

'I imagine he encourages you to find your

own amusements.'

Eleonore smiled. 'We are a most devoted couple. He can at all times have faith in me. So important, don't you think?'

'Indeed. As His Majesty himself commented when he urged me to accompany him to the wedding today since we both are without our dear spouses.' Louisa was wasting no time in letting everyone know that her hour of glory was about to dawn again.

Eleonore continued to smile. 'What a charming sentiment. Pray, do let us take coffee together this morning, Your Grace. I should so value your opinion of my gown.'

Belinda too had taken her breakfast in the breakfast room, but she was not thinking about the coming wedding, but of Thomas Entwhistle. He should know immediately of the outrageous discovery she had just made in her chamber. She cornered her host in the morning room after breakfast, quietly perusing his copy of *The Times*.

'Belinda?' Entwhistle rose to his feet, dropping the paper, for once in most disorderly fashion, through surprise. He was not pleased. First, he had heard some disturbing information, and secondly his aim was to remain completely anonymous in this household and to be singled out by a Montfoy was annoying.

'This is your house,' Belinda continued tartly, reading his expression correctly, 'and you and not Arthur would wish to be responsible, I trust, for what happens within it.'

'To a degree.'

'This, Thomas, comes within that degree. Someone has removed the Montfoy diamonds from my room. My maid has been with me many years and is above suspicion. Can you say the same of your staff?'

Entwhistle thought quickly. If that crook Tudor had been pilfering... No, he could not imagine he'd had the nerve, in view of what he paid him. 'I thought that I could,' he replied quietly.

'Or it may have been one of the guests,' Belinda said.

This was getting serious. 'Let us be quite sure they are not merely mislaid, Belinda. And then, could I suggest that we leave this unpleasant matter until after His Majesty has departed tomorrow? There is, after all, a wedding today, which I am sure you would not wish marred by the presence of police or indeed even by enquiries of this delicate nature.'

'Very well, Thomas, but then I shall insist on a full investigation.'

'Of course.' Entwhistle looked concerned, as indeed he was. 'We will see what has transpired, Belinda. And incidentally, I do trust you will give me the honour of escorting you to the wedding.'

There had once been a time when Belinda had thought how convenient, and indeed pleasant, it would be if she and Thomas could marry. It would seem a just step on the part of fate. Arthur's squandering of the Montfoy money (still unknown to Gerald) had been no fault of hers, and fate surely owed her something in recompense. However, delightful companion though Thomas was, their relationship had never grown closer. At first she had put this down to the fact that he lived abroad. This explained his occasional old-fashioned way of speech and his accent being almost too reminiscent of the era of the late queen; it might also mean his affections lay with another in France. However, by now she had come to the reluctant conclusion that he was one of those Englishmen who was simply not interested in ladies. Now, with this sudden warmth, she began to reconsider her verdict.

In the kitchens, the absence of the sun on this May Day morn was not noticed. There was heat enough from the huge ovens which had been hard at work since four in the morning. Auguste muttered a despairing prayer to *Le Bon Seigneur* since undoubtedly wedding banquets tasted better in the sun, but though the sun teetered on the point of emerging, it coyly refused to do so completely. The banquet, Auguste informed the sun, was not until two o'clock, and if it would kindly arrange to emerge by then he would be most grateful. Dancing round the maypole, which would follow the luncheon, was not so enjoyable in the rain.

Meanwhile, everything worked with precision in Mr Ethelred Perkins' kitchen under Auguste's direction – though he was forced to admit it would have worked as well under Mr Perkins'. One maid had been appointed simply to announce the deliveries shooting rapidly and continuously through the door: 'Two dozen turbot, fifty lobsters, eighteen salmon, two dozen halibut, twenty watercresses, ten bunches of chives, churn of cream...' Her voice was already hoarse but she was more efficient than most liveried toastmasters, relishing her moment of glory as kitchen staff hurried and scurried to her every announcement. Auguste worked with all the concentration he could muster, much relieved that he was not expected to attend the wedding. The greater the distance between himself and Gregorin, the better.

The best of English and French – his proud eye told him he had achieved this. The obligatory *poularde à la Derby* stuffed with truffles and foie gras (for His Majesty), bisque of prawn, *consommé Comtesse Eleonore* (his own invention) garnished with stuffed lettuce and *quenelles de volaille,* side by side with simple, colourful plates of asparagus, lobster salad, duck in aspic and egg and cucumber salad. And many, delightfully many more, both hot and cold dishes.

Auguste remained firmly on the servants' side of the baize door, but all the same each visit to a remote larder represented an act of courage. Checking the refrigerators brought the fear of being thrust within their heavy iron doors by Gregorin, each game room of being hung like a pheasant on one of those huge hooks.

There was one other unpleasant task he had to perform. His Majesty's breakfast still had to be presented to him. Auguste told himself he had nothing to fear; that incriminating plate of sandwiches had long since been cast into the cellar boiler. His Majesty could not possibly know of Auguste's involvement, and so the only remaining question was His Majesty's mood: was he furious at the thwarting of his night's plans, or happy in their resulting fulfilment with his former mistress? The arrival of His Majesty's breakfast was no simple matter. It was some way from the kitchens, involving a series of chafing dishes in a specially equipped service area next to his dining room. It also involved inspection by His Majesty's detectives, equerries, aides and valets, not to mention Gold Stick. Finally, he found himself alone with His Majesty, and the royal kidneys had been served and approved. Auguste studied the mood carefully: a certain abstraction maybe, but no rage could be discerned. He therefore decided on a bold move.

'Your Majesty enjoyed last evening's supper?'

'I did. You've got the *bécassines* for the wedding breakfast, I trust?'

'Yes, sir.' Auguste relaxed. All seemed well, and he awaited his dismissal from the Presence hopefully. He did not get it.

'You've met the Comtesse Eleonore, haven't you?'

'I have, sir.' Auguste trembled.

'Ah. Rum woman. I've asked the Duchess of Wessex if I can have the pleasure of escorting her at the wedding.'

So that was it. His Majesty had decided no French countess was going to make a fool of him. Auguste rejoiced. Eleonore would once more be available as his confidante. And *nothing* else, he assured his conscience firmly.

At eleven thirty the bridegroom left with his best man (if Cousin Gerald deserved the adjective best) for the wedding that was to solve all his problems. He was remarkably cheerful.

'What are you going to do with all that money, Arthur?' Young Gerald asked nonchalantly. 'I've one or two ideas that might help.' After his cousin was safely married to Miss Dollars-in-Plenty.

Arthur was never one for picking up hints. 'I fancy the gee-gees,' he announced cheerfully. 'And I'll buy a house.'

'A *house*?' Gerald was taken aback. 'Farthing Court not big enough for you?'

Arthur perceived he had made a mistake. 'Town house,' he amended hastily.

'You've got one.'

'Another one.'

'Ah.' Gerald said no more, but he sensed a mystery, and it was his experience that where there was mystery there might be money.

At twenty minutes to twelve His Majesty descended the staircase, silk top-hatted, frock-coated, pearl-grey waistcoated, and cane in hand. The assembled party bowed or curtseyed, and a small girl presented him with his buttonhole. The king nevertheless was deeply displeased. Louisa had not yet arrived. On the other hand, the Comtesse Eleonore, looking more winning than ever in a delightful lemon-yellow gown and matching muslin-swathed hat, curtseyed deeply, and stood demurely by, awaiting the party's departure. The king disliked un-

135

punctuality; it reminded him too much of Alexandra. Of all people, Louisa should know *that* after all these years. As he advanced towards Eleonore, however, he heard a commotion behind him; frowning, he looked round to see a distraught Louisa rushing down the stairs, and all eyes turned to her in astonishment. She too was immaculately dressed in pale-yellow silk – save for her head on which a housemaid's mob cap rested.

'Forgive me, Your Majesty. A domestic accident,' she babbled. 'My hats have been stolen.'

Apart from unpunctuality, if there was one thing His Majesty could not tolerate, it was a woman improperly dressed. 'Madam.' He bowed formally to the duchess, then turned to the Comtesse and took her arm. Mightily surprised that her own methods of ensuring this happy outcome had been unnecessary, Eleonore took her place at the King's side, comforting her conscience that the senna pods in Her Grace's coffee could now work their wicked will without undue embarrassment to the duchess.

Desolate, Louisa returned to her room, and met Auguste on the way – not entirely by accident on his part. 'It isn't fair,' she blurted out.

'What is wrong, Your Grace?'

'Every single hat,' she moaned. 'The big

one with the roses, the dear little cloche, the straw – all thirty hats *vanished*. Even the black one for mourning. It's that woman,' she confided. 'It must be. She didn't want to entertain His Majesty herself, but can't bear the thought that I did, so she stole my hats.'

'How could she do that, Madam?'

But to this there was no answer, as a glazed look came over Louisa's face, and without her usual merry laugh she hurried – almost ran – on her way.

'Vous êtes très belle, madame.'

In the bride's room Jeanne Planchet sent her lady to meet her destiny, with fewer cares in the world. This morning had been arduous, with the bride's aunt, the bride's sister, a duchess or two and several other guests all volunteering their unprofessional services. For some inexplicable reason, something blue had had to be provided, something old and something new – the latter, in mademoiselle's fortunate case, had proved no problem.

Mademoiselle Gertrude had said little. Nerves, thought Jeanne uninterestedly, much more intent on her own good fortune. She admitted her mistress made a lovely bride, and in her own miraculously restored good humour she devoted her best efforts to Mademoiselle Gertrude's hair. After all, it wouldn't be for much longer.

This morning Jeanne, too, had seized the opportunity for *un petit mot* with Mr Entwhistle, whom she had been most surprised to find at Farthing Court. She had quite calmly informed him that she could ruin this wedding if she were to speak of what she knew, and she was hardly surprised to find he agreed with her. What was it worth to him for her to say nothing? She suggested it would be quite a lot, and was hardly surprised to find he agreed with her again. The sum was easily enough to pay her passage to America, without Mademoiselle Gertrude, and what was all the more pleasant is that it had been instantly forthcoming and was already tucked inside her stays in crisp English twenty-pound notes. Revenge was very sweet.

At ten to twelve the bride descended the staircase and took her father's arm. Gertrude reminded herself that she had made her decision and Pennyfathers never changed their minds. She couldn't let poor Arthur down now; Farthing Court was crying out for a mistress, and the village of Frimhurst for a lady of the manor, even if she did intend to spend most of her time in parliament once she had won the vote for women.

They proceeded through the open doors, and she walked to the open carriage over a footpath of flowers strewn by village maidens. She had wanted to walk the whole way, but since the church was inconveniently nearly a mile away she had reluctantly changed her mind. At the church Bluebell, in a frock of the same colour as her name, would be waiting for her to perform her duties as bridesmaid, and His Majesty would have taken his place in the front pew. Not to mention three hundred or so guests who had made their way both from the railway station today and from the house this morning. Her path in life was set, and it would be as sunny, she vowed, as these lucky flowers portended. As if to reassure her, the sun at last emerged. Gertrude managed to smile. Marriage to Richard, she told herself, would have been very dull, and her fears over Arthur were merely last minute nerves to which all brides were entitled, even American ones, who knew exactly where lay their path through life.

Auguste flew round the kitchen with the ease of the daring young man on the flying trapeze. Never had his preparations for such a large wedding breakfast gone so easily. Aspics slid from moulds, *côtelettes de mouton glacé* glistened, stuffings remained obediently inside their hosts, instead of taking every opportunity of escape to the outer world, the huge sheaves of parsley detailed as emergency shielders of slight flaws in presentation were almost uncalled upon and cream remained good-temperedly un-curdled, as did the mayonnaise. The Sydney Smith Salad slid onto the lettuce leaves without a murmur of complaint instead of clinging in little balls of discontent.

May had arrived, spring could be greeted, the days of winter were past. Auguste rejoiced, humming happily to himself. So happily he even failed to notice he was humming the dance music from *Eugéne Onegin,* something he usually avoided since Tchaikovsky was Gregorin's passion – in addition to cheese.

Everything was now ready, down to the last truffle in the garnish. Soon the happy pair, His Majesty and the guests would be back, ready to celebrate the day with champagne and more importantly, an Auguste Didier banquet. He had noticed with some disquiet that the white may was still in the house, despite Mrs Honey's best efforts to remove it, but cheered himself by reflecting that if anything was going to prevent this wedding, it now had very little time left to bring it about. All the same, the disquiet refused to go away, and he found himself listening for the slightest sound of the guests returning. It must stem from Entwhistle – he tried firmly to think of him thus – and the general air of enchantment over Farthing Court, for he could not rid himself of the thought that something evil lurked here. However, it was too late now; once the ingredients were cooked, only tasting would tell if poison lay within.

He suddenly cried out in horror, 'What are you doing, Jenny?' The girl was actually decorating a trifle with caviare.

'I'm sorry, Mr Didier.' She was appalled at her mistake. 'My grannie says that this be an unlucky day.'

'It certainly would have been for those who like trifle,' he pointed out.

'She read the tealeaves, you see.' Her mind was *still* not on trifle. 'She's looking forward to today, she says.'

'We all are. A wedding is a happy day.'

'No. She's looking forward to the downfall of the Montfoys.'

'By his lordship's marriage?' Auguste was taken aback.

'Don't know. But something nasty,' said Jenny darkly. 'They can all sense it in the village. Delighted, they are.'

'But the Montfoys are popular surely. They've been in Frimhurst for hundreds of years.'

'My gran hates them. And so do the Spades. The Montfoys threw them out of their home.'

'Why does your grandmother hate them?'

'Her dad were one of them. Wrong side of

the blanket of course, but they did nothing for him. All the same the Montfoys, take what they like and give nothing back. That's what my gran says.'

'Not the present Lord Arthur, surely?'

'You ask Bessie Wickman, Mr Didier.'

Auguste decided not to. In his opinion, Bessie was hardly an innocent village maiden, and could well take care of herself. In half an hour not even Bessie Wickman could untie the knot that would bring prosperity back to the Montfoys.

The Frimhurst bells rang out joyously partly because of the knowledge of the imminent influx of new money, but mainly because the beer supplied by Mr Entwhistle to their ringers had been very copious indeed. The bride and groom were coming out of the church, closely followed by His Majesty the King. Frimhurst had a new Lady Montfoy. The bride retrod the flower-strewn path, and a shower of rice (carefully arranged by Bessie to hit her full in the face) rained down its promise of fertility. Over three hundred guests swarmed out into the churchyard, and the village people congregated on the green, waved hats and curtseyed to everyone and no one. They too were joyous. One more day, a few rounds of the Sellingers dance round the maypole, one more performance of the (newly) famous Frimhurst Horn Dance, and the White Dragon would be safe and not least they could all get back to work. Even the school had been given a whole day off today instead of the usual grudging hour to watch the infants dance round the maypole.

The bride, smiling in relief that the die had been cast, climbed up into the carriage, her groom beside her, ready to drive to the home she fondly thought was now hers. Arthur uneasily remembered the fact that sooner or later she had to be disillusioned, but congratulated himself that Gertrude, like all his ladies, would most certainly be his devoted slave after the events of the night to come.

Auguste greeted the sun which had now reluctantly decided to remain out. The champagne had flowed, the banquet was over, and the guests were gathering to walk to the maypole ceremony. Looking at the remains of a feast could be a mournful experience for a chef – or a joyful one. What had been eaten, what remained, could tell a poignant story or a happy one. Auguste surveyed the tables in the ballroom, where the gold and silver decorations and flowers (stripped of their green leaves)presided complacently over the empty fruit bowls and glasses beneath them. The plates from the main two-course dinner (consisting of forty alternative dishes each) had been removed together with the left-over food. He went into the serving room where many of the food dishes still remained. Why had the lobster salad been avoided, and the *caneton rôti* devoured? He would have expected the opposite, especially since diners were now unaccustomed to such a method of dining, where desserts, vegetables, salads and roasts could all make up a second course, and *assiettes volantés* – flying dishes – came straight from the kitchen with choice delicacies. The art of eating changed with the number of those dining, and according to the interest or otherwise of the conversation; after so long he thought he had grasped the principles but he was constantly surprised.

Today's remains showed little rhyme or reason, no overall picture of content. Yet why? No dire misfortune had overtaken the bride and groom, who were safely married. Short of the rector of Frimhurst turning out to be an impostor not in holy orders, nothing could now go wrong. In the light of his relief that the banquet was over, and he had given of his best in preparing it, it did not even seem so unlikely to Auguste that he had been entirely mistaken about Thomas Entwhistle, despite the fact that English cheese seemed to have been a most popular item on the table. Chesnais, after all, was a careful man, and would hardly have been mistaken in his identification of Gregorin. In fact, the only fly in Auguste's whole ointment was the unfortunate presence of large quantities of Pilgrim's Cherry Shrub at the banquet; huge jugs of evil red fluid still met his eye at every turn. Few people had been disposed to empty them during the banquet, he noticed, but there they obstinately remained for any persons seized of a desire to poison themselves during the afternoon.

The guests strolled in the grounds, returning at intervals for yet more champagne until the maypole ceremony should begin. Bored with the gathering, and unable to pick out any single heiresses by sight, Gerald went back to the house in search of Jeanne Planchet, with two objects in mind, the first that she might prove more generous than yesterday, for which he took along a bottle of Arthur's champagne, the second the pursuit of the mystery that he increasingly sensed existed.

First things first. 'Here's to Gertrude, and her poor sot of a husband.' Gerald opened the champagne with aplomb in his bedroom.

'Men,' Jeanne announced darkly, 'are *merde*.'

'Which bedroom did you see Arthur

coming out of yesterday?' he enquired somewhat later, caressing one breast.

Jeanne giggled. She had nothing to lose now. 'The third one along the ladies' corridor. The Rose Room.'

Gerald abruptly removed the hand and sat up scowling. 'That's his sister's.' No mystery there, but he was convinced there was one somewhere.

Jeanne thought of the money tucked inside the discarded stays. Never mind, the money – and America – were safe.

By the time he left, Gerald was reconsidering his disappointment and putting two and two together with some dexterity. Belinda had already confided in him about the loss of the Montfoy necklace and highly upset she had been. She must have been upset for her to talk to him about it, he reflected dispassionately. Belinda usually played her cards close to her almost nonexistent chest. Why, however, should Arthur take the necklace? The minute it appeared round Gertrude's neck, Belinda would see it and yank it off. There was only one way to find out, he decided. He would tackle the lady herself.

He sought Belinda out in the garden, admired her deplorable mauve gown, detached her from the deplorably boring gentleman (Thomas Entwhistle) to whom she was talking, and drew her aside. 'Your necklace, it's headed for Gertrude.'

'What *do* you mean, Gerald? I can't believe Gertrude would steal from my room. Why on earth should she?'

'Not Gertrude. Her newly acquired husband. Your dear brother Arthur.'

She stared at him. 'Why should he? He must have known I'd find out.'

'Why else was he in your room yesterday afternoon? He was seen leaving it.'

Belinda looked sharply at him. 'I don't believe you.'

'I can prove it.'

Belinda began to believe him very quickly, for a few yards away by the maypole she saw Arthur chatting to that terrible woman, Bessie Wickman. Democracy could go too far. Rage boiled up inside her as Belinda thought it through. 'Arthur must have found out it wasn't still in our safe at the Dower House.'

Gerald stared. 'The Dower House?' From the immediate reddening of Belinda's face, he suspected he'd played an ace without knowing it, and thus come close to the mystery. He grinned. 'Come on, Belinda. Fess up.'

Appreciating she had gone too far to draw back, and in the circumstances seeing no reason for further loyalty, Belinda announced furiously, 'He's nearly bankrupt, Gerald. Or was. If it hadn't been for

Thomas buying Farthing Court...'

Her voice went on but Gerald hardly took it in, for once completely dazed by the turn the situation had taken. He vaguely heard himself promising to mention this to no one, or at least until the king had left on the morrow. Justifiable anger (as the heir to the title and estate) seized him. 'Why wasn't I told about this?' he hissed.

'You were in South Africa, getting rich,' Belinda pointed out, amused now the truth was out.

Red-faced with fury, Gerald crashed his glass down on the serving table. 'What happened to the money?'

Belinda shrugged. 'A friendship with His Majesty can be costly, and Arthur is not the best manager in the world. Anyway, it's gone.' She began to regret, from the odd look on Gerald's face, that she had told him. 'You had to know some time. It doesn't affect the title, of course. That still comes to you. And now Arthur's married, you wouldn't have got the money anyway.'

'Yes, there's any future little Montfoys to consider, of course.' He thought of Gertrude's generously built figure, and railed against fate. Then a happy idea occurred to him, as it usually did when his own survival was at stake. If dear little Gertrude and her father were unaware of the situation, then there might be more to gain in keeping the

148

marriage happy than in his wrecking it even before its consummation. And thereafter Arthur could be milked by a careful cowherd like Gerald. Gerald disliked the word blackmail, but even he was forced to admit this was what he had in mind.

Like the sun, Auguste emerged, correctly attired, to join the distinguished gathering for the maypole dancing. For an hour or two his task was over, and he convinced himself that among three hundred or so people, Gregorin, even if a dagger were secreted about his person, would find his target a hard one. His Majesty, seated between bride and groom, looked distinctly trapped, and it was clear that maypole and morris dancing were beginning to have the same effect on him as cricket. At least this dance looked rather exciting, Auguste thought. For some reason all the dancers wore antlers on their heads, no doubt on loan from the folly. The leader's head had entirely disappeared, covered by the deer's antlered head that had hung over the folly mantelpiece. It was removed to reveal Bert Wickman's face.

'The Frimhurst Horn Dance,' he announced self-consciously, as the fiddler, fortunately without a deer's head, began to play. It was a very strange dance, and it took some time before Auguste realised the dancers must be imitating the escape of the deer from the hunt, and that Bert Wickman was not another deer, but Herne the Hunter.

The Sellingers' dances which followed and the plaiting of the maypole garlands by the schoolchildren were somewhat more conventional, but Auguste was not surprised when His Majesty rose to retire to his apartments, for the sleep which had been postponed too long. That meant that Eleonore would be available for consultation. She was, but he made the mistake of reaching her at the same time as Louisa, bent on vengeance. They paused as they saw each other, both rapidly readjusting their planned opening words. Moreover, Eleonore had not been alone. Bluebell was interrogating her on French life, and from what he could hear, they were animatedly discussing the relative merits of French Savoie, English Wensleydale and American soft cheese.

'Did you not like French food, Bluebell?' Auguste asked politely.

'I like American better.'

'I think you like everything American better, little girl. That nice young American man Harvey, for example.' Louisa, partly recovered from her indisposition, was intent on driving this child away. She could prove nothing, but she had strong suspicions as to whom she was indebted for her uncomfortable few hours. 'You think he would have been a better husband for your sister than Arthur.'

'No, I don't. I just don't like Englishmen.'

'Why not?' Eleonore asked curiously.

'They believe in fairies.'

'And you don't?'

'Gertrude does. That's why we've got this maypole.' Bluebell heaved a sigh. 'I think if there are fairies, they aren't pretty, but nasty. Don't you?' She appealed to Auguste.

'There are tales and legends all over Europe,' he replied diplomatically. 'All sprung from a common root.'

'There now,' beamed Louisa, conscious that this unattractive child might soon be her stepdaughter. 'Not for little girls to get upset about.'

Bluebell began to dislike England even more. 'That's what you think. Girls of my age have special powers, you know. That's what Bessie says. They can tell when there's trouble brewing for Frimhurst and old Herne is on the march.'

'*Hélas,*' cried the Comtesse 'And how can this be prevented?'

'There's only one way, Bessie says.' Bluebell felt important, with two French people and a duchess hanging on her every word. 'And that's for old Herne to have the lord of the manor in his power. That's why he must go to ask his permission when there's a wedding under his roof.'

'My dear child, I'm sure you're right,' Louisa drawled.

'I am,' Bluebell shouted, hating this woman. 'That way, the village will be happy again.' (And Arthur will look so silly, Gertrude will be sorry she ever married him.) 'At twelve o'clock, that's when old Herne will walk. You'll see. I'm going to tell everyone about the rhyme I heard about him. We'll *all* see him walk.'

Gerald was seething all through his tenth glass of champagne. How he'd love to set the cat among the pigeons so far as the Pennyfathers were concerned, but it simply was not in his own interests. He wished it were. Arthur deserved everything that would come to him and he, Gerald, would personally like to deliver the first kick, preferably where the production of little Montfoys might be thereby considerably delayed for some time. He might have a preliminary word with Arthur; that would spoil his maypole dance. He promptly set out in search of his cousin, but failed to find him, only an apparently empty conservatory where, in fact, Horace Pennyfather was secretly drinking a whisky, escaping from Louisa, the world and Gerald Montfoy, since his basket chair was higher than Horace's head. Then Gerald saw someone coming towards him and seized the opportunity to vent his anger on someone. 'I suppose you know about this, Didier?'

Auguste, on his way back to his room to change back like Cinderella into working clothes, did his best to pass by, but Gerald's clutch on his lapel prevented him.

Horace was about to stand up to make enquiry of his chef as to how the Pilgrim's Cherry Shrub supplies were doing when Gerald's next words stopped him.

'I suppose the king, you, everybody and his damned dog knew Farthing Court had been sold because the Montfoys are bankrupt – everybody except me and the poor old Pennyfathers.'

'I am here as a chef,' Auguste replied firmly, removing the hand from his lapel and hurrying away. He was in enough trouble with His Majesty without getting embroiled in a secret that had nothing to do with him.

Horace rose to his feet. 'And I'm here as a poor old Pennyfather.' Grimly he marched towards Gerald. 'Suppose you just tell me what all this is about.'

Caught, Gerald reluctantly obliged in full. He'd have to rearrange his plans; the prognosis for a happy marriage between Gertrude and Arthur now seemed doomed.

'Gertrude!'

Her father's roar brought the bride running from the charming sight of little girls, big girls and grown men all decked out in flowers and garlanded hoops, still twisting and turning under the maypole for those with enough stamina to watch to the end. Her father had only roared twice in her life before, once when she made a face as she drank Pilgrim's Cherry Shrub, the second time when she announced she was to marry a gigolo in one of those new-fangled moving pictures. Each time she had been impressed by what he had to say.

'Have I done something to offend you, Pa?' She followed him into the nearby folly where he slammed the door.

'I'll say you have, but it's not your fault, honey. It's mine. We've had the wool pulled over our eyes, and we're going to do something about it.'

Bluebell, scenting trouble and ever hopeful, crept up outside below an unfortunately closed window and listened with attention. To her great disappointment she could make little of the sounds she heard. There were odd murmurs and a scream from Gertrude, and something about the lord of the manor, or not the lord of the manor, and the importance of not telling His Majesty.

Then they came nearer to the window, and she could hear a little more. Gertrude

154

was wailing, 'It's my wedding night. What shall I do? Oh pa, let's talk to him now.'

'Listen to me, my girl. Tomorrow morning I can talk to my London lawyers, and then to His Majesty the King. Gertrude, you make sure you sleep alone, that clear?'

'But how can I–' She thought for a moment. 'Of course. Arthur must go to the maypole at midnight to seek Herne the Hunter's permission. I'll move rooms while he's gone.'

'You do that, my girl, and lock the door. The more people know, the more fools we look, and that isn't going to happen. We're going to keep this secret or it'll be all over town, and what's that going to do to sales?'

Bluebell was enthralled. Whatever had happened? What would Richard and Harvey say if they knew Gertrude was sleeping alone? Married people usually slept in the same bed, didn't they? Sometimes, anyway. A lot of fuss was made about it. So what had happened must have something to do with Lord Arthur and bed. Maybe the fairies had enchanted him, given him a monkey's body perhaps, so Gertrude wouldn't want to sleep with him. Maybe he had some dread disease? Maybe he was a frog in disguise? Even Bluebell realised this was unlikely. Whatever had happened, they probably wouldn't tell her. She peered round the corner to see Gertrude emerge. Would she

155

be in tears? She was not, but she was looking very, very angry.

Bluebell considered the one obvious fact: whatever had happened was to do with Arthur, and therefore was all a help to her plans (and to Bessie's). She decided to help out by telling everyone that tonight Gertrude was going to make sure that Arthur went to the maypole at midnight.

After all, she knew what was going to happen, thanks to Bessie. It might prove the nail in the coffin so far as Arthur was concerned. And then, oh joy, Gertrude would come back to America.

His Majesty was first mollified, then charmed. It had all been a mistake. Eleonore hadn't been so cruel as to suggest herself that Louisa had pinched the sandwiches she'd left as a signal, but that was undeniably what had happened. Hell hath no fury like a woman scorned. Only, Bertie reminded himself, Louisa hadn't been scorned. He had over the years given her some extremely expensive presents, and last night that had included the priceless one of himself. Tonight there would be another plate of sandwiches outside Eleonore's door, and that was that. It was true he wasn't sure he could manage it – the years marched on – but with some delight-ful help from Eleonore it might be possible.

He'd retire early from the ball and get some rest in.

At eleven o'clock, after an excellent dinner and an energetic ball, His Majesty retired and took a light supper in his apartments. The bride doggedly danced on, as did most of the guests. It was not polite (other than for the king) to leave before the bride. Gertrude retired at eleven thirty, having instructed Jeanne to remove her clothes and possessions from the marital chamber. Bluebell had already vanished. So, less forgivably, had the groom.

At twelve thirty a plate of cold quail sandwiches appeared outside the countess's door when her *déshabillé* was complete and she was ready to receive her royal guest, and this time it remained there until heavy footsteps stopped to claim his prize. Auguste Didier peacefully slumbered in his bed, Eleonore's charms completely forgotten after the glories of his achievements during the day.

At seven o'clock his lordship's valet found Arthur's bed unslept in, though this was hardly surprising since it was his wedding night. It was only by delicate discussion some time later in the servants' hall with her new ladyship's maid that it appeared that his lordship was not to be seen in the adjoining room either. It was agreed he could have been in the adjoining bathroom or dressing room. In any case, it was none of their business. It was therefore left to Alf Spade to come rushing wild-eyed into the manor entrance hall, still bedecked in its mocking white may, to raise the alarm.

Auguste, swiftly summoned by Mr Tudor, ran across the gardens, as did Harvey, Richard, Thomas Entwhistle and a large party of other men who were able to respond quickly to the summons on their bedroom doors. It seemed odd to be running side by side with Thomas Entwhistle, and he seemed to agree for his face looked extremely grim.

Alf led them to the maypole and pointed. There, firmly bound to the sturdy oak pole, was a figure identifiable, at first sight, only by his trousers and jacket for a deer's head, topped by splendid antlers, masked his face.

There was one other feature which sent a shiver of horror through Auguste. An arrow pierced the man's chest.

'Who is it?' Thomas Entwhistle asked sharply.

Auguste gulped as he rushed after Entwhistle to help remove the antlers.

The dead man was Arthur, late Lord Montfoy.

Five

Chief Inspector Egbert Rose did not care for the country. He missed the compact warmth of Highbury, the street lamps glowing on wet streets, the shops whose goods overflowed on to the pavements: brooms, brushes, vegetables, books. He even missed Mr Pinpole's appalling butchery: the carcasses hung in rows as a threat to every decent well-behaved stomach, and the pies which assembled themselves like cannon balls ready to attack the unwary. Edith Rose, unfortunately, was devoted to Mr Pinpole.

Even less did Egbert like being summoned to murder scenes where His Majesty King Edward VII was also present, especially when His Majesty was – if he interpreted Auguste's excited tones correctly – not officially present in England, but was popularly supposed to be in France. He had enough problems with Special Branch at the best of times, and he had been somewhat surprised that on this occasion it had been only too eager that he take up the formal invitation from the Chief Constable of Kent to investigate the strange proceedings at

Farthing Court.

He climbed down from the railway train at Cranbrook and looked around with little enthusiasm. From what he had heard, Cranbrook was a small town with a mill, houses and shops; what he had seen as the train steamed in, was fields, woods and narrow lanes. An occasional sheep condescended to raise its head at the disturbance to its grazing life. Egbert braced himself to meet the welcoming party awaiting him once his ticket was duly punched by the station porter. Three uniformed men, one not – and one of the uniformed men he recognised.

'Morning, sir.'

It was Naseby. Of course it was. This was Kent. Wherever he went in Kent, Naseby pursued him. Fifteen years now, and Naseby was drawn to his impending presence like a bloodhound.

'Ah, Naseby,' Egbert replied cordially. 'Where's Monsieur Didier? I was expecting to see him here.'

Naseby's face went blank. The unwelcome news that that Frenchie was around again had convinced him that he was intent on ruining Inspector Naseby's career. 'This is police business, sir.'

Egbert shook his head gravely. 'His Majesty won't like it if you've forbidden him to come, Naseby. They are related, after all.'

Rose was in fact uncertain as to how much help Auguste was likely to be in this case. He was worried that Auguste seemed obsessed by the belief that Thomas Entwhistle was Gregorin, and that a murder on the premises confirmed this thesis. Usually he trusted Auguste's instincts; on the question of Gregorin he did not. He preferred to believe Chesnais who knew Gregorin was safely in Paris. Unless he had flown over in the Messrs Wright's flying machine just to commit this murder, Gregorin had to be excluded from suspicion.

Naseby was now with Maidstone Borough Police. The other officers were introduced to him as the Chief Constable of the Kent County Constabulary, the inspector in charge of Cranbrook sub-division, and the fourth, in civilian clothes, who appeared to be doing his best to attain utter anonymity, was one of the two sergeants in the recently formed Kent CID. Detective Sergeant Harold Lyme seemed to Egbert to prefer mysterious lynx-eyed looks to contributing to the discussion, since he communicated only in monosyllables.

Rose looked unenthusiastically out from the carriage upon the delights first of Cranbrook and then of Frimhurst village. The latter was subdued by recent standards. News must have spread about the murder of their former lord of the manor, for there was a preponderance of black in the villagers' attire. Rose thought over Auguste's explanation that the bankrupt Lord Montfoy was no longer lord of the manor – save in the eyes of his wedding party – and that this Thomas Entwhistle had lent him Farthing Court in pursuance of the deception. It was a rum situation – and His Majesty was, according to Auguste, right in the middle of it. As soon as he had finished at the scene of the crime, and rescued Auguste from the oblivion to which Naseby had consigned him, he would have to speak to the king's detective, Sweeney, and to His Majesty. To cap his disapproval of the country, Farthing Court and all things royal, it began to rain.

News of the murder had indeed reached the village. It reached it very early, as Alf Spade burst in to the White Dragon where Bert was taking breakfast with the young Wickmans. There was no sign of Bessie, but the resulting pandemonium brought her down in her nightgown.

'He's dead,' Alf bawled at her. 'Lord Montfoy. Old Herne got him.'

'How?' Bessie asked sharply, leaning over the banisters for once oblivious of the increased display of her mature charms.

'Shot by old Herne, he was.'

'He can't be,' she shrieked.

'Don't be so daft, Alf,' Bert grunted. 'You ain't telling us there really is an old Herne, eh?'

Alf looked obstinate. 'His horns was over Montfoy's head, and his lordship were tied to the maypole.'

'You said shot, not suffocated,' Bessie said impatiently, coming down the stairs. 'You didn't mean that, did you?'

'An arrow through his heart.'

'Go on with you,' Bert jeered.

'I saw him. The police have been sent for.'

Bessie sat down heavily at the table, for once bereft of words, and it was left to Bert to be decisive. 'Call 'em all here, Alf. *Now*. We've got to talk this over.'

Alf's voice bawling down the village street was as good as a town crier's, and Adelaide, young Harry and even Jacob and Aggie obeyed the summons. Aggie was openly jubilant. 'Didn't I say 'twere wrong to mock the fairies?'

'Keep quiet, you daft old ha'p'orth,' Bert growled.

'She be right,' Jacob weighed in. 'Old Herne did walk. Just as I said he would. Farthing's lord be crowned with horns.'

'Montfoy's not the lord,' Bert pointed out.

'He was to us,' Jacob said sullenly.

'We've got to stick with it,' Bessie suddenly contributed. 'Eh? No telling the police about Squire Entwhistle's plans. Everything we done, we got to keep doing, till this is over.'

'Why?' Bert was astounded.

'We don't want them policemen thinking we had anything to do with it, do we?'

No one disagreed with her.

'Old Herne done it,' Bessie said forcefully. 'He walks every twelvemonth, don't he, Jacob?'

Jacob looked scared. 'Reckon he does,' he muttered.

'Well then,' Bessie smirked. 'That's that then.'

Even Aggie didn't dare say that the fairies usually had the last word.

'Murder, Tom?' His Majesty looked bleakly at his kidneys, eggs, bacon, kedgeree and pigeon breast. Suddenly they failed to attract him. 'But *I'm* here. Sure poor old Arthur didn't do it himself?'

'The circumstances suggest otherwise, Your Majesty, and your personal detectives from Special Branch agreed the police should be summoned. The local police are guarding the body now and a Scotland Yard Chief Inspector is on his way from London.'

'Not that fellow Rose?'

'I don't know, Your Majesty.'

'I hope not. He's worse than a bulldog once he gets on a case.' He paused. 'I have to be in Paris tomorrow.' His voice had a hopeful note.

'Yes, sir.' Thomas hesitated deferentially. 'With Your Majesty's consent, it could be arranged.'

His Majesty brightened immediately. 'I don't want to dishonour poor old Arthur, but it's not as though I have anything useful to tell the Yard. On the whole, it's best I don't bother the police. I wouldn't want to take up their time unnecessarily.' He eyed Thomas. 'You can tell him anything he needs to know about Arthur and Farthing Court.'

This was not what Thomas had had in mind, but he was a fast thinker. 'We had planned I should accompany you, Sir, but I realise it's better I remain here. There are the funeral and the inquest to consider. We can postpone our own arrangements. Perhaps later this month?'

'Splendid. And you'll do the explaining to Horace and Gertrude. Lady Montfoy, I should say. Poor girl.' His Majesty frowned. 'Her wedding night.'

'I gather from the new Lord Montfoy that Mr Pennyfather discovered the truth about Arthur's finances yesterday afternoon.'

His Majesty's brow wrinkled. Mornings were not his best time of day, but even so the unwelcome thought that there might be some connection between this fact and the death of Arthur Lord Montfoy forced its way through. 'In that case, I'm definitely leaving.'

Thomas Entwhistle nodded. 'I will arrange it now, sir.' He bowed and began to retreat, but was stopped by the roar of His Majesty's indignant voice. 'It's that dashed Didier's fault! Wherever he goes there's a murder. I'm beginning to think he carries them out himself. I'll have to do something about it. Can't have a murderer in the family.'

Thomas smiled gently. 'Leave it to me, sir.'

'Well?' Egbert Rose regarded Auguste balefully. Naseby and his colleagues had escorted him to the maypole, and expounded their own theories ad nauseam, which ranged from 'a tramp' to 'a poacher' or a vague 'someone in the village with a grudge against him'; the chief constable and inspector had returned to their head-quarters, duty done, and with difficulty Rose had persuaded Naseby and the monosyllabic Sergeant Lyme to arrange an office and accommodation within Farthing Court, and to explain to those guests who had remained overnight that they would be enjoying at least one more luncheon at the house. Doctor's and photographer's tasks had been carried out on the now heavily trampled ground round the maypole, and six local constables were mounting guard, as the body was at last untied for removal to the mortuary for a post-mortem.

Auguste explained as much as he could of what had been happening while trying to avert his eyes, and willing his imagination to believe the limp figure the straw-made carnival figure of fun it so closely resembled. The deer's head which was now being removed carefully to test for fingerprints made a mockery of death; who could have hated Lord Montfoy so much that that final scornful touch was added?

Other sets of deer's antlers, left over from the Horn Dance, lay disregarded to one side, as the head was taken away and a constable stood guard over a bow lying nearby them, obviously thrown down after the arrow had been shot. Auguste stared at the bow as though its slender wood would provide vital evidence of Lord Montfoy's murderer.

'You were right,' Egbert continued. 'There *was* trouble brewing, though not in the way you thought. Nothing to do with Gregorin.'

'How do you know that, Egbert?'

'Common sense, Auguste.' Egbert decided to nip this obsession in the bud right away, otherwise he would get no real help from Auguste. 'Why, even if you are right about his identity, should Gregorin kill Montfoy? He'd be putting paid to the foul plans you think he has for politically embarrassing His Majesty.'

Auguste hesitated, then plunged. 'Suppose

167

the deer's head was put on first, and Gregorin thought it was me? I am much the same build as Montfoy and one dinner-suited man is much like another.'

Egbert stared at him, even more concerned. 'Why on earth should he?'

'On Sunday evening he mistook me for Montfoy from behind. Suppose he did the same last night?'

'It's Montfoy's front he'd have seen last night, not his back.'

There must be a flaw in this argument, but Auguste reluctantly conceded Egbert was right in one respect. He must concentrate on facts. He made one last attempt. 'You don't think it an odd coincidence that I tell you a professional assassin is present and, lo and behold, there is a murder?'

'One could say the same of you: *you* are here and there's a murder. It follows you around.' Egbert looked pleased with this *bon mot,* enraging Auguste.

'I had *nothing* to do with this murder.'

'You've no motive that I can see.' Egbert decided he had thrown enough cold water on Auguste for the present. 'I'll have to see His Majesty now. Where will he be?'

'Taking luncheon very shortly. He has asked for it in his apartments today.'

'I take it he knows about this?'

'Mr Entwhistle–' Auguste emphasised the name heavily, – 'said he would tell him

168

about the murder.'

'Very well. I'll have a word with his equerry and ask to see him after luncheon.' Egbert heaved a sign. 'There are times, Auguste, when I could wish I had never met you.'

Auguste was hurt.

'Professional times,' Egbert continued hastily. 'And then only those that involve His Majesty. But now I'm here, tell me again about this wedding and Montfoy's masquerade as the owner of Farthing Court, and how Pennyfather took the news. I don't see Edith's father taking kindly to the deception if he'd discovered me pretending to be the Assistant Commissioner. I doubt if Americans are any different.'

It was some kind of olive branch, and Auguste took it. Edith's father had worked on the railways, a solid, down to earth gentleman, now well into his eighties, and he had certain similarities with Horace Pennyfather, though possession of a million dollars was not one of them.

Rose listened while Auguste talked on. Then he enquired, 'Why was Montfoy down here dancing round a maypole when he should have been in bed with his bride?'

'The villagers still firmly believe in their old traditions and legends. Gertrude Pennyfather, now Lady Montfoy, intends to write a book about English folklore. She was delighted to find such riches in Frimhurst.'

'Another coincidence,' Rose remarked idly.

'The old folk seem to be most know-ledgeable,' Auguste said uneasily, now that Egbert had put his finger on something that had been troubling him also. 'They teach the young ones. My kitchen maid practises the lore she has learnt from her grand-mother.'

'Including dancing round maypoles at midnight?'

'There seems to be a particular legend in the village that if there is a wedding at Farthing Court, the lord of the manor must ask the oaken maypole or rather its spirit, Herne the Hunter, for permission for the groom and bride to retire for the night.'

He thought Egbert might laugh, but he didn't. He stared at the huge pole. 'And Montfoy became Herne's stag? Herne shot him with an arrow and a deer's head and horns on him? Somehow I don't think any maypole come to life planted those. Where did they come from?'

'They were left nearby after the after-noon's festivities.'

'Strange sort of festivities. A hunt?'

'No. An ancient dance. The antlers and head came from the folly.'

'And the bow and arrows? We found them lying in the undergrowth.'

'From the folly too, I expect. They could have been taken at any time.'

'Show me this folly. There's nothing much to see here. Any footprints have been tramped on by the fellow that raised the alarm, together with all your eager sight-seers this morning.'

Auguste flushed. 'I tried to stop them.'

Egbert shrugged. 'You tell me every Tom, Dick and Harriet was dancing here yesterday, so I doubt if there would have been much to see anyway, especially with the earlier rain.' He cast a scathing look at the heavens, and put his umbrella up as they began to oblige with a further shower. That was another thing about the country he disliked: mud. The roads in London threw up mud, but he could deal with that. He could see where it was, whereas in the country every innocent patch of grass might be a bog in disguise. He marched beside Auguste over the grass towards the woods, on the edge of which stood the folly.

The inside walls looked barren, and the places where the deer's head and antlers had come from stood out, as did another space which had probably held the bow and arrows.

'Who had access to this place?'

'I gather it is usually kept locked, but with so many visitors this weekend who wanted to see it, Tudor tells me it remained open.'

171

'Very handy for old Herne.' Egbert paused. 'The doctor believes he was tied up to the pole alive and then shot. It would be easier than lifting him up as a dead weight.'

Auguste shivered as he thought of Montfoy dragged kicking and presumably gagged to the pole and strung up for death. 'Unless he went willingly.'

'Why should he? On the other hand, why bother to tie him up to kill him? Why not just shoot him?'

'To tie in with the Frimhurst legend of Herne the Hunter.' Auguste stated the obvious.

Egbert sighed. 'Why would anyone want to do that? It's beginning to sound like one of your fancy cases again. Are these grounds guarded at night?'

'Normally yes, but for this wedding only the grounds immediately surrounding the house were guarded, owing to the maypole celebrations, and the dabbling in the dew party and so forth.'

'The *what?*'

'And then of course the troubadour had to have access,' Auguste added innocently.

Egbert regarded him grimly. 'I'm almost looking forward to seeing the king. At least he doesn't believe in fairies.'

Louisa was bristling with fury. Her hats had all – save one – reappeared in her rooms as mysteriously as they had disappeared. The one that had not reappeared was the black one she needed to complete her deepest mourning ensemble. This was a plot, and one which had sinister implications.

'Are you quite sure you remember packing it, Wilson?'

Her maid glowered. 'Oh yes, Your Grace. I couldn't not.' Indeed she couldn't. The black plumes had caused her endless trouble in the packing; the end of one had snapped off and had been replaced only with great difficulty, by the promise of a kiss to the under-butler, and a solution of tragacanth gum paste.

Louisa was thus forced to go cap in hand to Eleonore, whose fair beauty black suited well she couldn't help noticing. It merely accentuated the fifteen years between them when Louisa wore it. Fond though she had been of Arthur, his death was highly inconvenient.

'Of course, dear Louisa, you may borrow a hat. I have several with me.'

'Just as if you had known you would need mourning,' Louisa could not resist pointing out.

'Indeed yes,' Eleonore agreed. 'It is always so wise to be prepared for all contingencies at these events. One never knows what attire one may need for day *or* night.'

Louisa's eyes narrowed. She was resigned

to being supplanted by Mrs Keppel in His Majesty's affections, but an upstart French countess was quite another matter. 'So tragic,' she murmured, 'for poor Arthur to die on his wedding night. I must offer my condolences to His Majesty, who must be greatly upset at the death of his friend. He was not at luncheon; an old friend such as myself understands his grief. We can mourn together. Have you spoken to His Majesty today?' She could hardly keep her eagerness to know out of her voice.

'Not since – that is to say, no.' Eleonore felt she could hardly be specific about the time His Majesty had left her company *much* earlier today.

Louisa went straight to the royal apartments, convinced of the purity of her motives. As she turned into the corridor that led to them, however, she almost collided with a strange gentleman in a homburg hat whom she could not recollect seeing before. He must, she deduced, be something to do with the police, and promptly donned her most gracious expression.

'May I help you, my man? This is the royal corridor, you realise.'

'I'm well aware of it, madam.' Egbert was on his way to keep his appointment with His Majesty, but saw no need to inform everyone of the fact. They arrived at the main door to his apartments together and in silence, and she stood impatiently aside as he rapped on the royal knocker, presumably installed for the visit, since it was an interior door. His summons was answered instantly by an equerry in court dress.

'The Duchess of Wessex to see His Majesty.'

'And Scotland Yard. Same errand. By appointment.' Egbert had seen Gold Stick before luncheon, and had almost been run over by the trolleys of food whisking by him to feed the royal palate.

'I regret His Majesty is resting. Might I ask you both to return later?'

The inspector from Scotland Yard and the Duchess of Wessex retraced their steps in the same silence in which they had arrived. The duchess was feverishly wondering whether Eleonore could possibly have beaten her to the royal presence. The inspector was annoyed at having to postpone the evil moment when he must face his monarch.

Gerald lay in wait for Jeanne Planchet, until she should appear from her mistress's room on some errand that would take her in the direction of the servants' quarters. He had a great deal on his mind, and in his anxiety he had almost forgotten he was now Lord Montfoy. When he did remember, the fact gave him little pleasure as he recalled that titles were all very well, but money was better.

He had spent the morning consoling Belinda who actually seemed upset that old Arthur was no more. He had done his best to grieve with her, but it surprised him that she should be so forgiving towards a rotter like Arthur, who had made her a pauper and then had stolen her necklace to give to Gertrude into the bargain.

At last Jeanne appeared. Again to his surprise she seemed in a good mood, and only too willing to allow him his *droits de seigneur* as he laughingly put it. He then listened patiently, and with some interest, to Jeanne's dramatic rendering of her breaking the news of Arthur's death to her mistress, his bride, early that morning. Jeanne had been most surprised to receive instructions from Gertrude to remove her possessions from the bridal chamber, and had performed these duties somewhat earlier than instructed. After all, it seemed from the gossip she had overheard there might be interesting events taking place at the time Gertrude had stipulated. She had been right.

A hand was now clasped to her naked bosom as she retold the tale. '"Thank the good *Seigneur* you are safe, madame," I cried.'

'From what?' Gertrude had asked.

176

'From the assassin of your husband, madame.' Jeanne had burst into dramatically timely tears, and Gertrude had spent some time wiping them up and comforting her.

'Didn't she cry?' Gerald asked curiously.

Jeanne shrugged. 'She is an English lady now. She has a stiff upper lip. It is we French who feel things deeply.'

Gerald decided enough time had been spent soothing French emotions. The problem of his own safety must now be solved. He had told himself it was highly unlikely that the story of his discovery of Arthur's bankruptcy would reach the police's ears, but he had then discovered that the crazy French chef was some kind of chum of the Scotland Yard man, and would undoubtedly relate all he had heard in the conservatory yesterday.

'*Chérie,*'he whispered, 'last night – shall we say we were together?'

'Why?'

'*Both* of us would have an alibi,' he pointed out. 'And however innocent we both are, that is no bad thing.'

'How much will you pay me?'

Gerald was hurt. Surely the privilege of sleeping with the new Lord Montfoy was payment enough. Apparently it was not.

'Six sovereigns,' he said reluctantly.

Gertrude sat in her room, quite still, and tried to make sense of her emotions. She was appalled to find she had none. The events of the last two days had rendered her completely numb. Now at last her brain began to work. I must have been crazy, she told herself slowly. Quite crazy. First there was Arthur's death to consider, then her own future. Should she pretend to be a grief-stricken widow? It would be expected. *Was* she a grief-stricken widow? No. Even that appalling fact failed to touch her. She looked up as her father came in. He looked tired, and still faintly unbelieving of the dire results of the wedding to which he had so much looked forward.

'The police are here, honey. Do you feel like seeing them?'

'I have to, Pa.'

'How are you?'

She made a gesture. 'I get married, I'm told I'm a pauper's wife, and that I have to sleep alone – and now I'm a pauper's widow.'

'They're going to say I – *we* – had a motive, honey. And we did.'

She shook her head. 'If he'd been found with a bullet in him, perhaps. But he wasn't. He had cuckold's horns on his head–'

'Gertrude honey! They were old Herne's horns. A cuckold's would mean you didn't love him the way you ought.'

'And did I, Pa? Answer me that. Because I surely can't.'

She was painfully aware that while her mind struggled to cope with Arthur, her heart was facing the same problem with Richard.

For once in his diplomatic life Richard was unable to think clearly. The Foreign Office, after all, was rarely called upon to deal with fairies, ghosts and murder, and he felt out of his depth. There was too much going on here that he could not understand. Auguste Didier, he'd heard from the king's detective, was under the impression their host was a Russian agent. The Dizzy Duchess was dashing around even more dizzily than usual, and to cap it all, Gertrude's bridegroom had been murdered. Arthur's death was part of a dark blur in his mind, where reason did not seem to be coming to his aid. The one thought that kept surfacing, quickly to be repressed, was that Gertrude was now a widow.

Much the same thought was running through Harvey's mind. He longed for the clean open spaces of America – or even its busy throbbing cities – where the convoluted ways of England would be far behind him. He felt lost in a land where the past, as represented by huge Elizabethan mansions, aristocracy and royalty, not to mention superstition, was so carefully cherished that there was hardly breathing space for a present, let alone a future. Harvey Bolland decided he'd had enough. The quicker he could get back to Denver and take Gertrude with him, the better. Gertrude's plans for writing books on folklore and standing for the English parliament would be doomed, he told himself, if only on grounds of taste, now that Arthur had died in such a way.

It occurred to him that he hadn't seen anything of Bluebell since the news broke. She was a smart kid, and he hoped she hadn't had a hand in this.

No longer was Farthing Court a Tir Nan Og: now uncertainties lurked round every corner, if not something more sinister. Nevertheless, as Auguste made his way back towards the kitchens, from another talk with Egbert in his hastily arranged office in the morning room, he felt on firmer ground. Food must go on, regardless of life and death, and so some semblance of normality must remain there. It had been evident as soon as he had entered the kitchen this morning that the news had spread long since. Work for dinner was now progressing, but a cloud was obviously lying over paradise. Signs of luncheon remained; His Majesty's dishes, all emptied, were still on their trolleys. Obviously His Majesty's appetite remained unimpaired, which was a good sign from Auguste's experience. Ethelred was quiet, however, and the happy hum to which Auguste had become accustomed was stilled.

There was a silence as Auguste whisked round in the hope that by focussing his mind on dinner, it might also be disciplined into order about the death of Lord Montfoy. He was horrified to find that the scorned lobster salad of yesterday was being reconstituted into lobster *à la cardinal*. If His Majesty's palate detected that, he, Auguste Didier, could expect no quarter. He promptly ordered it to be removed from the menu and allotted to the servants' dinner – an arrangement which caused no problems at all. Ethelred's excuse was that neither Auguste nor Mr Pennyfather had been available that morning to consult, and Mr Entwhistle could not be found either. Murder, Auguste almost said, was no excuse, and then realised it was. Even food must be put in proportion to the enormity of the tragedy that had hit Farthing Court. Nevertheless, His Majesty was present – it had to be thought of.

Ethelred retreated in dishonour, and then Jenny burst out sobbing.

'My grannie said there'd be trouble, and now there has been,' she informed them. 'It don't do to mock the fairies.'

'In what way have they been mocked?' Auguste asked quietly.

There was a slight pause. 'They didn't get their food the other night,' Jenny muttered in an anti-climax.

'And may in the house,' Mrs Honey added angrily, emerging from her stillroom. 'It's bad luck. I said so, and I'll say it again.'

'But that was brought in by your grandmother, Jenny,' Auguste pointed out, puzzled. 'Surely however much she disliked the Montfoys, she didn't want such a terrible crime to happen?'

'No,' Jenny agreed, somewhat reluctantly he felt.

'Is His Majesty much offended?' Ethelred asked gravely, regaining his composure after Auguste's rebuke.

'I haven't seen him,' Auguste replied. He could hardly say that he had been dreading a summons. 'I spent much of the morning with Inspector Rose, with whom I'm acquainted.' It seemed to him the whole of the kitchen was suddenly interested. 'I have had the honour of assisting him on a few occasions,' he added in explanation.

'But he's from Scotland Yard.' Ethelred's eyes grew round and the floodgate of babble was opened.

'Will they want our fingerprints?' Jenny asked in awe.

'Did you know Kate Webster, Mr Didier?' Mrs Honey enquired, as though famous murderesses automatically sought him out.

'What about Jack the Ripper?' was Ethelred's choice.

'Charlie Peace?' Stuart Tudor suddenly found the kitchen of more interest than his pantry.

'None. I met the Inspector at Stockbery Towers. The butler was murdered.'

Now his credentials were established, Auguste immediately found himself an authority on Fenians, forensic evidence, photography, Scotland Yard procedures and the Old Bailey. It was time to remember that Egbert would rely on him for help where the staff were concerned, and he should make that clear.

'Any information you may have about Lord Montfoy, or his family, or who may have wished him dead, would be much welcomed by the Chief Inspector.'

They looked at each other.

'We hardly knew Lord Montfoy,' Ethelred explained. 'We upper servants were employed by Mr Entwhistle, for Lord Montfoy naturally wished to take his own staff with him. Many of the lower servants – Jenny, for instance – were here in his time, but you will know how infrequently they come into contact with their employer.'

Auguste did know. The kitchen staff might

never see their employer in the whole of their service, and the housemaids very seldom, and then it was a case of 'Watch the wall, my darling, while the gentlemen go by'. So there was little point in asking Jenny or other kitchen workers about the Montfoys – or even about Entwhistle. Jeanne Planchet, on the other hand, had been only too eager to chat about her mistress at servants' dinner time. Egbert had taken lunch in the morning room with Naseby and Lyme, while Auguste had donned his chef's hat in Pug's Parlour. With the visiting servants still with them, it had been an awkward meal; the Farthing Court servants were trying to maintain the shreds of honour for their house by refraining from comment on the murder, and the visiting servants were only too eager to glean all the gossip they could.

'Mademoiselle, how is your mistress?' Auguste had asked Jeanne.

'Composed, monsieur. She is a brave lady.'

She must be indeed. Most ladies of Auguste's acquaintance would be prostrated in bed with tansy tea and smelling salts at losing their husband on their wedding night. But then yesterday had been no ordinary wedding day.

Jeanne stole a look at him, clasping his arm, as he escorted her to dinner, more firmly. 'Poor Lord Montfoy. Do you think it was Lady Belinda killed him?'

'His sister? Why should his sister wish to murder him?'

'He stole her necklace to give to his bride.'

He stared at her. 'Have you seen it in your mistress's room?'

'No. But I saw Lord Montfoy coming from Lady Belinda's room,' she informed him, gazing up at him with innocent large eyes. 'Naturally I told *no one*. It is not my concern, after all. Now the poor gentleman is dead, and–'

'You must tell the police,' Auguste interrupted firmly.

Jeanne had thought this over. Part of her said she had nothing to lose now; the other part said she might gain a little more.

Egbert looked up as Auguste entered the morning room. To Auguste's relief there was no sign of Naseby or Lyme. Egbert interpreted his look correctly. 'They're off interviewing guests. Half of them are declaring diplomatic immunity and saying they must leave immediately. I told them they can't.'

'The King is still here, and they couldn't leave before him.' Auguste paused. 'How is His Majesty?' He tried to sound casual.

'I almost wish I knew. But I don't. He's put off my appointment until late this afternoon.'

'He ate a good lunch.'

'I'm not surprised. Good cook they have here. He turns out a nice chicken pie.'

'His name is Ethelred Perkins.'

'Anglo-Saxon, eh? Better cook than King Alfred, anyway.'

'*Pardon?*' Auguste tried to recall a chef of this name.

'Great English king, whose chief claim to fame is that he burnt the cakes.'

'The English delight in bad cookery,' Auguste observed. 'Such wonderful food, such bad chefs.' He decided he could wait no longer in such irrelevancies. He had to know. 'Have you met Thomas Entwhistle yet?'

Egbert leaned back in his chair. 'I have. A very polite gentleman.'

'I trust he will be polite when he murders me.'

Egbert sighed. 'I grant you he's Gregorin's build, Auguste, and looks – from what I remember and from his photographs – somewhat similar. But I *have* to go by what Chesnais tells me. Or do you think the Sûreté is in this conspiracy too?'

'Perhaps Gregorin has a double.'

'A very elaborate conspiracy if so. Ent-whistle's servants all swear he's in England and Gregorin's that he's in Paris, a fact confirmed by Gregorin himself.'

'But a murder has taken place *here*.'

'We've been through this. I suppose you didn't decide to save His Majesty's honour, as you supposed, by bumping Gregorin off?'

'If I had,' Auguste, taken aback, managed to reply with some dignity, 'I should have made a good job of it, and not killed Lord Montfoy in his place.'

Although well used by now to such sparring with Egbert, he felt uncomfortable. Even Egbert could not deny there was unfinished business between him and Gregorin and that Gregorin was persistent. Auguste remained convinced he was living under Gregorin's roof, and was fully aware that with a murder having taken place there was little chance of escaping from it.

'Right,' Egbert declared. 'Let's assume that the murderer got the right victim, shall we, that he and perhaps others tied Montfoy up and then shot him – why put a deer's head on him?'

'Like a blindfold–' Auguste made an effort to be objective – 'before an execution.' *As Gregorin would do.* 'Perhaps there were two separate stages; Montfoy was tied up with the head on him, and someone came along and took advantage of the fact.'

'Why,' asked Egbert practically, 'tie up a bridegroom on his wedding night? To prevent him reaching his bride?'

'Or just to ridicule him.'

'Now you're beginning to think, Auguste.'

Egbert was approving. 'A jilted suitor. Why horns then? Because the jilted lover intended to step into his place?'

'Perhaps. Bluebell said she was going to tell everyone the rhyme about Herne and how the lord of the manor must seek Herne's permission for the consummation of the wedding to take place.'

'What did the bride think of that?'

Auguste hesitated. 'She is very enthusiastic about these traditions, as I told you. But yesterday might have changed everything.'

'In what way?' Egbert asked sharply.

'The Pennyfathers discovered about the true state of Arthur's finances, not to mention the true ownership of Farthing Court. Unfortunately they discovered it after the wedding. Also, Jeanne Planchet was telling me that Arthur Montfoy stole his sister's necklace to give to Gertrude. Has she mentioned it to you yet?'

'She has not.' Egbert thought for a moment. 'But I think it's time to talk to the grieving widow, don't you?'

Gertrude received them in the blue drawing room, and her father sat at her side. She was very pale, and the unrelieved black gown did little to help. There was no sign of weeping, however, though Auguste would have expected no less from a woman of

188

Gertrude's strength of character. Horace, on the other hand, was more clearly under strain, although he immediately looked at Egbert Rose with keen interest.

'Don't I recognise you?' he asked.

'You met Chief Inspector Rose at the affair of Lady Wantage's Temperance Soirée. Where we first had the privilege of drinking Pilgrim's Cherry Shrub,' Auguste could not resist adding.

'Sure.' Horace remembered that too. 'That's what launched it over here. Now what about this murder? I don't mind telling you it's been a shock.'

'So I gather. You discovered some unpleasant facts about your son-in-law after the wedding.' Egbert too could be a master of understatement.

The amiability vanished from Horace's eyes. 'I have good lawyers, Chief Inspector. They'd have had Gertrude out of that marriage in a flash without my needing to murder him.'

'Where were you last night, Lady Montfoy?'

'Must you call me that?' she pleaded.

'Why not, honey?' her father intervened. 'Face life straight on, that's what I always tell you.'

Gertrude gathered her strength. 'In my room alone, I retired at eleven thirty and found the new room ready for me. The door was bolted. Pa had advised I moved rooms after the shock we had yesterday afternoon.'

'Can anyone confirm that?' Egbert asked.

'My maid was there, when I came up from the dance.'

'But there was nothing to stop you going out though later?'

'Why should I?' Gertrude replied quietly.

'It's possible you might have wanted to follow Lord Montfoy down to the maypole. Did you persuade Arthur to go down there?'

'Originally, yes, I wanted to go together, but Arthur insisted we went separately for some reason. He suggested I came with the others at twelve o'clock.'

'And did you?'

An angry flush came to her face.

'What for? I had by then decided to sleep alone. I had, it may not surprise you to know, no interest in this particular tradition after our discovery yesterday.'

'You might have wanted to see him look ridiculous.'

'That may be the kind of joke you'd play in England, Mr Rose,' Horace declared, 'but we don't fool around when we've been deceived. We let the lawyers get on with the job, and move on to something new.'

'Then why did he go?'

'I've no idea. He did not mention it to me. Perhaps he thought it would please me. We had one dance together, for form's sake, on the Monday evening, and I did not speak to him alone after that.'

Egbert left the matter of the maypole.

'How well did you know the estate, Lady Montfoy?'

'It was my first visit. Arthur took me round it on Saturday.'

'We're interested in who could have had access to the folly. It was usually kept locked, but I understand it was unlocked all this weekend.'

'Arthur unlocked it on Saturday–'

'Gertrude!' Horace's voice was sharp.

'And he left it unlocked,' she continued calmly. 'He said it wouldn't matter for they'd need to get the horns out for the Monday dance.'

'So anyone could have marched in and picked up a bow and arrows?'

'Yes.'

Horace relaxed, though not for long.

'I've been hearing tales about Lord Montfoy giving you a diamond necklace, Lady Montfoy.'

Gertrude looked surprised. 'They are incorrect. The only necklace Arthur ever gave me was a string of red beads we won at a seaside fair. He told me my price was far above rubies. I guess I was taken in by that. Price was all that interested him about me. When was he supposed to have given it to me?'

'On Sunday or Monday.'

'Arthur gave me nothing.' Her voice suggested that was the end of the matter, and to Auguste's surprise, Egbert seemed to agree.

'May I ask you what your plans are now?'

'I shall stay here, with Mr Entwhistle's permission, until the funeral is over and then return to London.'

'And then,' Horace said grimly, 'we're going back to the States where there's less folklore and more sense.'

Gertrude did not comment.

At that moment, the door opened and Bluebell, clad uncomfortably in black, which she hated, marched in uninvited and with true Pennyfather determination. She had decided on a bold approach.

'What are you doing here, honey?' asked Horace kindly. 'It's no place for you.'

'I've got something to confess to the inspector.' Bluebell stood, hands clasped meekly before her

'Oh no, you don't,' her father informed her immediately. 'Not till my lawyer gets here.'

'No, Pa,' Bluebell pushed her spectacles further up her nose. 'I need to tell the inspector *now.*'

'And what's that, miss?'

'Bluebell–' Horace yelled, but his daughter took no notice.

'Gertrude had asked me to help her with the folklore book and to make a note of all the rhymes and superstitions I heard. Didn't you, Gertrude?' Gertrude nodded. 'Well, there was this rhyme about the lord of the manor having to ask Herne the Hunter's permission for there to be a wedding at Farthing Court.'

'We know about that, miss, and that you told everyone about it.'

'Oh.' Bluebell looked disappointed. 'I thought you'd want to know I had a special talk with a few of the guests, and some of them were very interested.'

'Who, honey?' Horace seemed to have withdrawn his objections.

'Mr Waites was–'

'Bluebell!' Gertrude cried in alarm. 'You're not suggesting–'

'He *was* interested,' Bluebell said defiantly. 'Others were too. Gerald Montfoy, the countess, the duchess–'

'Louisa?' Horace asked.

'Just interested, Pa.' Bluebell didn't want to go too far in dissuading her father from marrying the duchess or it might rebound on her head. 'Mr Bolland wasn't at all interested, though. He was so unhappy that you were married, Gertrude, he told me he was going to drink a bottle of whisky and go to bed. *He* didn't want to go down to the maypole at midnight just to see Arthur.'

This was a nice touch, she thought.

'Richard would *never* do such a thing.' Gertrude became animated for the first time, as she shot a venomous look at her little sister. 'I don't believe you, Bluebell. Make her tell the truth, Pa.'

'Are you, Bluebell?' Horace asked.

'*Sure* I am.'

'Who else, Miss Pennyfather?' Egbert asked.

Bluebell considered. 'I told your maid Gertrude, and Mr Entwhistle, and Lady Belinda. I looked for you, Mr Chef, but couldn't find you.'

'Are you sure this is the truth, young lady?' Horace asked.

'Pa, you brought us up to be like George Washington, so you always say.' Bluebell started to cry. Her conscience pricked her that she hadn't exactly told *all* the truth, but she hadn't actually lied so that was all right. She left the room and went in search of Harvey, who was looking extremely happy, as he contemplated a future life with Gertrude in a Denver mansion as big as Horace Tabor's, Colorado's Silver King.

'The police don't suspect you any more,' she reassured him.

The smile promptly disappeared from his face. 'What the heck do you mean, Bluebell?'

'I told them, the police, that you went to

194

bed with a bottle of whisky and not down to the maypole. That's right, isn't it?'

He stared at her blankly, then pulled himself together and agreed hastily. 'Sure, sure it's right, Bluebell.'

'Motive.' Egbert clasped his hands gloomily behind his back. 'The new Lord Montfoy had one presumably. The Countess Eleonore didn't have one, so far as we know, nor the Duchess of Wessex, but both Mr Waites and Mr Bolland seemed to be rival suitors for Gertrude's hand from what you tell me. The Pennyfathers have a motive, for all their talk of lawyers. What about the servants, Auguste?'

'The upper servants are all new since Gregorin – Mr Entwhistle came, so it's difficult to see what motive they would have. The visiting servants seem unlikely too. Only Jeanne Planchet, Gertrude's maid, would know Lord Montfoy at all well.'

'And the village? They've been eager enough to rove all over the place in doublet and tights.'

'And the ghosts.'

'Ghosts? You haven't told me about that.'

'By daylight I don't believe in ghosts. It must have been organised by the village for the benefit of the bride. Effectively, however.' Auguste remembered the eeriness of that wood at midnight. 'There was something very sinister there. But perhaps,' he added, 'that was because Gregorin was standing behind me.'

'Auguste!' Egbert said warningly.

'It's hard to see ghosts could have anything to do with it,' Auguste said hastily. 'They appeared on the Sunday night, not the Monday. For the benefit of His Majesty too.'

'Talking of whom, it's time for my appointment.' Egbert rose to leave for the royal apartments.

'I'll walk along with you.' To see Bertie with Egbert might save him from the worst of the royal wrath, Auguste thought hopefully.

The royal wing seemed deserted, though the door was opened rapidly enough. It was a different equerry and there was no sign of Gold Stick. He seemed somewhat surprised to hear Egbert had an appointment. 'His Majesty left this morning for Paris, sir. Reasons of state.'

'Left? I saw no signs of it.' Egbert was greatly annoyed. 'Why wasn't I told?'

'I can't think, sir. An oversight on Mr Sweeney's part, perhaps.'

Perhaps. Or perhaps not. 'I saw no signs of his leaving.'

'I believe he left by the rear door, sir. By arrangement with Mr Entwhistle, to avoid disturbing the other guests at such a terrible time.'

Auguste's first reaction had been relief, whatever subterfuge His Majesty had adopted. Then fear began to replace it.

'Where's Gregorin?' he cried. 'Egbert, this is *some* plot, just as I said.'

He almost screamed, as a hand tapped him on the shoulder from behind, and a familiar voice of Thomas Entwhistle asked pleasantly, 'Who, Mr Didier?'

Six

'Does that not convince you, my doubting friend?' Auguste watched Egbert anxiously. In this elegant morning room, with the obligatory oil paintings of dead stags and hunting scenes, he felt uncomfortably as though he were back in Stockbery Towers once again, meeting Egbert for the first time. On that occasion he had been a prime suspect for the murder under investigation, and he hoped the parallel had not occurred to Egbert as well. Had there been a note of genuine doubt in his jest that Auguste might have shot Montfoy himself under the impression it was Gregorin? If so, the sooner this Gregorin matter was settled, the better.

Egbert laid down *The Times* on the Wednesday morning. At Auguste's request he had just read the interesting news item that during his private visit to Paris, His Majesty had visited Madame de Stael on the previous morning at 11.30 a.m., a time when His Majesty was in fact still digesting his breakfast in England.

'Convince me of what, Auguste?'

'Madame de Stael is a former ambassador

199

to the Tsar of Russia.' The Dizzy Duchess had clearly seen in her another rival for she had made a point of showing Auguste the article earlier that morning.

'So *The Times* mentions. It also mentions that no political conclusions can be drawn from the visit.'

Auguste snorted. Why must Egbert be so blind? 'Everything to do with France and England has a political significance, Egbert – otherwise why does *The Times* bother to comment on it?'

'I don't follow your drift.'

Auguste tried to keep his patience. 'His Majesty could not possibly have reached Paris by eleven thirty. Therefore it is plain that Madame de Stael has agreed to someone's request to conceal his absence. That could perhaps be His Majesty himself, but if not, and remembering the lady's earlier connections with Russia, who is the more likely: an English gentleman called Entwhistle or a Russian called Gregorin?'

'Forget about Gregorin, Auguste.' Egbert's voice was sharp. 'I've a murder to solve here, and at the moment you're off chasing butterflies. I may *want* your help, but I don't *need* it. Clear?'

'Very well, Egbert.' Auguste was bitterly hurt. 'Nevertheless, as someone you've been good enough to admit has been right in the past, can I ask you whether you think there

200

is *any* possibility that there is a link between Montfoy's murder and his host? Do you not think it at all strange that Mr Entwhistle should be quite so generous towards his friend in lending him his house and his servants?'

'Where His Majesty's involved, I've noticed quite a lot of people tend to act in odd ways. Including me. Including you. And I daresay including even Mr Entwhistle.'

Auguste was silenced.

'I'll bear it in mind though,' Egbert added, just as Detective Sergeant Lyme entered, now even more unnerved by this case – Scotland Yard was on one side, the aristocracy hounded him on the other, most of them demanding permission to leave. Some had been granted it, but others not.

'Lord Montfoy to see you, sir.'

'*What?*' The word was out before Egbert realised his mistake.

Gerald gave a careless laugh, as he came into the room behind Lyme. 'Don't worry, Chief Inspector. I haven't quite got used to the name myself.' He injected a slight apology into his voice. 'Doesn't seem right, not till the dear old fellow is buried, and Horace informs me that can't be until after the inquest tomorrow.'

Egbert did not comment, a gambit that he often employed.

'So I thought I'd come to see you, before

you came to see me,' Gerald added less certainly.

'What about, Lord Montfoy?'

'The necklace.'

'Ah.'

'The one valuable Montfoy heirloom we have left.' Gerald ignored Egbert's lack of surprise. 'Diamonds, given to the tenth earl well over a hundred years ago by some grateful natives out in India.' Given was not strictly accurate, but sounded rather better than 'extracted from a local Maharajah as a bribe'. 'It was stolen from my cousin Belinda's room on Sunday.'

'Why didn't she report it?'

'Because I told her who was responsible. It was Arthur.'

'It's hardly a theft if her brother took it, is it?'

'Arthur was seen leaving her room, Belinda wasn't in it at the time, and says she didn't give her permission for its removal – and now it seems to have vanished. That's theft.' Gerald displayed all injured innocence. 'I expect he gave it to Gertrude.'

'Very good of you to notify us, Lord Montfoy, but Lady Montfoy denies having it.'

Gerald was deflated. 'I thought it might have some reference to his death. Gertrude's maid, Mademoiselle Jeanne Planchet told me about it.'

'Why did she do that?'

Gerald looked becomingly modest. 'She and I are – well – on good terms. In fact such good terms that in case you might be wondering where I was at midnight on Monday, she would be able to tell you. And I was not dancing round the maypole with poor Arthur.'

Egbert left him to spell it out. 'Where was that then?'

'A gentleman should not specify precisely...'

'You can tell us, Lord Montfoy.' The neutrality in Egbert's voice took the insult out, but Auguste knew him well enough to know that he had taken an aversion to the new Lord Montfoy.

'In bed.'

Egbert ostentatiously wrote this down in his notes. 'Would you say you had any reason to kill Lord Montfoy, even though you say you can prove it was impossible for you to have done so?'

Gerald promptly looked virtuous. 'Absolutely none. I've inherited a title, but no money. What would be the use of killing for that?'

'Anger? To acquire money from a sympathetic sister-in-law?'

Gerald was greatly injured. 'That,' he announced, 'is not the sort of thing the Montfoys do.' Even he seemed to think this fell short of the truth, for he left hastily.

Egbert studied his notes. 'Lady Montfoy claimed her maid could give her an alibi.'

'She only said, if I recall, that the maid saw her. Not when. Or if she was there all night.'

'So she did. Glad to see Gregorin isn't entirely addling your brains.'

'They can still produce the occasional good egg,' Auguste managed to reply humbly.

'Either way, it will be interesting to have another word with her ladyship. If she doesn't have the necklace – who does – and does it matter?'

'It could matter very much if Arthur Montfoy was giving gifts to another woman.'

'Perhaps he wanted to pawn it?'

'That seems all too likely. In which case it probably still has to be in the house. I suppose we'd better search Farthing Court as well as the Dower House. The Commissioner will be only too pleased, I'm sure. It has to be done, though.'

'I'm sure Mr Entwhistle will be most obliging.'

'Glad somebody is.' Rose idly flicked through his notes. 'What do you make of Bluebell Pennyfather?'

'A highly intelligent young lady, obviously devoted to her sister. It seems odd to me that she was so eager to tell the company that Arthur Montfoy would be down at the maypole at midnight. How did she know for sure or was she guessing her sister would talk him into it?'

'Arthur must have told her himself. What matters is which of these people decided to end their evening with a trip to the bottom of the garden to see the fairies.'

Auguste was still following his own thoughts. 'But *why* was Bluebell so interested in Herne the Hunter?'

'She's at a romantic age.'

'Yes,' Auguste agreed, 'but what is romance for her? Perhaps it isn't fairies, but her sister's romantic affairs.'

Egbert seized on this. 'Mr Richard Waites,' he said meditatively. 'I suppose we'd better ask him where he was at midnight.'

In search of Jeanne Planchet, they found Gertrude in her room as well, now looking more strained, Auguste thought. 'Perhaps a cup of camomile tea' he suggested sympathetically.

'Thank you, Mr Didier. But no. It's merely the worry of the whole situation.'

'Of course.'

She smiled slightly. 'Not just Arthur's death. It's being here – as an enforced guest of Mr Entwhistle's.'

'That I do understand,' Auguste agreed all too well.

'He was so generous to Arthur; it seems too bad to have to extend the same generosity to me, my family, and those guests whom I gather you've asked should remain.'

'Murder makes few friends,' Egbert commented.

'Just at the moment,' Gertrude said, 'I've had enough of quaint old English legends and traditions. I guess I'll come back to it. What is it you want, Inspector?'

'To see your maid, Jeanne.'

'Oh.' Gertrude seemed taken aback, and somewhat reluctantly summoned Jeanne in from the dressing room, where she had been using the flat iron. Or should have been. In fact she had been listening at the door. Jeanne was not at all happy, for she had made a terrible discovery last evening. Her American money had disappeared from beneath her mattress, and she was furious; she knew very well who had taken it, and she intended to get her revenge. Fear had given way to anger.

'Miss Planchet, isn't it?' Egbert summed her up quickly, and to her surprise did not question her about Lord Montfoy and the necklace. 'You seem to be a most popular young lady. Not only Lady Montfoy, but the new Lord Montfoy claim that you can give them an alibi for Monday night.'

'*Quoi?*' Now her American money had vanished, Jeanne needed Milady Montfoy

206

more than a penniless English milord. At present, anyway. She opened dark indignant eyes widely. 'How can he insult me so? Of course I was with my mistress, monsieur.'

'In the same room?'

She hesitated. 'In the dressing room. I heard heavy breathing – very heavy.'

'I was snoring?' Gertrude was stony-faced.

'*Oui*, madame. All night.'

Lady Belinda was in the library, standing on the steps and searching amongst the bound copies of the *Gentleman's Magazine* from the eighteenth century. She was entirely clad in black and unlike some of the ladies had not bothered with any tiny relieving touches of grey. Not even a brooch enlivened the expanse of black, and her pale face looked sallow against it.

She closed the volume when she saw Egbert and Auguste and reluctantly descended the steps, indicating to them that they could be seated. 'Forgive me, Inspector, it is rarely that I have an opportunity to consult this library so regularly. Mr Entwhistle is most generous, but I am reluctant to take advantage too often of his kind invitation to me to consult it whenever I wish. I recalled there was a reference in a volume of 1792 to prehistoric drawings found in flintstones at Margate, and pursuing my theory that the well-known shell grotto at Margate discovered last century is not an eighteenth-century folly but a prehistoric temple founded by Phoenicians, linking up with art forms in Egypt and Crete, I naturally wish to gather all the supporting evidence I can.'

Egbert was taken aback, recalling the jolly visit he and Edith had paid to the grotto, after which Edith had been so enthusiastic about shell-lined walls she spent the remainder of the holiday with her eyes permanently fixed on the beach, and a large reticule at her side into which she surreptitiously popped her trophies. Edith hadn't said a word to him about prehistoric Phoenicians.

'I take it you've no news of your necklace, madam?'

Belinda flushed in annoyance. 'I suppose Cousin Gerald has been talking.'

'He told me your brother had removed the necklace. You confirm that?'

'Yes, but I was not able to confirm it with Arthur. It hardly seemed a suitable subject for his wedding day. Nor, for the same reason, could I approach Gertrude.'

'She denies having it.'

'In her place, I might too.'

'What were your views about your brother's masquerade of still being the owner of Farthing Court?'

'Strong disapproval, but I could not betray

him. I respect Gertrude, and disliked her being deceived by Arthur. However, he refused to risk telling her the true state of his affairs – and see what has happened.'

'You think his death was linked to it, then?' Rose asked mildly.

Belinda opened her mouth and shut it again.

'Can I ask where you were at midnight, Lady Belinda?'

'In bed. And before you ask, I have no maid of my own who could confirm my presence there. Equally no one could prove my presence elsewhere.'

'She has some sort of motive, though,' Egbert commented, once they were back in his temporary headquarters. He suddenly pushed back his chair, marched over and turned an oil painting of a particularly dead stag to the wall. 'Doesn't seem decent to me in the circumstances,' he muttered

'Only if you agree that Lady Belinda was so furious with her brother she took the opportunity to shoot an arrow through him when he was helpless.'

'But how did he come to be helpless? That to me still seems the crucial question.'

'Good morning, sir.' Inspector Stitch's face fell as he bounded eagerly into the room only to find Auguste Didier in full spate. He was well aware of Auguste's presence at Farthing Court but Twitch (as he was privately dubbed by Rose) had nursed a vain hope that on this occasion Didier would once again be top of the suspect list, since he was clearly trying to pervert the cause of justice with all this nonsense about the owner of Farthing Court being a Russian spy in disguise.

'Ah, Stitch. There you are at last. Join Naseby and his team in the house search, will you? A diamond necklace is what we're looking for. Here it is.' Egbert led the way to the entrance hall where Belinda had pointed out an oil painting of her mother wearing the necklace. It was the only object of interest in a highly gloomy picture, in Auguste's view. The lady's ample girth, in full, purple evening dress, had been painted with one hand resting on her late husband's memorial stone, rather like the famous picture of her late Majesty Queen Victoria, though the latter at least was wearing her widow's weeds.

Auguste would be the last to deny Stitch's value in tasks demanding such painstaking care as a house search. Particularly of this one, where the remaining guests querulously questioned the need for them to vacate their rooms, while still clad in their walking instead of their luncheon dress. That they did so at all was thanks to Thomas (Auguste grudgingly admitted) who tactfully suggested the quicker the unfortunate matter of Arthur's death was cleared up the better, no matter at what sartorial cost. Auguste quickly built on this position by suggesting that several bottles of champagne should be taken to the dining ante-room, since this was a well-known medicinal remedy for shock, and that luncheon could then be immediately taken. He himself would see to it.

He hurried to the kitchen, still unbelieving of his good fortune in that instead of the usual waves of hostility from the resident staff, he could look forward to instant co-operation.

All eyes were on him as he came in. 'Luncheon, Mr Perkins. Is it possible to advance it by one hour at Scotland Yard's request?'

Ethelred Perkins blenched only for one moment. 'Certainly, Mr Didier. It will mean slightly narrowing the choices on the menu. The *filet de boeuf rôti* must be set aside, and the *gigot*. The *pommes de terre soufflés* may also prove a problem. However, in order that we may retain a choice of *six plats* for each course, we could substitute *gratin dauphinois* and perhaps a hot dish of ham in Madeira sauce might be acceptable – as a last resort in such circumstances.'

'Certainly, certainly,' Auguste would agree to anything at the moment, though at another time he might have queried the substitution of another fish dish instead of a *gigot*.

Underchefs flew to their stations, kitchenmaids rushed to the stillroom, and it was left to the butler's boy, stopped in his usual tracks, to ask plaintively, 'What about servants' dinner?'

Auguste was aghast at his having forgotten all about it. Servants' dinner was sacrosanct. Not even a plea from Scotland Yard could change that. Servants' dinner was at twelve; the upper house's luncheon followed at one. It had done so for centuries and would continue to do so. The kitchen stopped as the entire staff waited to see whether the stars would stop in their courses, as servants' dinner changed its time.

'Servants' dinner will be at one thirty today.' A gasp of horror ran round the kitchens, while Ethelred held up his hand. 'Today, its menu will include *filet de boeufs rôti, pommes de terre soufflés, gigot d'agneau*.'

All opposition was stilled.

In his relief, it was only after Auguste had left to accompany Mr Tudor bearing the champagne to the ante-room that he realised what had been overlooked. At some point Mr Ethelred Perkins' kitchen, Mrs Honey's stillroom and laundry room, and Mr Tudor's cellars must be searched.

He decided he would prefer not to be present.

Farthing Court already bore traces of disruption. As Auguste went upstairs, curious to see how Stitch was progressing, he passed housemaids dismayed at being seen in their print gowns after twelve o'clock, piles of linen removed from Mrs Honey's closets, and more housemaids turned out of bedrooms in the midst of their cleaning. An irresistible idea came to him, as he caught up with Stitch, whose opening words were, 'I can manage without you, thank you, sir.'

'Of course. I wondered, however,' Auguste asked anxiously, 'if you had considered the dirty laundry – so many guests left yesterday and this morning. It would make an excellent, if temporary, hiding place, would it not?'

Stitch glared at him, and Auguste immediately summoned Mrs Honey to lead Stitch to the huge collection of linen and towels assembled by the housemaids in the laundry closet ready for despatch to the laundry. Quietly he slipped away, well satisfied. After all, it was time for luncheon, and today Auguste decided he should dine as a gentleman.

In the relative informality of this meal, he managed to sit at Eleonore's side, even though this meant facing Louisa's disapproving eye, not to mention her neighbour, Thomas, alias Pyotr Gregorin, with whom she appeared to be in deep conversation.

'Farthing Court is not the same without His Majesty,' Eleonore remarked gloomily.

'No,' Auguste agreed, though not for the same reasons.

'Such a charming gentleman.'

'Could you not have left with him?' Auguste asked somewhat crossly.

Eleonore laughed. 'My dear Auguste, I am a married lady.'

'And I a married man,' he muttered, wondering whether by any chance he *had* mistaken her invitation to him.

'However, I do live in Paris,' Eleonore ignored Auguste's wedded state, 'and as His Majesty is a great admirer of our city, I have little doubt that we shall meet again. In any case, I must stay for Arthur's funeral, and the good Inspector Naseby has told us that, in any case, we cannot leave before the inquest, because we knew that poor Arthur was likely to go to the maypole at midnight. I am a *suspect*,' she added almost proudly.

'You were a friend of Arthur Montfoy?'

'No. Of Gertrude, whom I met in Paris.'

Gertrude, reluctantly joining the company, sat flanked by Pennyfathers and Harvey Bolland at one end of the table. She caught Eleonore's eye and smiled in acknowledgement, but her crab soufflé did not seem to be receiving the same attention, Auguste noticed.

'She shows great fortitude in the face of a double shock,' he observed.

'Double?' Eleonore repeated. 'Ah, the money! Yes, Arthur was really very naughty. It seems terrible to say so, but I never thought him worthy of her. Auguste,' she added, 'I know you are fond of His Majesty–'

This was more than Auguste knew, but cautious acquiescence seemed the right attitude.

'I am concerned for him,' she continued. 'Politically.' She suppressed a laugh in case Auguste could mistake her meaning.

'I don't think *you* need worry about that.' Auguste knew he was being churlish, but found to his horror that he still felt distinctly jealous of being ousted by Cousin Bertie. Moreover, he was aware that Gregorin had very sharp hearing.

'Ah, but there are many interests at stake. Many believe the safety of Europe is balanced on a knife edge ever since the Kaiser's rash intervention in the Morocco question. Believe me, Auguste, as I tried to tell His Majesty, the Kaiser will stop at nothing to break up the alliance between England and France for which His Majesty has worked so hard.'

Chiefly at the Folies Bergère and the

215

Restaurant Voisin, Auguste thought irreverently, but all he said was, 'He won't succeed, surely?'

'That we still have to see. Delcassé's position is still threatened.'

'But I read that the French parliament is standing by him,' Auguste said idly. For a while it had indeed looked as though the French Foreign Minister would be forced to resign – which would greatly please the Kaiser – or rather his *éminence grise* Von Holstein – since it was Delcassé who was doing his best to further international acceptance of French influence in Morocco.

'His position is still tenuous. The Kaiser wants him forced from office, and then he will achieve what he wants.'

'Morocco?'

'No. Morocco is a pawn in the game between Germany and France. The Kaiser is intent on breaking the alliance between England and France and what better way to do so than force France to go to war over an issue on which England will not feel strongly enough to stand by her. And if France will not fight over it either, he will get his way by demanding an international conference, to diminish France in the eyes of England and Russia, his new friend.'

'You are a diplomat, Eleonore.' He was impressed.

She shrugged. 'I only know what my

husband tells me.'

Aware of Gregorin, despite the fact he appeared only to be interested in Louisa, Auguste tried to whisper. 'But Russia has enough on its hands with its war with Japan. Nothing but disaster after disaster, and still it refuses to negotiate.'

'Ah. Now there is some hope. Perhaps our host has mentioned to you that he is to hold a reception in Paris shortly, which he expects His Majesty will attend. There he will meet President Roosevelt's personal envoy. Perhaps you have heard that President Roosevelt feels that America should enter upon the world stage as a peacemaker?' Eleonore broke off. 'You seem surprised, Mr Didier, that our host moves in the highest circles.'

'You know him in Paris?' August whispered.

'Not well, but I have met him.'

'Do you also know a man called Gregorin?'

She thought for a moment. 'I do not think so. Why?'

Auguste decided discretion was best, and reverted to her original comment hastily. 'Why are you worried about His Majesty?'

'My husband tells me that there are those who would not hesitate to discredit the king in any way possible at this delicate time for international relations.'

'The Kaiser?'

'Not necessarily, Auguste. Shall we say those with a grudge against His Majesty, especially if they can maintain their anonymity?'

Louisa leaned forward. 'My dear Eleonore,' she said warmly, 'I gather we are to meet later this month in Paris. Thomas has just been kind enough to invite me to his reception for His Majesty and the American envoy.'

At her side Gregorin looked blandly at Auguste.

'And yourself also, Mr Didier. You would be most welcome.'

'None of these is mine, Inspector.' Belinda looked at the collection of jewellery produced for her inspection by Stitch, of which few bore much resemblance to the necklace in the painting.

'Are you sure, miss?' In his disappointment Stitch clean forgot about the 'ladyship'.

'I am quite sure I know the difference between diamonds, glass and crystal,' she declared somewhat tartly. 'And now, Inspector, no doubt you will wish to search the Dower House, although it's hard to see just what motive I could have had for pretending my necklace had been taken in order to blame my brother.'

'I'm sure I'd find your job in Egyptian mummies just as hard to understand.' Stitch indulged in a rare fit of repartee.

'Touché, Inspector. However, someone did steal my necklace and it must be in the house – or the Dower House – since it seems highly unlikely anyone would choose to break in from outside when the house was full of detectives this weekend.'

'Unless it's the Hindoos,' Stitch leapt in eagerly and unwisely, being fond of reading tales of derring-do about stolen holy jewels to the younger Stitches.

'I don't have a lot of faith in Special Branch, Stitch,' his superior informed him, 'but I think they'd have noticed if a band of Hindoos came marching up the drive to Farthing Court to reclaim their lost property. What do you think, Auguste?'

Auguste jumped. He had been miles away – in Paris, in fact, locked in mortal combat with Pyotr Gregorin. Eager as he was to put as much distance as he could between himself and Farthing Court, when Egbert ordered a search of the kitchens, a certain wistfulness overcame him at abandoning an opportunity to suggest to Twitch that the necklace might well be buried in a large canister of ground white pepper. Should he tell Egbert where he thought the answer to the necklace mystery lay, having given much thought to it? He decided not to, until he knew for sure. Meanwhile Egbert was looking at him expectantly.

'Unless the Hindoos were disguised as smugglers' ghosts,' he offered feebly.

'Take Inspector Stitch and his team to the kitchens, Auguste,' was Egbert's only reply.

He thought rapidly for a way out, and found one. 'I fear I cannot. I do not have the authority.'

'Then who does?'

'Mr Entwhistle.'

Richard Waites, striding through the woodland on the Farthing estate, was none too pleased to meet that gangling American Harvey Bolland coming towards him. He wanted to be on his own, so that he could consider the startling events of the last few days, and think about his next move rationally instead of following his first instinct to lay tactful court to Gertrude instantly.

Harvey bowed briefly, even less pleased to see that prim Englishman in his path, and wishing he could trample over him like he was these wild blue flowers. Then he reconsidered. Might it not be the action of a subtle man to talk to the fellow? There was no sign of Gertrude, and the longer Scotland Yard were in the house the more, it occurred to him, they might think he, Harvey Bolland, had a motive for getting rid of Arthur Montfoy. If he did, then Richard

Waites did also, according to Bluebell. He couldn't seriously believe that this slightly-built serious-faced Englishman was a rival for Gertrude, but if he thought he was, then he was, Harvey reasoned. It wouldn't matter to Richard that there was no chance of Gertrude's accepting his hand – and with Harvey on offer there *was* no chance. Bluebell saw that right away. He stopped.

'Mind if we talk a while?'

'Not at all.' Years of diplomatic experience suggested to Richard this was the quickest way to get rid of him.

'Seems to me,' Harvey began carefully, watching a vole scuttle back to its hole, 'we've a lot in common.'

'Have we?'

'Gertrude. She'll be coming back to the States now.'

'She's told you so?'

'Doesn't have to. You don't think old man Pennyfather would let her marry another damned Englishman, do you?' Harvey was irritated.

'Gertrude is twenty-five.'

'Not much money of her own, though.'

It was Richard's turn to be annoyed. 'The British Foreign Office does pay me enough to marry upon.'

Harvey eyed him thoughtfully. 'So you are thinking of it.'

Richard suddenly grinned, realising he

had been guilty of the worst diplomatic crime, that of underestimating his opponent, and put out his hand. 'May the best man win.'

'Sure.' Harvey did the same. He grinned too. 'And I've got one advantage you don't have.'

'America?'

'Bluebell. She's taken against you.'

'I'm terrified.'

'You'd be right to be,' Harvey replied seriously. 'Bluebell doesn't believe in fighting fair, only hard, and she's getting mighty pally with that Scotland Yard fellow.'

There was a pause. 'She can't prove anything,' Richard said at last.

'The trouble with Bluebell is,' Harvey informed him gloomily, 'that her being on your side can be worse than her not being on your side.'

Another pause. 'She still can't prove anything.'

Harvey looked at him. 'Did Entwhistle invite you over to that reception of his in Gay Paree in three weeks' time?'

'He did; as a diplomat he thought I'd like to be there.'

'I'm going because the Pennyfathers are going.'

Richard was startled. 'Not Gertrude surely?'

'Yes. It's Horace's doing. Entwhistle told

him about that king of yours and the American envoy being there, and Horace seems to think he ought to lend support. He's got political ambitions, has Horace, and he's an old hunting pal of Roosevelt's.'

'But Gertrude–'

'Because of the bereavement, she and Bluebell will disappear well before the dancing begins. I'll escort her, of course.'

'Don't bother. I will.'

'You're a diplomat. You can't leave if the king is present.' Harvey seemed amused.

'Look,' Richard tried to control himself, 'Gertrude will be in mourning for a year.'

'In the States, six months deepest mourning – and then–'

'Six months,' Richard said angrily. 'We'll both agree not to approach her within six months, and not to ask for a public declaration for a year after that.'

Harvey thought. 'It's a deal. Unless, of course,' he added offhandedly, 'one of us is removed from the scene for any reason.'

'What reason?'

'Murder, I guess I meant.'

'I've no intention of being murdered, and the only person I feel like murdering at present is you,' Richard assured him.

'I must have meant Arthur Montfoy's murder, Dick.' Harvey sauntered off, well pleased.

'And don't call me *Dick!*' His Majesty's

diplomat, highly regarded for his calm, yelled after him.

Auguste walked along the footpath to Frimhurst village. It was a quiet footpath, passing through meadows where only sheep and cows took any notice of him, and only a frisky bullock distracted him from his main concern – which was not the murder, but the terrifying prospect before him. Having bypassed the bullock, he was free to try to think. All that kept nagging at him was the conviction that there was no way whatsoever that he was going to be a guest under Entwhistle/Gregorin's roof again, whether it be in the Avenue van Dyck or the Place Vendôme. Not Eleonore, not His Majesty, not even Tatiana could drag him there. Egbert might not be much of a help here, but in Paris he would be even less of a help.

That decision made, he felt better and prepared to soothe his conscience by devoting the afternoon to following up a theory of his own. The footpath was disappearing into woodland, and he had to suppress a slight fear that hobgoblins, even on this bright day, might be lying in wait for him. He would return to Farthing Court well before dusk, he decided. He made a supreme effort to take his mind off the woodlands around him, whose trees seemed to be eyeing him speculatively, weighing up his possibilities as their next victim.

'I am making an *aioli*,' he diverted his imagination furiously. 'Concentration is everything. Drop by drop the oil must be added, the temperature is all important' In such a way he escaped the perils around him, and arrived safe from hobgoblins at Frimhurst village.

It seemed sullen and suspicious, however, for here too there was a feeling of tense waiting – natural enough, he tried to convince himself, with the inquest and funeral still to come. Some of the coroner's jurors would be drawn from the village, and whatever their opinions of their late lord, the Montfoys had led the village for centuries.

Most signs of May Day jollity had been removed. Some curtains were drawn, the flag on the church steeple was at half mast. The formerly merry village girls had sprouted black bows and aprons and, at the very least armbands adorned each masculine arm. Not that there were many villagers to be seen. A few people emerging from shops and houses took one look at Auguste and changed their minds. Auguste glanced curiously at the thatched roof of the pub, a corner of which had escaped from its concealed bands, and was flapping in the wind, as he went into the post office.

'Where may I find Mrs Aggie Potter?' he enquired of the postmaster.

'At home.'

A young postman come to collect his afternoon delivery sack shot Auguste a nervous glance and disappeared into the back regions.

'Shall I inform Chief Inspector Rose of Scotland Yard that she is keeping her address secret?' Auguste asked amiably.

The licking of a halfpenny stamp to place upon a postcard received from the hands of his predecessor in the queue seemed to take an extraordinarily long time.

'Primrose Cottage.' It was a reluctant growl, but all Auguste needed. Murmuring his overwhelming thanks, he left, having purchased half a pound of jelly babies for his hostess-to-be.

The sweets appeared more welcome than he did, when he arrived at Primrose Cottage, and he sat in the ancient armchair while she noisily sucked at first a green, than a red offering.

'Your granddaughter Jenny is an excellent worker.'

A loud suck agreed with him.

'And very impressionable.'

Not such a loud suck.

'Why do you fill her head with legends and superstitions and tell her they are true?'

Aggie delicately removed the remains of a red baby from her mouth and prepared to speak.

'The fairies will not be mocked,' she intoned, sitting back to see what effect this might have.

'Nor will Scotland Yard.'

The cannibalised jelly baby was replaced.

'Nor the Cranbrook Police.'

Aggie nearly choked in her haste. Cranbrook was near at hand whereas Scotland Yard meant little. ''Tis all true, mister.'

'I think not.' He reached out and gently removed the jelly babies.

'Nearly true,' she amended, eyeing her lost booty.

'You all knew that Lord Montfoy had sold Farthing Court?'

'Yes. Ain't our business though what the manor does. They be gentlefolk, so dey be entitled to be crazy-mazed.'

'So you knew he was no longer lord of the manor, yet the village does all this for him. Why?'

'I be old now. I don't rightly know, mister.' She grinned, and snatched the bag back in triumph.

'Come now, you're the village wise woman – everyone says so.'

'I just tell folk what I remembers.'

'About may being taken into the house bringing good luck?'

'Ah well, I might not have remembered that right,' she conceded. 'Brought bad luck, didn't it?'

'It did indeed,' Auguste said pointedly.

'I just did it to welcome Lady Montfoy,' Aggie choked piteously.

'You must be a very good-hearted village.'

'Yus.'

'Now tell me whether you made up the legend of the Montfoy wedding and Herne the Hunter.'

Aggie looked cross. 'Dat's Jacob's job.'

'Job?'' Was he getting somewhere? 'Jacob who?'

'Mus Jacob Meadows, and I don't want you a-bothering him, I don't.'

'Then tell me who I can bother. Whose idea was it to think up a legend? Alf Spade?'

She snorted. 'No.'

'Who then?'

When she did not reply, he said gently, 'Mrs Potter, you don't want to be suspected of murdering Lord Montfoy yourself, do you?'

Still no reply, but he had her attention at least.

'It's said that you have a grudge against the Montfoys.'

'So's everyone,' she snorted. 'You'd best see Mus Wickman at White Dragon.'

'Thank you, Mrs Potter – and just to cover everything: where were you at midnight on Monday?'

She cackled. 'In the bed the Good Lord sent me.'

'And no doubt Jacob Meadows would say the same,' August said resignedly.

'No, he wouldn't, cos he were in mine.' She looked pleased when she saw Auguste's flabbergasted face. 'You young folk don't know what life's all about.' She crammed two jelly babies into her mouth. 'Keeps the fairies away, don't it?'

Auguste tried to refocus his thoughts on Herne the Hunter, though it was difficult. It was even tempting to think that Mrs Aggie Potter was quite astute enough to have introduced this interesting alibi to distract him from her own involvement in any conspiracy to murder Lord Montfoy. The problem with a conspiracy theory was that though there might be individual motives for villagers to have hated Arthur Montfoy, there was no discernible reason that he could see for the whole village to have a collective motive. (Now if it had been Squire Entwhistle they hankered to murder...)

And yet he was almost sure there was a conspiracy of some sort. He had come across quite a lot of English villages, not to mention French ones, and experience taught him two things: firstly sweetness and light, whether May Day or not, were not an atmosphere that prevailed for very long, and secondly, villages only acted in complete unity when something serious threatened their collective existence.

Even the rector was part of a conspiracy, though his was the conspiracy to murder him, Auguste Didier. Or was it? Had he iced the cake before baking it, and in his pre-occupation with Gregorin jumped to an unwarranted conclusion? But the name Entwhistle had been mentioned, hadn't it? Auguste frowned at elusive memory, as he arrived at the front door of the White Dragon.

He glanced up at the creaking inn sign, not faded and weathered like most inn signs, but bright and newly painted, and carrying the Montfoy arms. And then he began to see light. This pub was rented; it was still part of the Montfoy estate. No wonder Bert Wickman was so anxious to give the new bride such a welcome. No, that couldn't be right either, for the Montfoys were no longer his landlord. Entwhistle was!

He changed his mind about entering the pub and sauntered down to the small river that trickled past the back of a nearby row of cottages, and continued through the White Dragon's garden. A whole new idea occurred to him... Had Entwhistle's generosity to Arthur Montfoy in loaning him the house been extended to 'persuading' the village to please his bride with a suitable array of, among other things, ancient legends and superstitions, whether true or false? Could this have been to suit his own purpose: that Arthur Montfoy and not Auguste Didier was to be the turtle slaughtered for his soup?

Auguste turned this over in his mind, though still not under any illusion that Gregorin would have forgotten his delightful promise of premature death to him. Perhaps, however, Auguste had merely proved a fly in the turtle soup in Gregorin's more immediate plans to kill Arthur Montfoy.

Why? He decided he did not know enough about their relationship to answer this question, but a most unwelcome idea came to him. Cousin Bertie. Arthur Montfoy was a friend of His Majesty's before Thomas Entwhistle came on the scene. Did Montfoy know something about Entwhistle that should not, in the latter's view, reach His Majesty's ears? Yes. *He had discovered Entwhistle was Gregorin.* Perhaps he was only holding his peace until his wedding was safely over.

Flushed with pride at his detective prowess, he marched up to the White Dragon and found it closed. He walked round to the back of the building, and there found Bessie Wickman involved in mangling the weekly wash, postponed from its usual Monday timetable.

'He's not here,' she said promptly, recognising Auguste and heading off trouble.

'Perhaps you could help me, Mrs Wickman.'

'You could turn this dratted mangle.'

Normally, Auguste's gallantry towards a still highly attractive woman would have propelled him rapidly into agreement. Not on this occasion.

'Or perhaps you could abandon your washing and talk to me – instead of the police?'

'What about?' Her voice was sharp, but she promptly dropped the mangle arm. He also noticed her voice acquired a certain seductiveness as she said, 'You'd best come inside, mister.'

He followed her swaying body into the rear of the public house, averting his eyes from the kitchens, whose state confirmed the provenance of the terrible pies he had seen on offer in the bar. He knew that the best of succulent fare could come from a village range, and the worst from a highly sought-after Paris chef, but he had few doubts about this one. Bessie was more interested in her own charms than in those of what might charm the palate, and he remembered the rumours he had heard about her association with the late Lord Montfoy.

'I want to know whose job it was to make the Herne the Hunter legend about crowning Lord Montfoy's head come true.'

'Don't know what you're talking about.'

232

'In that case I'll wait till your husband returns and ask him.'

'You can't. He doesn't know.'

'But you do?'

'Only because there's nothing to know,' she flung at him.

'There I disagree, madame. The village conspires to produce among other things an entirely false legend about the Montfoy family, as a result of which his lordship is found dead.'

Bessie decided on wheedling. 'An honest gentleman like you wouldn't tell her new ladyship a lot of it was made up. His lordship wouldn't like it.'

'The present Lord Montfoy?'

'No, squire. He be lord of the manor.'

'It won't be up to me. The inquest is tomorrow morning.'

'They won't be asking that, will they?'

'Why not?'

'Bert's on the jury. Half of them are from the village.'

'But they're interested parties.' Auguste was aghast. 'The coroner should be told.'

'He's a pal of Bert's.'

'He still has to ask the right questions. I'd remind you, Mrs Wickman, that it's no ordinary inquest – Scotland Yard, the Chief Constable, the Cranbrook Police, to mention but three important bodies will be present.'

'Makes no difference,' Bessie said smugly.

Auguste tried again, and this time more boldly, since he had nothing to lose. 'There's no reason the coroner should ask questions about everything the village organised to please Lady Montfoy, but he's certainly going to want to know about that deer's head and the Herne legend. I think you were there, weren't you? You were furious, not so much that Lord Montfoy was marrying, but that he abandoned you so easily. You wanted to make him look ridiculous, didn't you? So you appointed yourself guardian of the legend – which I've little doubt you helped Jacob invent.'

'No, I didn't.' she interrupted fiercely.

'Then you took advantage of it. You informed him he should be tied to the pole, then you placed the deer's antlers over his head.'

'Not me,' she shouted.

'Suppose we have a witness.'

'You can't have. There was no one there but us two and–' Bessie broke off with a most unfairylike comment on her own stupidity.

'What about Bluebell? She knew of your plans, didn't she?' How else, he had reasoned, could she know about Arthur Montfoy's intention to visit the maypole that night? He would hardly have confided in her, and nor would Gertrude. Once he had discovered that Bluebell attended Bessie's dabbling party, the solution emerged like a soufflé from the oven, cooked for exactly the right period of time.

Bessie looked sullen. 'I told her to tell as many people as possible. I wanted that bride of his to see him looking so stupid. But as soon as I put the head on and made sure he could breathe, I was off. Nothing to do with the bow and arrows. *And* she saw me go.'

'Bessie Wickman was going to be a witness anyway, so her husband's off the jury, and the coroner isn't going to be the one she's expecting. The chief coroner will be here conducting the inquest instead.' Egbert paused after listening to Auguste's eager recital. 'You've done some good work. Glad you've taken your mind off Gregorin.'

'It explains more of what happened,' Auguste said, unreasonably ruffled. 'We know now there were two involved, the person who tied Lord Montfoy to the pole, and the actual murderer.'

'Do we know that?'

'I can't see Bessie risking murder,' objected Auguste.

'Can't you? Let's have another word with Miss Bluebell Pennyfather.'

Accepting the olive branch, Auguste waited while Rose rang the bell for his constable to take a message to Miss Pennyfather, and five minutes later, Bluebell, accompanied by Horace, entered the morning room, somewhat less confidently than on her earlier visit.

'Miss Bluebell, Mr Didier here tells us that Bessie Wickman claims that as well as telling people about Lord Montfoy's likely visit to the maypole at midnight, you were present yourself. Is that right? You didn't mention that to us.'

'Now see here–' Horace interrupted angrily.

'Yes, I was,' Bluebell said aggressively. 'But there was nothing to tell you, so I didn't.'

'I'm not accusing her of anything, Mr Pennyfather, but there's been a murder done and we need to know what she saw.'

Rather reluctantly, Horace postponed his immediate plan of sending for every American attorney in London, but continued to listen very warily.

'Why did you go there?'

Bluebell hesitated. 'I thought Gertrude might be there, since the old legend involved her bridegroom.' Her eyes shone with innocence behind the heavy spectacles. 'And I thought *everyone* should be there, since it was so important a legend.'

'And who was there?' Auguste asked quietly.

'When I got there, Bessie was just leaving, and Arthur–' her voice faltered a little '–was tied to the maypole with the deer's head on. He did look funny.' The voice quavered and she looked to her father for reassurance.

'So you knew Herne hadn't appeared himself, honey?' Horace intervened.

'Fairy forces have sometimes to work through human hands, that's what Bessie said. Herne had used *hers*. Human hands carry out the rituals *because* they are true. The spirits inside the oak were calling to her, she said.'

'And what about Lord Montfoy?' Rose asked. 'Was he making any sound?'

'He was *alive*,' she said quickly. 'He was wriggling and seemed to be saying something but his voice was muffled. Bessie said it was the call of the oak, and it was time for her to leave. So she did.'

'Then whose human hands did you think would remove the head?'

'I asked Bessie that,' Bluebell said with some pride. 'She told me the bride would claim her bridegroom.'

'Did Gertrude know that?'

'Oh yes, Bessie said she'd told her.'

Horace's face grew black.

'And everyone else,' added Bluebell hastily, seeing where this would lead.

'Then what did you do? Try to talk to Lord Montfoy?'

'No. I was scared. Just a little bit, so I came back to bed. I thought Gertrude would be coming – in any case someone was moving through the trees.'

'Who?'

'I don't know.' She shut her mouth obstinately. 'It was a *man*, though. That's what scared me.'

'No idea who it was?'

'No. I know he wasn't tall enough for Harvey though.' She assuaged her conscience by telling herself that she really had seen someone, and had thought it was a man. 'Did I do wrong, Pa?' She looked worriedly at her father.

'I guess it must have been Old Herne, honey,' Horace said comfortingly.

'Ah, Mr Didier, I am so pleased to find you here.'

Et in Arcadia ego. The Latin tag came chillingly back to Auguste as he entered the former Arcadian paradise of the kitchens. Today the serpent had wriggled his way in. Pyotr Gregorin (he still could not think of him as Thomas Entwhistle) was talking to Ethelred Perkins, Mrs Honey and Stuart Tudor. They must indeed be angelic for what servants would tolerate the intrusion of their employer at such a crucial time for dinner? Tudor should be supervising the setting of the tables, and Ethelred in the final delightful stages of touring the kitchen, checking and tasting. A *Sauce Dugléré* did not reach perfection by itself.

'You will recall,' Gregorin smiled at him (as did the wolf when Little Red Riding Hood trotted in), 'I invited you to join my reception for His Majesty in Paris later this month on May the twenty-third. That is a Tuesday, and my guests are joining me on the previous Saturday. As his cousin by marriage, you and your wife would be a glittering addition to our gathering.'

The only thing that would be glittering, in Auguste's opinion, would be the knife that flashed into his back.

'I am honoured,' he replied, 'on behalf of my wife and myself. Unfortunately she – and indeed I – will be absent at the Gordon Bennett trials in the Isle of Man, to which she is committed.'

Never had motor racing been so welcome in his eyes. In fact the trials were a week or so later, but he hoped that Gregorin would not know the niceties of the motor racing scene.

'That is indeed unfortunate.' Gregorin looked disturbed. 'I shall have to explain to His Majesty.'

'Why?' The question was bald, but Auguste was immediately suspicious.

Ethelred Perkins replied. 'It is my fault, dear Mr Didier. Please blame me. Mr Entwhistle has kindly suggested that since the American envoy is to be present, and many English dignitaries, many of whom live abroad, it would be a courtesy to them if I were to travel to Paris, accompanied by Mr Tudor, to organise the banquet, since his French chef, excellent though he is, cooks only in the French mode.'

'And does that affect me?' Auguste asked warily, and aware of Gregorin's watchful (mocking?) eye upon him.

'I felt I was not sufficiently experienced to undertake a banquet with American and French dishes in it, and suggested to Mr Entwhistle he might request your gracious assistance in helping me run it.'

A prickle of fear ran down Auguste's spine as he heard Gregorin reply, 'And since you are an honoured member of the royal family, I naturally had to mention this to His Majesty. He was most eager that I persuade you.' He provided Auguste with another smile, as he placed the cheese in the mousetrap. 'Indeed, he all but insisted, since he laughingly joked that he had this arrangement whereby if he requested it you should cook for him at such banquets.'

There seemed to be some amusement on Gregorin's face as he added gently, 'He does request it, Mr Didier.'

Snap! The mousetrap held him fast.

Seven

The inquest into the death of the late Lord Montfoy was held, with great reluctance by Chief Inspector Egbert Rose and great eagerness by Naseby, in his own former ballroom; the drawback that many of those most closely involved in the death were still residing under the same roof was overlooked, since Farthing Court was the only building in Frimhurst, save the church, large enough to hold the hordes that might be expected to attend. The press had held back many of the more lurid facts of Lord Montfoy's death, but nevertheless his death in what was described as a 'fatal shooting accident' on his wedding night was bound to attract some attention. Even the village hall, a proud edifice painstakingly transformed into a mediaeval relic for the Montfoy wedding, though in fact constructed only forty years earlier, was dismissed as unworthy for the event.

The inquest began at ten o'clock on Thursday morning, with no deference to the fact that many guests in the house would normally still be at breakfast at this hour and far from suitably attired for such an occasion. Gertrude, however, had decided that the funeral should take place later that day, and Gerald, whose permission was belatedly sought as present head of the Montfoy family, was eager to agree.

Auguste was surprised to find no sign of Egbert in the room, only Naseby who graciously awarded him a scowl. Puzzled, he saw a vacant chair, and made his way to it, only to find he would be delicately positioned between Eleonore and Louisa. Too late to draw back, he sat down, and the feathers in their respective hats stuck out towards each other over his head like a triumphal arch.

'What happens if the jury thinks one of us is guilty?' Eleonore enquired.

'Worried, Comtesse?' Louisa asked sweetly.

'Ah, Louisa, let us not trifle so on this solemn day,' Eleonore replied gravely.

Point to Eleonore, Auguste decided.

'My apologies if you mistook my meaning.' Louisa looked most hurt. 'As a stranger here, I thought you might have a natural suspicion of our splendid police system.'

Or perhaps it was a draw.

The jury, seated on the platform – if Auguste remembered correctly from the May Day cavortings at least one of them

242

would be more at ease playing in a band – stared stiffly ahead as though a glance at the packed audience might prejudice the course of justice. The coroner, having lodged for the night with the local registrar, after his journey from Maidstone, was wishing he didn't have to view dead bodies so soon after eating badly cooked kidneys.

Little emerged from the technical evidence that Auguste did not already know. However, the time of death was now fixed at between eleven and one o'clock, which was new, and he waited with impatience for the coroner's questions on the presence of the deer's head. He waited on the whole in vain for after Alf Spade had explained how he found the body, had denied that he himself had placed the head on the dead man, and explained that in visiting the maypole at seven in the morning he had not been returning to the scene of his own crime but merely coming to tidy away the remaining deer's antlers, the only question the coroner asked was whether Lord Montfoy could have suffocated.

Assured by the police doctor that the arrow had been the cause of death, he asked no more save for details of where the bow had been found and where it had been obtained. However, Auguste noticed that various members of the press were showing a great deal more interest than hitherto.

Where was Egbert? he wondered. Bluebell was taking the stand now, with Horace and Gertrude in the front row, anxiously watching her. As the only person who had admitted being anywhere near the scene, Bluebell appeared now to be relishing her position as principal witness, and her accent brought even more avid scribbling in press notebooks. Only one of the principal witnesses, Auguste qualified. Where was Bessie Wickman?

'Just tell us what happened, young lady. No need to be nervous,' the coroner told her kindly but unnecessarily.

'My sister is very interested in your English legends, so when that old gentleman from the village told us the legend about Herne the Hunter and Montfoy marriages, I guess I thought I'd go down and see if Arthur and Gertrude would come down to the maypole in case old Herne did walk. So I left the dance, went back to my room and washed up, ready for–'

'Washed up, young lady? In the kitchens?'

Bluebell was nonplussed. 'No, the maids bring the water up to the room.'

'And what do you do with the clean dishes?'

Richard Waites stood up. 'A difference of language, sir.'

Bluebell proceeded to explain that when she got there, her new brother-in-law had been tied to the maypole, with the deer's head on, but there had been no arrow in his chest. 'My friend Bessie was talking to him.'

'Through the deer's head?'

'Yes. Then she patted it, said goodbye, and left.'

'Why didn't you remove the head?'

Bluebell replied quickly enough, having been prepared for this. 'Oh, I couldn't, sir. It was an old English legend you see. I thought it might bring bad luck to interfere, and that my sister would be coming to do it.'

The coroner nodded approvingly at such sensitivity to English ways. 'And you and Mrs Wickman were the only people there?'

'Yes.'

'Your sister didn't come?'

A very decided 'No.'

'Or anyone else?'

Bluebell hesitated. 'I didn't stay very long, but I thought someone was coming. It scared me, because it was a man.'

The coroner's endeavours to establish the identity of anyone else present at the scene proved fruitless, and the jury brought back a verdict of murder by persons unknown. It took them some time to reach their decision since several jurors (those from Frimhurst) stoutly maintained either that it was an accident, that he did it himself or that that American young lady had more to do with it than she was letting on. Fortunately for international relations reason prevailed.

There was still no sign of Egbert, although a late and speedy luncheon was now being served, before the funeral at three o'clock. Ethelred had earnestly consulted Auguste last night over what might be a suitable luncheon menu to intervene between an inquest and a funeral. Auguste's mind, naturally enough in the circumstances, had not been fully on the subject and all he could suggest was that venison should not be on the menu. Ethelred had given him a look of deep reproach and pointed out that buck venison had just come into season. Auguste had pulled himself together, and between them they had composed a menu of light, cold dishes, since it was not known how long the inquest might take, comforting soups and a good-tempered hot dish that would not object to a long wait in the chafing dishes. More attention was paid to the funeral tea which must, it was unspokenly agreed, in no way resemble the wedding breakfast.

'Cakes, sandwiches and *no* ices, Mr Didier,' Gertrude had decreed, though whether she was in a position to decree anything was a moot point, Auguste had reflected. Farthing Court at present had three persons to issue orders, Thomas, Gertrude and the new Lord Montfoy, and two chefs to carry them out.

At least, Auguste realised thankfully, that whether Egbert liked it or not, he could escape from Farthing Court tomorrow, as could the other guests. Egbert – where was he? Just as his eye fell on a most interesting locally made goats' cheese, Mr Tudor whispered in his ear that the bell had been rung in the servants' hall from Inspector Rose's office, and he hurried to find him.

'Ah.' Egbert looked up as Auguste rushed through the door. 'I thought you might have been my dinner.'

'I can arrange a lobster salad immediately. Perhaps some soup to precede it? Egbert, where–?'

'And one of those bavarois things?'

'Certainly, Egbert. Egbert, where–?'

'And a spot of cheese. I'm partial to Wensleydale.'

Auguste surrendered and ran the several hundred yards to the Farthing Court kitchens. He reappeared ten minutes later, accompanied by two footmen and a trolley of food, and waited impatiently while the table was set and the first pangs of appetite assuaged.

'I hear the verdict was murder by persons unknown,' Egbert said at last.

'Yes.'

'It's not unknown now.'

'Who?' asked Auguste sharply, running his mind over his own luncheon table to see if there were any absentees.

'Naseby has arrested Bessie Wickman.'

'*What?*' Auguste was puzzled, not that Naseby had arrested her, but that Egbert had presumably agreed. Auguste didn't like Bessie, but didn't see her as a murderess. She was far too fond of her own seductive skin. 'I am sure she would have no reason to kill–'

'She had every reason, Auguste,' Egbert interrupted.

'Just because Lord Montfoy rejected her? Surely the idea of the deer's head was simply revenge to make him look foolish on his wedding night – even to miss it perhaps. And, besides, Bluebell saw her leave, and Montfoy was still alive.'

'What would you do if you were set on murder and a young girl came along? Say, sorry, my dear, go away because I'm about to commit a murder? Bessie went away all right, but then she returned. She had more motive than hurt pride.'

'What was that?' Auguste asked with an unpleasant foreboding he was not going to like this.

Egbert flourished a large canvas bag. 'This is her peg bag. We found it hanging on her mangle.'

'What have pegs to do with it?' Auguste recalled having seen the peg bag and Bessie's hand upon it. No wonder.

'It's what else it contains besides pegs that's interesting. One diamond necklace. *Now* do you see her motive?' Egbert flashed the diamonds before Auguste's eyes.

'No,' Auguste obstinately maintained. 'If he gave her that necklace, she had all she wanted.'

Egbert sighed. 'You're still hoping the murderer is Thomas Entwhistle, aren't you?'

Auguste reluctantly admitted it, especially in view of the terrifying prospect before him. He realised he was clutching desperately at straws, at *anything* that could prevent his having to leave for Paris in just over two weeks' time.

'Bessie had been given the necklace all right,' Egbert continued, 'but it was an heirloom, remember. Arthur Montfoy was sure to demand it back once his marriage was established. He might even accuse Bessie of stealing it, even if she sold it immediately. With Montfoy dead, she was at liberty to do what she liked with it. We searched the house this morning; it was Twitch who found it.'

Of course, Auguste thought, tiredly. He himself had been within a few feet of that mangle, not knowing what it hid. He grappled to find a flaw in Egbert's argument, and succeeded. 'If she had murder in mind, why get Bluebell to spread the word so that more people would arrive?'

'It would provide more suspects.'

'Why tell Bluebell in the first place then? Egbert, it doesn't make sense.'

'Look, Auguste, you're prejudiced,' Egbert said kindly enough. 'Perhaps she only thought of killing Montfoy on the spur of the moment. Perhaps they had an argument. She's admitted their appointment was eleven thirty, not at twelve as everyone else was told. Evidence and facts, Auguste. What matters is the quality of the meat, not the way you cook it.'

Auguste disagreed. Cooking *was* important. 'We've proof that someone else did go down there.'

'We've no proof who it was. Bluebell might have been mistaken. Badgers are large creatures. Old Herne, perhaps. Everyone claims to have been in their beds–'

'Or someone, else's,' Auguste said savagely. 'Even His Majesty can claim that alibi.'

'You're never going to convince me that the King took a midnight stroll to see if Herne the Hunter was out, and then decided to play Robin Hood with a bow and arrow.'

Auguste surrendered. 'You're right. Your theory fits the facts, it fits everything.'

'Except for your nose, perhaps?'

'You may laugh at it, but my nose–'

'Keep your nose for Paris, Auguste.'

Last evening, Auguste had consulted Egbert about Gregorin's implied command to him to cook for the reception. Egbert had been on the whole sympathetic, but had pointed out that he would be in an excellent position to settle once and for all whether Entwhistle was Gregorin. It had been three years since Auguste had last seen Gregorin, and that was only a passing glimpse; it was five years since he had been face to face with him, and over a period of time memories could play tricks.

'It doesn't worry you that he has inveigled me under his roof once more?' Auguste had asked a little sadly.

'If I thought Entwhistle was Gregorin, yes, it would.'

'Would you not even try to come over yourself?'

'Special Branch wouldn't like that.'

'Even if you were on holiday.'

Egbert had wavered. 'I'd like to – but what use would I be? I can't stay at your side all the time, because if I were on holiday I couldn't stay under Entwhistle's roof. I'll ask Chesnais to keep a watch on you. If you're really worried, why don't you invent some excellent reason why you can't go? It's all very well saying that the King might be in danger politically, but there's nothing you could do to prevent it, even if it were true.'

Auguste began to feel heartened. 'What excuse could I give His Majesty?'

'Tell him Tatiana's ill.'

'Egbert, that is *magnifique*.' Tatiana would be home by then, and would most certainly insist he went nowhere near Gregorin.

The funeral was an awkward occasion. The newspapermen had stayed on, partly in the hope of noting the widow's demeanour under her thin black veil. They then repaired to the White Dragon where Bert, torn between his personal horror and commerce, decided he could do more good for Bessie by announcing the iniquity of her arrest to the world than by closing the shutters. Now that his worst suspicions had been so dramatically confirmed, he felt almost fond of Bessie again and managed to convince himself of the truth of his words.

'Them Montfoys always were crafty,' he informed press and villagers alike. 'He wanted to seduce my Bessie, he did, so he lured her down to the old maypole, and tried to have his way with her. Only she were stronger than him, so she tied him up and left him there.'

'Who do you think really murdered him, Mr Wickman? Old Herne the Hunter?' came the first eager question.

Bert paused, thinking his way through this one.

''Tis a powerful old legend in the village,'

252

he informed them, 'but old Herne never be known to kill with bow and arrow before. No, I reckon 'twas–' his audience waited expectantly, as he paused impressively – 'One of dem foreigners.'

'The widow?' one asked hopefully.

'Could be. I'm not saying, mind. Just one of them as don't know our ways.' A dim recollection of squire asking him something about whether a foreigner had been asking questions came back to him. 'That chef, maybe. The Frenchie.'

Several notebooks were whisked into play.

Louisa selected another dainty cucumber sandwich at the funeral tea.

'Dear Mr Didier, what a comfort it is to know you will be with us in Paris.'

'Comfort?' Auguste's conscience pricked him since he had no intention of going. 'Indeed I shall enjoy sharing responsibility for the cuisine with Mr Entwhistle's own excellent chef.'

'Not for the *food*, Mr Didier.'

Auguste was startled. What other comforts had Louisa in mind? With His Majesty so devoted to Eleonore, had she alternative pleasures in mind for herself? He began to edge away, when her next words stopped him, 'His Majesty's comfort.'

'He could take the Buckingham Palace chefs, of course.'

'No, no. At this time, this delicate time for international relations, I feel His Majesty might be – shall we say – a little blind to the uses to which unscrupulous persons might put their proximity to him.'

'*Je m'excuse, madame?*' Auguste was cautious. Did she speak of Eleonore or of Gregorin?

Louisa looked cross. 'Do I have to explain further?' she hissed. 'Your very telephone conversation last Sunday night – which I happened by the merest chance to overhear as I was emerging from an adjacent room – suggests you are as aware as I of the dangers.'

It was Gregorin then. But what was her interest? Did she hope to restore herself to His Majesty's good books? From her attention to Horace, he thought her strategy lay in that direction now.

'I might not go,' he said. 'I have family commitments.'

'You must, Mr Didier. Nothing is more important than England.'

Auguste slipped away from the gathering, with this thought on his mind, though not convinced of its truth. He reminded himself firstly that he was French, for only half of him had English blood, and secondly that he was extremely important to himself. He had promised to discuss the reception menu with Ethelred this evening after servants' supper, since he would be leaving early on the morrow, but his conscience troubled him that he was obliged to deceive Ethelred into thinking he would still be going. He told himself that safety and prudence demanded it.

Ethelred looked up eagerly in the midst of his preparations for this evening's dinner. 'I have spoken to the fishmonger. He can arrange for samphire to be delivered to Paris. He has an arrangement with the Dieppe market.'

He could cook fish on a bed of samphire! His eyes brightened. Already he could smell the crisp pungent aroma, taste its delicious sharp freshness. How could he give up such an opportunity?

Yet how could he go?

The dilemma stared him once again in the face. To cook for the reception was tempting, even without samphire. A *Menu d'Unité* had been agreed, the tables would be decorated with flowers massed in the colours of the three flags, French, American, British, and dishes from each country would be presented in a choice of soups, fish, removes and *entremets*. The menu cards would be held aloft by miniature Statues of Liberty, and three ornate meringue *flancs* – of Versailles, of Windsor Castle and of the White House – would adorn the table. And to think he might not be part of it!

At the buffet supper late that evening a compromise occurred to him. He would ask Eleonore's opinion. As the wife of a French diplomat, she would understand the issues involved, since she would – he tried to ignore a slight pang of jealousy – be close to His Majesty.

He managed to find her alone, engrossed in the choice of cheeses before her.

'I recommend the Stilton, Eleonore, though perhaps your preference is for Port Salut?'

'Stilton suits me excellently, thank you, Auguste. I would most certainly take the recommendation of the house here above all places.' She paused. 'And in Paris too, I trust? You can arrange that?'

He could hardly have sought a better opening. He explained at length to her about Entwhistle and Gregorin while they ate, and she showed instant concern. 'You mean, if you are correct and this Entwhistle *is* Gregorin, His Majesty could be in political danger at this reception.'

'Yes.'

'It seems unlikely.' Eleonore pondered. 'However, I have never met this Gregorin though I know many Russians in Paris.'

'Because of his travels he does not lead a life in the public eye.'

'No. So let us suppose you are right, and

that he did try to kill you here, and killed Arthur by mistake. Is that not at odds with his planning a political downfall for His Majesty? Your death would be a distraction and draw attention to his household, which is the last thing he would want with the king present.'

This was not quite the way Auguste would have put it himself, but he reluctantly agreed with her.

'After all, Thomas had to change his plans at the last moment, because of the funeral,' Eleonore continued. 'The same would have applied if *you* had died. The same will apply in Paris. If he plans the downfall of the king, then he will not have a murder take place in the house, which could upset the reception.'

'You are right. Dear Eleonore.' He kissed her cheek, greatly relieved. The samphire could win and he do his duty without over-much worry. 'I will come to Paris.'

'I want that very much, Auguste.'

It wasn't till he climbed into bed and blew out the candle that he realised he had a vague feeling of discontent – and not one caused by his unaccustomed eating of cheese late at night. Could it be because he could spot a flaw in Eleonore's argument? What if he were wrong about Gregorin plotting the king's downfall, and his whole intention had been and still was to murder Auguste Didier? Auguste told himself not to be so absurd. These were but night-time fears, and would soon be digested along with his supper.

'What's that collection of white turnips over there?' Ethelred craned his neck out of the window as the Calais Engladine express drew close to the Gare du Nord.

'The Basilica of Sacré Coeur,' Auguste replied, deducing the subject of the question from the direction of Ethelred's eyes rather than his description. Built just after he had left Paris, its dominance on the hilltop of the small lively village of Montmartre had taken a little time to blend in to his own private vision of Paris, but Paris was a beautiful woman who could wear her new clothes with the same grace as she displayed the old.

'Mr Entwhistle,' Ethelred declared fervently, sinking back into his seat, 'is a splendid employer.'

'Who else would send his servants first class?' agreed Stuart Tudor. 'A most worthy gentleman.'

Auguste's views remained unspoken.

Despite his lack of relish for what lay ahead, excitement seized him as they descended from the train, each clutching precious luggage containing his own tools of the trade. He and Ethelred clung to their own knives and notebooks; Stuart Tudor to his silver polishing cloth and corkscrew. The rest of their luggage had been registered through in advance, but no one, in Tudor's view, entered unknown territory unarmed with the means to carry out one's profession. (Or, rather, present profession.)

Emerging from the railway station, Auguste sniffed an intangible quality in the air that spoke to him only of France. If he had stopped to analyse it, he could perhaps have identified the smells of mingled coffee, hot bread, tobacco smoke and perhaps a hint of bowls of steaming *moules* emanating from the many cafés clustered round and in the station, but he did not bother to do so. It was enough that it was familiar, that it spoke of his younger days, and that its message was: Paris.

Even as two *fiacres découverts* transported them ever nearer to whatever fate might await him, Auguste enjoyed rumbling over the narrow *pavé* roadways often half obstructed by barrows and markets and Parisians, with their eyes only on food, spilling into the roadway after them. Watching the eagerness of the shoppers, he reflected how strange it was that for some years French chefs had been bemoaning the fact that society no longer appreciated its own cuisine because its life had become so busy that proper meals taken in relaxation, comfort and respect for the *estomac* were no longer possible.

His reception dinner, Auguste vowed, would be a different matter. All fifty guests would remember the *Menu d'Unité* for ever. Not, it belatedly occurred to him to hope, because the chef was murdered as soon as the last *entremet* had been placed on the table. He firmly put this unpleasant thought from his mind, for he had resolved to get through this ordeal by assuring himself that he was safe provided he remained under Gregorin's or rather Entwhistle's roof. He was, it was true, not sure that it would be Gregorin and not whoever the true Thomas Entwhistle might be, at the Place Vendôme, but he was so near to certainty that he decided he must proceed on that assumption. Expeditions out would only be undertaken with the greatest precautions.

His Majesty, Auguste had been relieved to hear both from Eleonore and from Gregorin before he left for Paris, would be staying at the Hôtel Bristol in the Place Vendôme, and not with Gregorin. Eleonore's mocking glance had dared him to voice his instant thought that this was a great deal handier for a *very* private visit than staying in the house where the *very* public reception was to take place.

'I am looking forward so much to Mr Entwhistle's reception, *naturellement*.' Eleonore's eyes had gleamed when he said goodbye to her at Farthing Court. 'And even more to the weekend before it. I have promised to show His Majesty Paris.'

'I think you'll find he knows it,' Auguste had pointed out sourly.

'But not *my* Paris. That will be an entirely new experience for him,' she retorted demurely.

'Are you not concerned about your husband?' Even in France, husbands did not stay away indefinitely.

'He's in Russia now.' Eleonore looked surprised. 'As you know, France is anxious that we, and not President Roosevelt, should be the brokers of peace between Russia and Japan. Moreover,' she laughed, moving closer, 'where is your wife, Auguste?'

Where indeed? At the time of that conversation she had been in Paris; now he had with some difficulty persuaded her to participate in the British Eliminating Trials for the Gordon Bennett Cup in the Isle of Man, which would take place a week after the reception, and which would, he assured her, necessitate hard practice in England. The lure of the track had proved greater than her suspicion of his motives. He had decided that the name Gregorin should not pass his lips, in case she insisted on accompanying him. He did not want Tatiana in Paris if he were to confront Gregorin,

261

although Egbert had suggested that since Gregorin was her uncle she should put Auguste's theory to the test. He would not do so, and besides, he was still convinced he was right. The aura that hung around Entwhistle every time he met him still shouted Gregorin.

As the *fiacre* rattled down the rue de la Paix, he could see the classic perfection of the Place Vendôme before him. On the right the luxurious hotels, the Ritz, the Bristol and the Vendôme. In between them or on the left would be Entwhistle's house, or *hôtel*, as the Parisians referred to these grand homes. There were fewer of them now that so many people were moving into apartments for convenience. Entwhistle must indeed be a rich man. Did Egbert not even think it was strange that no one seemed to know where he had come from, or how he had acquired this wealth? When he had asked Egbert, the answer had merely come back from the Sûreté that he had come from India. That apparently explained all – except to Auguste.

In his preoccupation he handed over too much money to the *cocher*, and demanded change from his two hundred centimes. A heated discussion ensued to Ethelred's lively interest. Auguste won and went his way triumphantly to see how Stuart Tudor was faring in the other *fiacre*. Mr Tudor was having no problems at all. His paragon, Mr Entwhistle, had both told him and provided him with the correct fare.

Stepping inside Hôtel Entwhistle to be surrounded by a bevy of impassive liveried servants was not to be compared with the comfortable smell of ancient wood and leather emanating from Farthing Court. Perhaps it was the high rooms and the white paint everywhere, from moulded ceilings to carved doors, relieved only by touches of gold, that gave it a remoteness that was not reassuring for one come to stay under the same roof as his would-be murderer. The house spoke of money but little atmosphere. Auguste was just contemplating the reason for this when Thomas Entwhistle suddenly appeared from one of the salons leading off the foyer. Or was it once more Gregorin? Auguste's heart lurched uncomfortably, but he beamed a welcome. The beam's warmth did not penetrate the barrier of cold that enveloped the man who was undoubtedly Gregorin.

'My dear Mr Didier, welcome to Paris. Perkins, Tudor,' he nodded. 'My resident staff here are greatly looking forward to your visit.'

Probably with carving knives in hand, was Auguste's instant thought. Surely there could not be a second Ethelred Perkins in the world?

'Naturally, Mr Didier, your room will be on the guest floor.'

Why? What had Gregorin in mind? Auguste was instantly suspicious, but as it might suit him to be on both sides of the Great Door between upper and lower houses, his dry lips managed to murmur thanks.

The semi-basement kitchen area was as impressive as the Farthing Court kitchen, though in different style. Where black lead ruled at Farthing Court, gas ovens gleamed here, and marble tops replaced English oak. In one other respect also it differed. Instead of an array of aspiring Ethelred Perkinses, there was a bevy of kitchenmaids, even the underchef was female. Even more to his astonishment the chef was a woman. In the closed world of French cuisine, how was this tolerated?

'*Enchantée,* Monsieur Didier.' Madame Thérèse Lépine proved to be considerably older than Ethelred, but somewhat after the same style; thin, eagle-eyed and with the same air of general importance.

'I have heard much of you from Madame Pryde,' she continued. 'It is a pleasure to meet you, Monsieur Didier.'

Emma? Auguste warmed to Madame Lépine immediately. He had never been able to convince Tatiana of the essential charm of Emma Pryde, unlike some of his other *amies*. Dear Maisie was a friend to them both, as was Natalia Kallinkova, but at the name of Mrs Pryde, or even of Gwynne's Hotel in St James, which she owned and ran in her idiosyncratic way, a distinctly frosty Russian look came over Tatiana's usually amiable face. Auguste was forced to admit that Emma did not put herself out to endear herself to ladies, since gentlemen were more in her line, and it said much for Madame Lépine if she were part of Emma's *coterie*.

'If you are a friend of Emma's, you would be able to cook for His Majesty superbly,' Auguste assured her warmly.

'Indeed no, monsieur. We live simply here unless Monsieur Entwhistle entertains, and it will be an honour to work with you, and with Mr Perkins too.'

Thomas Entwhistle was, Auguste realised after a most delightful *suprême de volaille en Belle Vue*, a most extraordinary gentleman. Only with difficulty did he recall that he was indeed extraordinary. He was Pyotr Gregorin.

Auguste awoke early next morning with a feeling of restlessness, perhaps of unfinished business. Was it the list for the *marché*, was it the arrangements for the ices, His Majesty's *bécassines*? No, for once it was not food, he decided, it was something to do with this

265

house. Then he remembered. At Farthing Court a murder had taken place, for which he was by no means sure that the right person had been arrested. And many of the other persons involved were now staying under this roof: Gertrude, Gerald and Belinda Montfoy, Louisa, Richard, Harvey, the Pennyfathers. Moreover, once again, His Majesty would be present, at least at the reception. Surely this was no coincidence? The guests were arriving today, as was His Majesty, but with Eleonore's home in the Boulevard de Capucines so conveniently close, it seemed highly likely that they would be seeing little of His Majesty, even though he was staying so close in the Hôtel Bristol. Was that part of Gregorin's plan too?

He decided he would go for a walk, although it was only six o'clock. Outside he would be exposed to any designs Gregorin might have on his life, but on the whole it was unlikely that he would be standing guard at the front door with a dagger quite so early in the morning. Dismissing the unwelcome notion of hired assassins, he hurriedly washed and shaved, dressed, and went downstairs where only a bleary-eyed kitchenmaid greeted him with some nervousness. He would take a cup of coffee in a café rather than here. Where should he go? Les Halles Centrales, of course. To the market where– No, he would walk to the river instead, and he retraced his first steps. Working Paris was beginning to wake up, the gutters ran with water, tradesmen already added colour to the grey streets with their wares, and in the cafés, full of smoke, *ouvriers* were taking their first *marc* of the day with coffee. The smell was too enticing and he went inside the next café to present itself for a coffee, before continuing to the river.

The Seine was the lifeblood of Paris, fuller of traffic than the highways at this time of the morning. As he reached its familiar beauty, he wondered what he was doing there so far from Tatiana. Tatiana, not France, was home now. 'I could not love thee dear so much/Loved I not honour more.' Was that, in the poet's words, why he was here? To protect Cousin Bertie? Or was it the magnet of the banquet that had drawn him here? On an impulse, he jumped on to one of the *bâteau* omnibuses that served the Seine. He knew now where he wanted to go. He alighted at the Pont D'Alma and began to walk up to the Arc de Triomphe, and then on beyond that into familiar territory indeed. At this early hour the children, nannies and society ladies were not yet to be seen in the Parc Monceau. The houses of the great overlooking the parc were still silent, only the basement areas showing any

267

signs of movement from the road outside. He stood in the parc and looked up at a house he knew very well. Was Gregorin behind those closed shutters, or the real Thomas Entwhistle – if there was such a person? Or was there no one save servants here? He stopped a milk cart, who had just finished its deliveries, and bought a cup of milk to drink, suddenly aware that the coffee – it must be the coffee – was making his heart beat uncomfortably loudly.

'Who lives there?' he asked.

'*Russe,*' was the milkman's grunted answer. '*Très gentil, très riche.*' Guffaw of French laughter.

The Tsar paid his Okhrana well, as Auguste knew. A great part of the Imperial wealth or, as Tatiana pointed out wryly, of the country's wealth, was spent in maintaining it while the peasants starved. Fond though she was of Cousin Nikky, one day she was sure there would be more than just a few anarchists.

'Is he at home?'

'Now he is at home. I saw him only last evening.' A slightly suspicious look now, and the milkman rapidly took his departure.

Auguste had learnt nothing that he did not know already.

Then he saw a familiar figure emerging from the tradesman's entrance to Gregorin's house. It was Gertrude's maid, Jeanne

Planchet. How could she know Gregorin? He remembered the look of surprise she had given at Farthing Court at seeing the owner in the kitchen domain – had he been wrong in his conclusion that she was shocked at the breach of etiquette? Had she looked startled because she too had recognised Gregorin? Perhaps his visit here had been far from wasted.

'Bonjour, Mademoiselle Planchet. You are up early to attend mass, perhaps.'

Guilt, anger, obstinacy, shock – all these were reflected in her expression as she realised the identity of the gentleman who had apparently sprung from nowhere. Jeanne Planchet was well equal to the occasion. She simply replied, *'Oui, monsieur.'*

Begin with surprise, but not too great a surprise, like the perfect menu. 'When you told me at Farthing Court, mademoiselle, that you had worked briefly in this area, where was that exactly?'

'Rue du Faubourg St Honoré.' She began to walk speedily away from him, not into the Parc Monceau, but towards the Faubourg she had mentioned, where the many small shops would provide an excellent escape for her, he realised. He accompanied her.

'And not at the house of Mr Pyotr Gregorin, which you have just visited?'

Sudden wariness on her face. *'Non.'*

'You were there to see him, were you not?'

'*Non. Ma soeur.* She works in the kitchens.' A look of triumph.

He tried another tack. A gentler one. 'Mademoiselle, it is important for England and France that you tell me what you know.'

'It is even more important for me that I say *nothing.*'

'So you do know Gregorin, for otherwise you would not be scared.'

'Why *should* I be scared?'

'For your life. As I am.'

Even this failed to move her. 'He fears me.'

'Then he most certainly has reason to kill you. And knowing him, he will.'

At last he had succeeded, for she said almost pleadingly, 'If I say nothing, he will do nothing. And soon I will be away in America with Miss Gertrude.'

'She has decided to return home?' Auguste was surprised.

'Of course. Why not?'

'Suppose she marries another Englishman?'

Jeanne considered this. 'It would not be proper for her to do so for at least a year and a half. So she must go to America first. And once there, monsieur, I shall be safe.'

'Nowhere can one be safe from Gregorin, even in America. Assassins can work anywhere.'

'I will be. You do not know him, monsieur, as I do. He has a tender, loving side, and I have seen it.'

'Even though he dismissed you – from his employment, and, if I may guess, his bed?' He knew from Tatiana that Gregorin's tastes in women were as diverse and curious as his tastes in food – and also that one meal when concluded, was swiftly forgotten.

Jeanne marched straight ahead, and at last spoke. 'I will tell you this, monsieur. I can do *nothing* for Monsieur le President de France, or for the King of England, but you can. This reception tomorrow night is the climax of long, long planning for the person by the name of Entwhistle.'

'There is no real Thomas Entwhistle. And what is going to happen at this reception?'

'I can't tell you, except that his enemy is England.'

Never had the menu blackboard looked less attractive. A special kitchen leading off the main one had been prepared for him, Madame Lépine had informed him, a new gas pipe and stoves erected, new cupboards built, newly equipped with cutlery, pots and pans, mincing machines, even ice chests, not to mention his own staff seconded to carry out his every whim – or rather in the case of this menu, whim-wham, the English dish selected for the traditional English *entremet.* Tudor had a room leading off this new kitchen which was to be his own domain.

Auguste felt as if he were in the Grand Exposition of 1900, the kitchen of the future. It should be another paradise, but somehow it failed to be. The menu facing him on the blackboard seemed to be staring back at him menacingly, devoid of life, partly perhaps because his staff, instead of devotedly following their duties in silence or discussing in subdued tones the relative delights of *soufflé de loup de mer* as against *soufflé de turbot* were chattering about *le roi britannique*, Cousin Bertie, who had dined in full public view with the Comtesse Eleonore at Maxim's last evening, having enjoyed an equally public appearance with her at one of the jollier Champs Elysées theatres. Auguste had never known the King display his illicit preferences so publicly; he must indeed be smitten with Eleonore.

As soon as he had organised the preparation of the stock for the consommés, and prepared the final delivery lists for the Monday and Tuesday, encouraged the *patissier* chef in the early stages of the three great *flancs* which were to adorn the tables, he would go to see Richard Waites, he decided. The Sûreté did not believe him, Egbert did not believe him, but the Foreign Office would at least listen to him. There was no time to lose.

'Monsieur Didier.' The pert voice of the vegetable maid addressed him. 'Did you say spinach for the Potage Tranquille?'

'Non!' Auguste's shriek stopped the kitchen not in awe, but to giggle. One glance from his indignant eye quelled them. *'Laitue, s'il vous plait.'* He remembered his old adage: *menu mal fait diner perdu.* Tuesday's dinner would *not* be lost. He would have to work hard to bring this menu to life; and he would work as though it were to be the last banquet he ever cooked. Perhaps, he remembered gloomily, it would be.

To Auguste's relief, Richard Waites cordially agreed there was nothing he wanted more than a stroll along the boulevards and would be glad of company. Furthermore, he had been on the very point of suggesting it, should Mr Didier's work permit.

Auguste handed over to Ethelred the foundations of the *flanc* of Buckingham Palace, and the final checking of the menu to be sure the cardinal rule of no ingredient save truffles and *champignons* appearing twice on the same menu had not been broken. On being questioned as to the reason for his absence, Auguste had muttered a desire to seek out the finest snipe available at Les Halles, and prepared to do his duty by Cousin Bertie in a direction other than his stomach.

There was no doubt that a stroll along the Champs Elysées on a Sunday afternoon was a cheering experience, the boulvardiers and street entertainers were in full post-luncheon jollity, the plane trees out in their green spring dress.

'I wanted to talk to you, Mr Waites, about Pyotr Gregorin.'

Richard's face retained its usual impassive, somewhat amused, expression. 'And I wanted to talk to you about the Comtesse Eleonore.'

'*Quoi?*' Auguste quickly apologised for this impolite reaction, but it was the last thing he had expected.

'I see you are surprised. However, the Comtesse Eleonore will be a guest at the reception on Tuesday night.'

Auguste thought he understood. 'But His Majesty is a politician of much discretion. In the presence of the President of the Republic, Monsieur Delcassé, the Prime Minister, and the American envoy, surely you can have no fears that he would allow his private feelings to influence his behaviour at state functions, particularly one so important as this?'

'Hitherto,' Richard agreed, 'His Majesty has maintained a perfect balance between his public and his private lives. On this occasion he may believe he has done the same, since only on Tuesday will his 'official' visit to Paris begin. Nevertheless, having appeared publicly with the Comtesse at Maxim's and at the theatre, and by lunching with her today at her home, all Paris is talking of it, thus making it much more public than private.'

'You are worried news will reach the queen?' Auguste was puzzled. 'Paris has often talked before.'

Richard sighed. 'I don't know quite what I'm worried about, but–' he hesitated – 'people other than myself are concerned. I sense that Paris is for once deeply disapproving, and that cannot be good.'

'But she is married. Moreover her husband is a French diplomat.' Why did he feel bound to defend Eleonore? 'Is that the reason, do you think?'

'I don't know, but I intend to find out. I can't very well go straight to the *Deuxième Bureau,* but I shall make enquiries through the Embassy.'

'And why did you wish to talk to me about her?'

Richard laughed. 'Just as you as a keen detective may have observed an attraction on my part to Gertrude, I observed, as a trained diplomat, a similar attraction when you were talking to Eleonore. I wanted to ask whether she had ever mentioned anything that would lead you to suspect her motives in her *tendresse* for the king had any political ingredients.'

Had he been so caught up in his own emotion towards Eleonore that he had overlooked something? 'My first answer is no, but I will think very carefully.'

'And very quickly, if you will, please.'

'As I hope you will about Pyotr Gregorin.' Auguste waited to see whether this name had any effect on Richard.

'I heard about your theory that Thomas Entwhistle was a Russian spy in disguise.'

'And it amused you, no doubt.'

'I am never amused when the Okhrana is mentioned. Do you believe that poor Arthur was murdered by our host?'

'I can't see a motive for his killing Arthur, but I do believe he could have mistaken him for me.'

'So you don't believe in Bessie Wickman's guilt?'

'Only my sense of smell about the case tells me she is innocent.'

'Coming from a *maître chef*, that is a powerful argument. I presume the smell comes from the deer's head which deceived the murderer into thinking someone else, perhaps you, was beneath?'

'No. I think – I hope – it stems from elsewhere.'

Richard smiled. 'From the direction perhaps of myself? Like several other people, I could cheerfully have killed Arthur, were I a murderer. However, fortunately I am not.'

'I am more concerned at the moment with preventing trouble than solving it. If you accept the possibility that I am right about Entwhistle being Gregorin, then I beg you to think about the reception. Gregorin, not Eleonore, is our immediate problem.'

Richard flipped a coin into a street acrobat's collecting box.

'Perhaps it's both.'

Horace Pennyfather was extremely bored. For some mysterious reason Gertrude and Bluebell had managed to disappear to visit some museum on folklore, as soon as he expressed his own wish to sit in a nice café on the Champs Elysées and watch the world go by. Louisa equally mysteriously had then declared she knew where to find the best drink in the world, and would conduct him to it. This proved to be a long, undiluted, drink of culture. The Louvre was a mighty big place, and coming round in front of a struggling stone Laocoon for the fourth time in Louisa's indefatigable search for some lady with no arms, he went on strike.

'How about some tea and chocolates at Rumpelmayer's?'

Louisa, being British, knew all about strikes. She was also a shrewd judge of gentlemen, even Americans, and in any case it suited her plans. 'Why don't we go to some nice backstreet café where you can smoke and take a brandy?'

Horace warmed to her. These English duchesses weren't so bad when you got to know them.

'How is dear Gertrude?' Louisa asked solicitously, eyeing the patisseries wistfully and contemplating the stern reaction of her corsets if she were to indulge in them.

'Mighty shocked still, but my guess is it is the murder and not losing Arthur that's the cause.'

'She must be so relieved the murderess is found.'

Horace frowned. 'I don't mind telling you, Arthur wasn't the man I thought he was. A mistress is one thing, but meeting her on your wedding night is some weird English custom. Gerald tried to tell me it was called *droit de seigneur*, but it wouldn't happen in Ohio, I can tell you.'

'I gather Mrs Wickman was blackmailing Arthur.'

'I'm not surprised. Making out he was loaded with money, and as rich as Croesus, and all the while he was as broke as most of that stuff we saw in the museum.'

'So many English aristocrats have been marrying American heiresses, I suppose poor Arthur thought he could get away with it.' Louisa remembered who it was she claimed invited her to Farthing Court in the first place, and decided some defence of poor Arthur was called for. 'Consuelo Vanderbilt didn't find out until her wedding day that Blenheim didn't belong to her.'

Belatedly, Horace thought that even with a listener as sympathetic as Louisa it might not be wise to build up too much resentment against the late Lord Montfoy. 'I daresay he had his good points, of course. Too bad that woman took her revenge.'

'You're right, Horace. Will dear Gertrude be at your side on Tuesday?'

'Not for dinner. Far too soon, she says. I guess I'll be sitting with the US envoy and His Majesty.'

'How interesting,' Louisa said warmly. 'I do hope you are not embarrassed if you have that French diplomat's wife Eleonore sitting between you and His Majesty.'

Horace was horrified, not having thought of this possibility. The purpose of his presence was to further good relations between Britain and America, without all eyes being on that damned attractive countess. He needed an Englishwoman.

'I'll check with Thomas that she's well away from the king,' he said grimly. Then he looked more carefully at the Dizzy Duchess who was gazing at him in admiration. It was a long time since a woman had done that;

their gaze was usually directed straight at his pocket-book.

'Would you do me the honour, Louisa, of sitting with us at the reception?'

Louisa appeared overcome with surprise and gratitude. 'Oh, I *would*.'

'Generous fellow, Entwhistle,' Harvey remarked gloomily. He too was in the Louvre, only not with the lady of his choice. Gertrude had said it wouldn't be proper and had disappeared with Bluebell. Belinda Montfoy, on the other hand, seemed eager to come out even though she was still in deepest mourning. He took it she wanted a stroll in the Tuileries, but she, it appeared, had ideas of her own.

'Yes,' Belinda agreed without enthusiasm. When she explained that she would be unable to appear at the dinner on Tuesday, although like Gertrude she would join in the prior reception for Mr Smith, the American envoy, Thomas had commiserated with her so sweetly that she had believed their old relations were quite restored. However, when she had asked him to accompany her to the Musée des Antiquities Egyptiennes, he had refused almost abruptly, and she was forced to fall back on this odd American who didn't know a sarcophagus from a sarsen stone.

Harvey stared gloomily at a bas-relief of

Nekhtharheb of the XXXth dynasty, and wondered why Belinda thought it so entrancing.

'And now,' she declared with a deep sigh of regret at having to leave, 'we must find the Queen Karomana. And the bronze collection is said to be very fine.'

Harvey tried his best since he knew Europeans always seemed more enthusiastic about bits of old statues than newly carved ones. 'Amenmes and his wife Tepit,' he read on the label. 'A happy marriage,' was all he could find to comment on this representation of connubial bliss. It did nothing to lessen his depression.

'What a pity our host is not married.' She seized the opportunity to voice what was on her mind. 'You don't think there's anything *strange* about Mr Entwhistle, do you?'

'How do you mean?' Harvey replied guardedly, having the firm conviction that many unmarried Englishmen were distinctly strange, but unaware of whether Belinda would know about the obvious conclusion.

'He seems different.'

'Well, I guess some men prefer men to women. More fools they,' Harvey declared heartily, though he was beginning to think it might be a lot simpler.

Belinda stared at him deflatingly. 'I don't mean homosexual.'

281

Harvey was shocked at such outspokenness, for he had taken Belinda to be the epitome of an English lady.

'When I first met him in Paris and Arthur sold him Farthing Court,' Belinda continued obliviously, 'he was most friendly, but now in England he seems polite but distant. Does he appear so to you?'

Harvey pondered this. 'I guess I wouldn't like to have been in Arthur's shoes if I'd been tied to that pole and Entwhistle came by with a grudge against me.'

'That's what I feel too. You don't think he has any ulterior motive for inviting us all to this reception, do you?'

'What kind of motive?' Harvey stopped in front of a picture of some dame smiling.

'I don't know. But it was remarkably generous of him to loan the Court to Arthur for the wedding and pay for the village to–' She broke off very quickly.

'Pay the village to do what?'

'Buy new bells for the church,' she finished lamely.

'What's up, Bluebell?' Gertrude asked briskly. 'I thought you were keen on seeing these tapestries?'

Bluebell was. The calm lady in the Cluny Museum's treasured mediaeval tapestries of the Lady and the Unicorn somehow reminded her of Gertrude. 'I guess I'm still worried about Bessie,' she said reluctantly. 'I like her.'

'Even though she killed Arthur?' Gertrude showed her annoyance. The matter was over and done with until the trial.

'I don't think she did.' It was more of a mutter than a definite assertion.

'*Why?*' And when her sister did not answer, 'Bluebell, *tell* me.'

'I just wish I knew who that man was I saw coming through the trees.'

'Don't worry about him,' Gertrude said firmly. 'It's over. Do you hear me?'

'Yes. Gertrude. *Did* you go down to the maypole?'

'Of course not.' Her sister's anger showed momentarily before she controlled herself.

'If only I'd waited a few minutes I might have saved Bessie.'

'But you might make it worse for someone else.'

The unicorn gazed out peacefully from his centuries-old red tapestry home. *He* didn't have problems like this.

'Like Harvey?' she wanted to ask, but instead it came out as, 'Like Richard?'

Twelve hours to go. At six thirty this Tuesday evening Cousin Bertie would be sitting down to a dinner which might in some way represent the culmination of Gregorin's current mission, and that mission was to discredit Britain. Auguste tried to put out of his mind the still possible thesis that Gregorin's mission was to rid himself of the chef, not the guests. Already the last deliveries were beginning to arrive, carp, *écrevisses*, prawns for the bisque, turbot, salsify, snipe... Suddenly he felt the old excitement as one by one ingredients obediently presented themselves. His *Menu d'Unité* was all beginning to come together to form one glorious whole. Yet it could be ruined if Gregorin did indeed have political plans for the reception. Think, Richard Waites had said. *Think* about Eleonore, as well as Gregorin. He went over carefully, as best he could, each conversation he had had with her, every impression he had in watching her with other people. Lovingly he smelled the white truffles for the garnish. Perhaps, as so often, he would find the answer to the evening's problems by his work in the kitchen today, for there were many similarities between detection and the creation of a perfect menu. It might help if he added another blancmange to the menu. There was certainty in a blancmange. It would remain a blancmange and not suddenly transform itself into a jelly. It seemed a good starting point for the day.

Ten thirty. Eight hours to go. The heat was

rising from the ovens; *poulardes* were being stuffed ready for the grand dish *poularde Edward VII*, *canetons* were vigorously glazed, jellied and garnished, prawn after prawn surrendered its shell to the kitchenmaid's practised hands.

'Shall I start on the *crème comtesse* or the *pommes de terre duchesse*, Mr Didier?'

As he was about to answer the kitchen-maid's question with 'The *crème comtesse*, if you please,' he had a sudden memory of that embarrassing night when he had foiled His Majesty's plans, to the great benefit of the duchess, and a long unanswered question, apparently so insignificant, had come to mind: who was it who stole Louisa's hats?

He gathered up the bundles of asparagus for the crème. 'Yes, purée this now.' He would start with the *comtesse* and examine every little piece of this asparagus to check it was unflawed.

Twelve o'clock. Eleonore had been exonerated from the matter of the hats. Eleonore herself had taken breakfast and then coffee with the duchess. She had departed from the duchess's rooms to change for the wedding, and the duchess's maid had this morning informed him that the hats were still present then, and that she had been told by Eleonore's maid (interrogated at Louisa's insistence) that Eleonore had not

285

left the room again. With the time available and the intricacies of ladies' formal dress, there was no reason to doubt her. Moreover, Eleonore's lady's maid had escorted Louisa's maid all round Eleonore's room to prove her mistress's innocence. The duchess's maid had only left the room for a few minutes to answer a summons from Mrs Honey. The *crème comtesse* was innocent in respect of hats.

What, Auguste asked himself, had been the result of that fiasco?

Eleonore and not Louisa had been escorted to the wedding by His Majesty. It had restored their good relations. But that had nothing to do with politics or Gregorin, had it?

Or both? Richard Waites had asked. *Or both.*

Ignoring the kitchenmaid's request to check the *pommes de terre duchesse*, Auguste rushed to the grand dining room where Tudor and his French counterpart were busily polishing silver and placing plates on the two already splendidly decorated long tables and a third high table. Red, white and blue flowers to honour the three flags were woven on hooped arches over the tables, and in defiance of any French fairies that might be lurking in the Place Vendôme, greenery was clustered at the bottom of each arch. On the tables Sèvres china gleamed and crystal shone. The menu cards, each supported on their miniature Statues of Liberty carved in ivory, were already in position. What had he come to look at? What did he hope to find? Tudor did his best to prevent Auguste looking at anything at all, but before he physically evicted him from the room, Auguste had seen the high table – which had ten place settings.

Mr Entwhistle, as host, was at one end of the table, with the President's wife on his left and Louisa on his right; at the other end, with the French president on her left and His Majesty on the right, was the place card for the Comtesse Eleonore.

Tudor, following at his heels, explained. 'In the enforced absence of both Lady Montfoy and Miss Montfoy, the comtesse is kindly acting as hostess. Now, Mr Didier, if you would leave us to our work–'

Hostess? There was nothing wrong with this; if she were the formal hostess, the president would obviously be on her left and the king would naturally as the highest ranking personage present be on her right. And yet...

Three o'clock. Preparation of the garnishes and beginning of the *délices à la Russe*. All in due order, one by one. *Due order!* Of course! Now he knew what had been troubling him.

287

The guest of honour, the American envoy, should have been on Eleonore's left. And why was Eleonore hostess when she hardly knew Entwhistle, let alone Gregorin? Why not, on the other hand? He indecisively hesitated between *truffe* and *champignon* to garnish the *volaille*. She was French, she knew His Majesty... He had just decided to have another look at the table, Tudor or no Tudor, when fate in the form of a summons to His Majesty at the Hôtel Bristol intervened.

Fuming, he obeyed. As if there were not enough to think about. This was probably to check *Poularde Derby* was on the menu. It was not. It was an irate monarch.

'I hear you've been interesting yourself in the placing arrangements for this evening, Didier.'

'Yes, sir.' How did he know? Had Tudor bothered to tell Gregorin? If so, *why?* There was only one answer. It affected Gregorin's plans. 'And I am worried–'

'Not still on about Russian spies are you?'

'Yes, sir. Furthermore the comtesse is Mr Entwhistle's hostess. Or, as his real name is, Pyotr Gregorin of the Okhrana. And she is sitting between you and the President of France.' He'd gone wrong somewhere, he realised.

His Majesty turned an interesting hue between red and purple. 'Look, Didier, there's an alliance between France and Britain. Just what harm can the Comtesse Eleonore's friendship do to that? And just what do you think my private life has to do with you? The press understand the difference between private and public, why don't you?'

'But tonight will be a public occasion.'

'Certainly. Eleonore is my public hostess.'

'And your very public – er – companion, sir, this weekend. There is talk...'

He thought His Majesty was going to explode like a pressure cooker, but to his relief the temperature moderated just in time. His Majesty never forgot his public face, he merely laid it aside from time to time. 'Very well. I'll tell *Entwhistle*, not Gregorin, mind, that I want Mrs Smith, the US envoy's wife at the head of the table, etiquette or no etiquette. That do?'

'Thank you, sir.'

'Don't thank me, Didier. Just thank your lucky stars I don't kick you out of my sight for ever.'

'I do, sir.'

'Moreover,' the King rumbled as an afterthought, 'don't think I don't realise your interest in all this. Damned attractive woman, Eleonore. One word to Her Majesty and quite a few reach Tatiana. That clear?'

'Quite clear, sir.'

Six o'clock. He should be feeling overjoyed. He did not. The *poulardes* were about to go into the ovens, the soups to be gently reheated. The footmen were even now collecting the trays of *délices* à *la Russe* for the reception before the dinner. Bottles of champagne were being transported in ice up to the serving side rooms. Since even Gregorin would not dare defy the king's wishes, there was surely nothing to worry about. Somehow Auguste could not convince himself. If Eleonore was part of Gregorin's plan, it would mean that she was far from being the delightful lady he had thought her. He had no proof at all that she was anything other than she appeared. So why did he feel as though the soufflés were all about to sink beyond salvation?

'Tarte oh pomme's ready,' Ethelred cried. His mastery of French left much to be desired.

'Tarte à *l'oignon?'* Auguste was miles away.

'Haven't done one of them, Mr Didier. Not on the menu.'

Auguste pulled himself together. What had he said? *Tarte à l'oignon.* How ridiculous. As though he would have put that Alsatian speciality on his menu this evening of all evenings. Alsatian... Think over every conversation with Eleonore: *bergamottes, quetsches,* both from that area, that husky voice, the French almost too beautifully spoken. Could it be that Eleonore was not from Normandy but from Alsace-Lorraine, once French and now German? Even so, she was married to a French diplomat now, he told himself. Then he remembered, sickeningly, they only had her word for that. Why hadn't Richard Waites come to tell him about his enquiries through the Embassy? If by any chance he was right, and even if *tarte à l'oignon* were not on Gregorin's menu tonight Eleonore undoubtedly was. She was and always had been the main course in his plans.

He rushed into the main house, only belatedly remembering to remove his hat and apron lest the Sûreté who were already here in full force to protect the guests, arrest him on suspicion. They would be looking for gunmen, or bombs, not for Gregorin's more insidious methods of assassination. Auguste found Richard Waites in the delicate process of tying his own tie, and poured out his fears, appalled that ties appeared to have taken precedence over Gregorin.

'The Embassy have telephoned London,' Richard explained, somewhat annoyed at the interruption. 'They haven't come up with anything new on Gregorin or Eleonore.'

'It's Paris we need to ask if I'm right,'

Auguste said, explaining his reasons as rapidly as he could.

The tie promptly lost its precedence.

A quarter to seven. Auguste fidgeted, unable to settle, aware that even now the reception was under way and he had heard nothing yet from Richard Waites, who had disappeared once more to the Embassy.

'How is the reception?' he asked Tudor anxiously as he rushed through the door to collect more *délices.*

'Not too well.' He seemed almost pleased. 'The French and the Americans are standing on one side of the room, and the British, Russians and Germans on the other.'

Why should that be? Auguste worried. Or was he imagining things, and such a social pattern was merely coincidence.

Coincidence? No such thing where Gregorin was concerned. He could wait no longer for Richard. He must check the place cards to ensure Gregorin had had them changed. The Sûreté detectives would throw him out if he went in in chef's garb. Should he ask Tudor to do it? No, everything and everyone to do with Entwhistle must be suspect at this late stage. He rushed to the footmen's dressing room, praying that as in England a spare costume would be hanging there. There was, and ten minutes later, a somewhat flustered footman in full livery and imperfectly powdered wig marched confidently into the dining room, bearing the only thing he could find to explain his presence.

'His Majesty's horseradish,' Auguste announced to the assembled panoply of footmen and detectives, then advanced to the table to place the unlovely root on it. He had been right. According to the place settings, His Majesty was seated opposite Monsieur Delcassé, the French foreign minister and *bête noire* of the Kaiser, and between the two was still the place card for the probably German Eleonore, with whom the king had all too publicly spent the preceding three days. The *entente* would be *cordiale* no longer unless he acted immediately.

Seven thirty. The doors were flung open and a third footman attached himself to the two gentlemen who stood to attention to usher the guests in. He tried to make himself conspicuous. First came a smiling Pyotr Gregorin, bearing on his arm the president's wife, and behind him the other guests in order of precedence. Precedence broke down, for at the end of the procession, Eleonore, bewitchingly glowing in white satin, was on the arm of His Britannic Majesty. Amongst the guests, joining the procession belatedly, was a white-faced Richard Waites, whose attention to his initial astonishment Auguste managed to attract, drawing him aside.

'I'm sorry, Didier,' Richard said immediately. 'You were right, but we can do nothing now.'

'It's done, sir.' Auguste was aware of the Sûreté detective's suspicious eye upon him, and quickly whispered instructions to Richard.

Working at a speed unusual to the Foreign Office, Richard immediately approached one of the guests, firmly escorting her to her new position, just as the rest of the procession arrived in the dining room.

Auguste bowed deeply to His Majesty, as Richard with practised ease drew Eleonore aside to allow His Majesty to take his place next to his new dining partner.

His Majesty Edward VII looked round in satisfaction. He'd told Entwhistle in a few well chosen words that Eleonore was on no account to be seated near him, and she wasn't. Then the satisfaction vanished. He was, as he had expected, facing the President of France, but between them at the head of the table was the over-familiar face of Louisa, Duchess of Wessex. Looking around briefly, apoplectic with rage before he could arrange his features into a public expression of agreeable cheer, he saw another familiar face. It was blasted cousin-by-marriage Didier dressed up as a footman.

Eight

'The trouble with you, Didier, is that you have spies on the brain.' His Majesty, reclining in the luxury of his suite at the Hôtel Bristol, regarded Auguste with a complacent eye, no doubt comforting himself that the previous evening had gone off rather well.

And the trouble with Cousin Bertie, Auguste thought savagely, was that he was seldom predictable – save where his mutton chops and other assorted culinary delights were concerned. Having been summoned to appear before His Majesty, he had naturally expected to receive His Majesty's grateful thanks at being saved from a potentially highly embarrassing international situation. Unfortunately His Majesty possessed an uncanny knack of seeing matters entirely differently from Auguste Didier.

'Mr Waites will tell you that the comtesse is not what she seems.'

'The Foreign Office will tell me what suits them.' His Majesty looked rather pleased at his own ready wit. Then he remembered his cause for annoyance.

'You put me in an embarrassing position,

Didier. The Duchess of Wessex is—'

'Preferable to the German wife of the Kaiser's envoy at this delicate moment, sir.'

There was a silence, until His Majesty produced his masterstroke. 'I'd remind you I'm German myself, Didier. The comtesse and I have much in common.'

'I beg your pardon, sir. I assumed you did not know her background.'

'I have to admit that I was under the impression that she was from Normandy, and her husband Russian.' Coming from Bertie, this was a generous concession.

'As she told us, sir.'

'Us?' His Majesty turned a delicate shade of puce.

'Me, sir,' Auguste added hastily. 'I had assumed foolishly – Eleonore used her Norman title because her husband's Russian title was unpronounceable.'

The puce lightened a little. 'Very understandable, Didier.' Another heavy silence as His Majesty sought a path out of this thorny wood, then he pronounced judgement. 'On the whole, Didier, you did the right thing, in the particular circumstances of last evening.'

This was munificent praise indeed and Auguste glowed with pleasure. 'Have you seen the comtesse since, sir?' he asked, emboldened.

'Certainly. She explained to me that she

does not use her married name in Paris, since being born in Alsace only a few years after the war, she always considers herself French. You can understand that, can't you?'

'Yes, sir.' In this new-found amicability between them, Auguste decided to risk one further step. 'And does she admit she knows Pyotr Gregorin?' It was a mistaken one.

'I told you. You've spies on the mind,' His Majesty roared. 'She doesn't know this Gregorin. She hardly even knew Entwhistle before she went to Farthing Court, and, I tell you this, Didier, you're worse than Sweeney for asking impertinent questions.'

At least Auguste felt he was in good company if Cousin Bertie's loyal detective was concerned about the situation.

'But Mr Entwhistle did ask her to be his hostess.'

'Because he's English, and she was French, so he assumed, and it seemed good manners.' He managed to imply this was something alien to Auguste.

'However, Mr Entwhistle lives in Paris too and he, like the rest of Parisian society, must have known she was not.'

Bertie gazed at him, and Auguste held his breath. Would he explode? Order an immediate annulment of marriage for Tatiana? Forbid him his presence for ever (oh, happy thought)? None of these.

'If *you* think that way, Didier, I suppose others might get the wrong impression too.' The comment, however welcome, was grudging and there was a clear implication that the world was full of imbeciles and Auguste was in the upper echelons of their ranks. 'Very well, I'll invite the comtesse's husband.'

'To what, sir?'

'I expect it's escaped your attention, Didier, but there's a state royal wedding on the 15th June. My niece Princess Margaret of Connaught is marrying the son of the Crown Prince of Sweden. Tatiana's coming, and I presumed you would be good enough to join us too. You needn't cook,' he added kindly.

Auguste had a dim memory of Tatiana having mentioned it, but higher in her social calendar for June had come the Gordon Bennett eliminating trials on the Auvergne circuit. Besides, if one were to attend every royal wedding in Europe, one would spend one's entire life travelling between weddings. The Crown Prince of Germany was marrying in Berlin in a week's time, and that, he knew, His Majesty had skilfully avoided attending, so bad were the current personal relations between the two Emperors.

'It will be an honour, sir.' He bowed deeply, and retreated, every backward step taking him back through the looking-glass into a saner world.

The day after a banquet was normally a pleasant day of relaxation and assessment, of noting tiny details that might improve on reflection for the future, and above all, of glorying in the achievement of the preceding day. Auguste walked back to the Hôtel Entwhistle in some trepidation. The guests, he knew, would be leaving on Thursday, as would Ethelred and Tudor. The latter had asked most specifically whether he would help them today in checking the bills to be submitted to Mr Entwhistle.

Auguste's instinct was to leave as soon as possible, but he consoled himself that if he remained close to Ethelred, there was little Gregorin could do. He had seen nothing of his host, though he had lain awake last night behind the locked bedroom door, expecting that Gregorin might appear at any moment to take his revenge as promptly as possible. Now he had double cause, for in addition to his temerity in marrying Tatiana, he had foiled Gregorin's political plans. He had waited on edge. How Gregorin would come he did not know, but he was convinced that come he would. Down the chimney perhaps, bearing the gift of death.

Nothing had happened. Had his and

Richard Waites' fears of what might have happened at the reception been over-estimated? Had this whole thing been – as His Majesty implied – a blown-up figment of his imagination? He went to his bedroom to change from his best Bertie-visiting suit to working clothes, and even refrained from his recent, rather shamefaced search under the bed for assassins. He had almost convinced himself that he had been suffering from an overdose of imagination. With his familiar working suit and carrying apron and hat until he had reached the servants' stairs, he turned along the corridor, turned the corner to the stairs, his confidence growing with every step. Then he came face to face with Gregorin.

'Good morning, Mr Didier.'

'*Bonjour,* Monsieur Gregorin.' The shock made him blurt out the wrong name.

His host looked puzzled. Could it be genuine? Auguste thought, heart thudding, waiting for the panther to pounce. If this *was* Gregorin, he had ample opportunity to kill him here. He waited seemingly interminably for Gregorin to speak.

'I must congratulate you on your achievements last night.'

'Achievements?' Auguste stuttered. 'The – er – table arrangements, sir?'

That puzzled look again. 'The *bécassines à la souvaroff* in particular were superb.'

Gregorin – or could it possibly be Entwhistle – passed him and continued on his way.

Auguste decided he must leave, and soon. Never had he wanted the comfort of Egbert's dry advice and support more. In the kitchens he found Ethelred and Tudor packing up their personal implements before these disappeared into the drawers and cupboards of the Place Vendôme. Glad of something definite to do, Auguste found his own precious knives and lovingly stored them away in their own carrying bag. Tomorrow evening his knives would be back in their home kitchen at Queen Anne's Gate in London, and the only distance he intended them to travel thereafter was to Tatiana's Ladies' Motoring Club restaurant in Petty France.

'Where will you go, Gerald?' Belinda asked idly. 'You can't live in the Ritz forever.'

They were sharing a *fiacre* to the Gare du Nord, both preoccupied with their own position. Belinda with true historian's precision had hit the nail on the head. Young Gerald most certainly could not afford the Ritz forever, and so far no alternative plan seemed ideal. As for Belinda, she was experiencing a distinct sense of anti-climax. Once again, just as her friendship with Thomas seemed on the point of bursting into bloom again, he had withdrawn behind his barrier of reserve. She tried to tell herself without success that it was due to shyness.

Gerald grinned, deciding now was the time to explain to Belinda what his obvious, even if temporary, plan should be.

'Dear Belinda. I have no choice. I shall move into the Dower House.'

'*What?*' Belinda felt the shock like a physical jolt far worse than the *fiacre* bumping over the *pavé*. 'But it doesn't belong to you, Gerald.'

'Nor to you, Belinda.'

Belinda had long since faced the unpleasant fact that she would be dependent on her new sister-in-law to keep the Dower House roof over her head, since Arthur had in the euphoria of his coming wedding given no thought to wills. It was true she had a two-roomed flat at the top of a house in Doughty Street, but few Egyptian remains could be stored there. No, the Dower House it must be – but *not* with Young Gerald. She must speak to Gertrude at the first opportunity.

Gerald looked amused. 'Don't worry, Belinda. I'm sure Gertrude will see things my – or rather *our* way. After all, there's some unfinished business at Farthing Court.' He paused. 'Pay the cabbie, will you, there's a dear girl?'

It lay on Auguste's conscience that because of his own preoccupations he had not taken Ethelred round the delights of gastronomic Paris. He had not escorted him stall by stall round Les Halles market or introduced him to chef and kitchen at Voisin, or lunched with him at La Coupole. Even as the cab bore them along the Boulevard des Italiens and ever closer to the railway station, he found himself torn between pleasure at escaping with his life and reluctance to be leaving so many culinary delights behind with which he had failed to renew his acquaintance.

'I did not see Mr Entwhistle before I left,' Ethelred commented regretfully. 'I hope he is not displeased with us.'

'He complimented us on the dinner when I met him yesterday,' Auguste mumbled.

'And us as well. However, he had told us he would see us this morning about arrangements for Farthing Court.'

'What arrangements for Farthing Court?' Auguste was instantly suspicious.

'I don't know,' Ethelred explained patiently. 'I didn't see him.'

'His plans changed.' Tudor eyed a pretty French mademoiselle emerging from a boulangerie, and dragged his thoughts back to work. 'My apologies, Ethelred. I forgot to tell you. I took a telephone message for him while he was at breakfast. He had to go out to meet a friend of his at noon at Denfert-Rochereau. He often goes there, so the Frenchie told me.' (The Frenchie was his Place Vendôme counterpart, Auguste guessed, rather than himself on this occasion.)

'That wouldn't be,' Auguste asked, feeling there was nothing to be lost now, 'a Mr Gregorin, would it?'

'I believe so.'

Snap! Back into the jaws of death once more. How could he miss this opportunity? There were other trains and boats to England, but only this one fragile chance of seeing Entwhistle and Gregorin together. Hardly thinking how odd his behaviour must seem to Ethelred and Tudor, he leapt from the cab as the horses halted at the Gare du Nord, prepared to rush to the underground railway station. He was stopped only by the driver's less than polite demand for payment. He threw him two francs, and with a muttered excuse of the sudden need for a visit to Fauchon, and still clutching his precious bag of kitchen knives, he hurried to the *chemin de fer metropolitain*. Fortunately Place Denfert Rochereau was on the same line as the Gare du Nord, a new one since his days in Paris, which meant that if he was lucky he could be there by midday.

He fidgeted impatiently on the underground train, wondering what this would achieve. It would prove to him at least there were two Entwhistles, and also therefore two Gregorins, one standing in for the other as and when needed. Eleonore once more came into his mind and refused to be banished. Which of the gentlemen did she know? Or think she knew. And how well did she know him?

Coming up from the underground railway at Denfert Rochereau, Auguste blinked in the sun, and walked into a scene of such normality he could have thought himself a boy again in Cannes. In late May the plane trees were adorned in their fresh green leaves, the women and children had a spring in their step and summer colours in their clothes. Already in the cafés the bread was being cut for luncheon, and the smells of *coq au vin* and *tripes* à *la Caen* were mingling with those of coffee and hot bread. The idea of sitting in a café with a bowl of *moules,* a glass of wine, and a crust or two of bread was almost irresistible, and had to be replaced firmly by that of Gregorin.

Where, he asked himself, would he find Gregorin and Entwhistle in this late morning hubbub? Their clothes alone would help mark them from the *ouvriers* of the Place Denfert Rochereau. In the centre of the *place* the magnificent Lion de Belfort gazed down impassively on his problem. Not so very long ago this area had been outside the Paris boundaries, but now it was swallowed up into the city, and though the Seine and its bridges were far from here, it had the style of Paris. People sat outside and inside cafés watching the world pass by. A café was surely the most likely rendezvous point.

He decided to choose the grandest, and went in to stand at the bar where he had a good view of those outside as well as inside. Almost immediately he saw him. At a table by the window Gregorin sat impassively smoking a cigarette and drinking a small coffee. He was alone, clad in top hat, grey morning coat and striped trousers, the epitome of a gentleman. Only he wasn't. He was a ruthless murderer. Or was it Entwhistle? Auguste was too far away to be certain. Through the main door came another identically clad gentleman to join him. As Gregorin stood up to greet him, he saw that he was slightly the taller of the two, perhaps by an inch. Other than that, they were remarkably similar, lean of body and face, and the same sharp features. Relief swept over him. He had, he congratulated himself, been right. The junket had set, the *aspic de volaille* had unmoulded perfectly, there *were* two Gregorins. Whether Entwhistle belonged to the Okhrana or was merely Gregorin's paid tool was immaterial – for the moment.

Fear left him now, as he realised the two men were leaving. Of course he would follow them. It was easy enough in the crowded square. He merged with the crowd waiting its chance to cross the Boulevard St Jacques, amid the heavy flow of horse and motor traffic, then the Avenue Montsouris; he could see his quarry walking towards the building that used to be the tollgate for the old road south, the Avenue d'Orleans, pausing only for a moment for one of them to buy a flower from a rose seller. Such innocuous business. Surely it was hard to believe at least one of these men was a murderer several times over, and the other one his willing accomplice?

Barrière d'Enfer, they called it, Hell's Gate. And with great reason Auguste thought, for it was the entrance to the catacombs, the vast underground charnelhouse of bones taken from the overflowing putrefying cemeteries of Paris in the eighteenth and nineteenth centuries and stored in the ancient limestone quarries that underlaid this whole area. Although the catacombs were only open two Saturdays a month, to Auguste's curiosity the two men appeared to be going inside. Nor, he could see, as he reached the pavement not far from them, were they let in by a concierge either, but were unlocking it with a key. Perhaps they had special permission from the concierge, or more likely they had stolen or been given a key by a workman, as he recalled a group of bohemian artists and writers had done a few years ago when they decided they would like to hold a grim service in the crypt.

Gregorin and Entwhistle had disappeared now, but the door was ajar.

What should he do? Auguste hovered momentarily in indecision. He would be a fly walking into a spider's web if he followed them inside and they saw him. If they did not see him, however, he could not only learn something about them but, more importantly, what their future plans might be. An alarming thought had come to him. If Eleonore was going to the royal wedding, suppose Gregorin also had plans to attend, under the guise of Thomas Entwhistle?

He knew from his visit to the catacombs years earlier that there was a maze of cross-way passages down there of which King Minos of Crete would have been proud. Even if many were barred to the public, they still provided alcoves for hiding places. But it was a terrifying place, especially alone and in all but pitch dark. Candles carried by visitors were the only means of lighting. With his heart in his mouth he slipped through the door, telling himself that if the two men were still in the small entrance hall inside, he had time to retreat. He relaxed slightly when he realised it was empty. The light flooding in from outside revealed only a deserted *guichet* and a box of candles for the use of visitors, and matches.

Now was the moment of decision. If he was to try to catch up with them, he must descend into the deep darkness beneath, with only a candle to light his way. He knew it was sheer foolishness, yet obstinacy sent him on. Realising he was still clutching his precious bag of kitchen instruments, he placed it on the counter of the *guichet* with some reluctance, for he could not carry both it and a candle and still have a hand free. Feeling absurdly melodramatic, how-ever, he slipped one of the smaller knives into his jacket pocket, then lit a candle. Prudence suggested he put another in his pocket, together with the matches, and thus equipped he began the journey down seventy spiralling steps which led to the catacombs beneath.

At the bottom he stopped for a moment to listen to the silence. One could tell much from silence; it could speak of emptiness, of tension, of someone waiting to strike out from its depths. Ahead of him he knew there was a long, perhaps half a mile, narrow passageway, and he had only his own flickering candle to guide him.

Wherever Gregorin and Entwhistle were,

he did not sense them nearby. He seemed to remember that this passageway bordered by its stone walls led to the ossuary, some way away, but that there were one or two changes of direction in it which might account for the fact he had no sense of Gregorin being nearby. A thick black line painted on one wall provided a guide for visitors as to which way they should take, for soon the crossway passages would start.

Auguste began to feel like Hansel and Gretel in the Grimm Brothers' fairy tale making their way to the witch's house. Should he leave a trail behind him to show the way he had gone? He reminded himself that dozens of visitors passed this way each time the catacombs were open to the public, and none had ever been lost, but it failed to cheer him up.

As he walked along the passageway running directly beneath the Avenue Mont-souris, his feeling of running into danger intensified. What could Entwhistle and Gregorin be doing here? If Tudor was right and they often met here, why? It seemed a lot of effort merely to find a place to be alone.

At last the candle revealed that the passageway was opening into a rounded chamber but it, too, was empty of life, only stone inscriptions reminding him that men had worked down here – and died too –

during the Revolution and the Commune. Auguste decided to stop thinking about massacres as the passageway led him into the entry chamber for the ossuary. The candlelight revealed starkly black-painted pillars, but more chillingly it revealed to Auguste's eyes the discouraging inscription over the doorway *'Arrête; c'est ici l'empire de la mort.'*

Beyond here, he would find himself in a tangle of interwoven passages, each one lined with skulls and bones arranged in artistic patterns of death; only the inscriptions of which churchyards the bones had come from, or a line from a French poet or from Virgil's *Aeneid* enlivened this city of the dead. Taking a deep breath, he plunged forward; he must go on to the furthest point of the catacombs, the crypt of Sacellum, for there, if anywhere, Gregorin and Entwhistle must have halted.

Bones seemed to stretch out to him in mute appeal as he passed, and fanciful ideas flashed through his mind. What if they reached out further and barred his way, if the dead rose up to protest at his intrusion from life and sought to make him one of them? How easy it would be to lose the comforting black line on the walls, and plunge by mistake into a side passage. Perhaps he was already alone here; perhaps Entwhistle and Gregorin had finished their business, gone out through the exit door and vanished. He almost hoped they had – until he recalled they might have locked him in, and it would be ten days until the first Saturday of the month would bring the concierge and his visitors here again. Auguste battled with his instant desire to flee from this charnelhouse and reach the blessed air, for he realised the crypt of Sacellum now lay just ahead.

He could hear the sound of his own breathing, but nothing else. No voices, no other breath, no light. Opposite to where he stood, on the other side of a central block of stone, he could see the passage that led out of the crypt of Sacellum towards the catacombs' exit door; on his right, at the far end of the crypt was a rough-hewn altar. His heart seemed to be thudding like a mallet pounding on a steak. He must go in, he *would* go in.

'*Arrête-toi, Didier!*'

The scream just behind his right ear deafened him, terrified him; but what terrified him more was the mocking laugh of Gregorin which followed. Snap; the mouse had fallen into the cat's trap. As yet there was no touch on him only the sound of breathing and the sense of fear.

He would not turn towards Gregorin; instead he catapulted into the crypt followed by Gregorin's mocking voice:

'Ici l'empire de votre mort, Didier.'

Auguste reached the far side of the crypt and, hearing nothing, bravely stopped, swinging the candle up to see Gregorin's pale face grinning at him only a few feet away. Did the man see in the dark? Had he no need of candles? Even as the thought crossed his mind, he knew the answer. He was going to take Auguste's – after its present holder was dead.

'Pray don't be so alarmed, Didier. I prefer to kill from the front; so much more sporting, as I'm sure you will agree. So good of you to obey my summons.'

Auguste could not reach the passage he had come in by. All he could do was to spring forward down the exit passageway. And here, he instantly realised, Entwhistle might be waiting, or was it Gregorin's plan to let him run as fast as he could to the exit door – and then find it locked against him? He would turn – to find himself face to face with Gregorin.

'Alors,' Auguste managed to make his voice sound steady, 'what do you mean, your summons?'

'Through dear Ethelred. He has the makings of an excellent agent, rather better than you, Didier. Your profession seems to attract criminal minds.'

'So Ethelred and Tudor work for the Okhrana, or for the mysterious Mr Entwhistle?' Auguste's heart sank. He had been sent to his death by those he trusted most.

'For me, Mr Didier. Money smoothes most palms. I discovered Ethelred on the streets of London, and Tudor in Wormwood Scrubs.'

'And Mrs Honey?' Auguste asked bitterly.

'Running a brothel off the Haymarket.'

The last vestiges of Tir Nan Og crashed around Auguste in an inglorious *Götterdamerung*.

'Shall we both stroll towards the altar, where there is more space and we can continue our business more easily?' Gregorin asked gently. 'And this time, I can assure you, Mr Didier, your last prayers, which as a good Catholic I must permit you, will not be answered by the redoubtable Inspector Rose.'

'Are you, as a good Catholic, permitted to take life?' Auguste managed to reply coolly.

'Ah, that raises a moral question I have devoted much thought to: should my religion or my duty to my country come first?'

There seemed little point in not following Gregorin's suggestion to move nearer the altar, Auguste decided cautiously. It might indeed offer more flexibility. He remembered the knife in his pocket, which no longer seemed melodramatic, and it comforted him as he took the fateful steps.

316

There was no doubt now that this was Gregorin; the invisible barrier of chill around him surmounted even this cold atmosphere.

'You wish to kill me because I married your niece.' How odd, Auguste thought. His voice sounded quite calm. 'That is hardly a duty to your country.' What weapons did Gregorin carry? None that Auguste could see, but he was well aware that Wyatt Earp would have envied Gregorin's sleight of hand on the draw.

'My family is Russia.'

'Then the Tsar knows of your plans for me?'

'It is my duty to guide His Serene Highness, not to inform him of my methods. Some of course he is aware of. For some years the Okhrana has had a policy of providing its agents with as near a double as possible; they remain passive themselves, merely obliging in delicate situations, with a convenient alias or alibi. Dear Thomas is *always* obliging.'

'And where is dear Thomas now?'

'Long since left these delightful surroundings for my home at the Parc Monceau. When your body is discovered and the time of death ascertained, Gregorin will have been entertaining French diplomats for some hours. Had Tatiana still been in Paris I would have suggested he entertained her to give myself the perfect alibi. You understand I am only speaking so freely because what I say will die with you.'

'Is it you or Entwhistle who have so carefully sought the king's acquaintance?'

'Myself, naturally. I flatter myself I have had quite a rapport with His Majesty, a rapport which you have annoyingly smashed. I think we will find it will return when you are no longer alive. I deal you a spade, Mr Didier, the card of death!'

His hand flicked like lightning into a pocket, and in the dim candlelight a playing card fluttered to the ground. Gregorin began to hum from *The Queen of Spades*, and the sound seemed sacrilegious in this place of death. His own death. *'Principium et finis. Eternité'* as the inscription above the altar reminded Auguste only too vividly.

'Come, Mr Didier, do not look so glum. It is a fair fight, for you tried to kill me at Farthing Court.' He gave a shriek of maniacal laughter.

'Moi?'

'Why look so surprised? Poor Arthur. You thought it was me beneath that deer's head, did you not, and killed me perhaps with some thought of saving not only the king, but yourself.'

'You killed Montfoy,' Auguste said vehemently. What trick was this?

'I?' Gregorin laughed. 'I am glad you can

318

still jest, Mr Didier. Or can you?' He paused, coming close so that he could see Auguste's face behind the candle. It was all Auguste could do not to step back, but he held his ground. 'Are you telling me you *didn't* kill Arthur? Remember, these are your last words before you face your God, Didier.'

'I did not. You know full well that you did, believing it was me.'

'Dear me. Suppose for the sake of argument neither of us killed poor Arthur. Who did?'

'The police believe it was Bessie Wickman.' Oh, how far away Frimhurst seemed now that all that was real was this darkness, this candle – and the certitude of imminent death. Then he remembered the knife. How could he reach it with a candle in one hand, without Gregorin being on him before the knife was out of his pocket? Only by keeping him talking.

'And Eleonore. Did you plot with her to seduce His Majesty?' The free hand crept to his side.

'It was her idea. She speaks most highly of you, incidentally. Another reason to kill you.'

'Why?' Slowly the hand inched up towards the pocket.

'Firstly, since you have clearly been unfaithful at least in your heart to my niece;

secondly and more importantly that while I can for my country's sake tolerate the idea of sharing my mistress with the King of England, I have no intention of sharing her with a *cook!*'

Sheer instinct made Auguste swerve as Gregorin leapt forward.

He blew out the candle, dashed it in Gregorin's face, and then fell back against the wall, creeping along it towards the passageway out, but as he felt rather than heard Gregorin coming after him, he began to double back, manoeuvring his way back through the crypt of Sacellum in the hope of reaching the entrance passage. A sixth sense warned him that Gregorin had anticipated his plan, and he stopped and took the knife from his pocket. He would never have time to use it if Gregorin found him again, but it comforted him nevertheless. He forced himself to retreat slowly back across the crypt to that comforting wall and exit passage. Feeling his way along, he found he was in another crypt, a circular one, and he began to work his way round the walls, bumping into a pillar. At his muffled intake of breath, Gregorin laughed. He could only be a yard or two behind.

'Look around you, Didier,' he shouted. '*A la mort, on laisse tout.* Reflect on death, my friend.'

Then all fell silent as Auguste worked his

way on, longing, in this pitch dark, to get the other candle out. Light, oh blessed light. But he dared not.

'During the Commune soldiers hunted men down. They died like dogs, as will you, Didier.'

Gregorin seemed further behind now, and his next shout was comfortingly distant. Should he have cautious hope? No, that was when Gregorin was at his most dangerous.

'Did you see that inscription we passed? Of course not, it is too dark. But I know it well. It reads: Reflect every morning that by night you may be dead.'

Surely further away. Auguste crossed the passage to the inner wall. If only there were a cross passage that might lead back to the entrance corridor. There was, but even as his hand reached out, out of the enemy darkness came a hand clutching. Gregorin was on him pressing back against the wall, so that he was unable to use the knife, and the bones of the dead were pressing into his body behind him.

Then the hands were on his throat choking him, but his legs and knees were free, and forgetting the Queensberry rules of gentlemanly behaviour he used them.

'*Salaud!*'

A howl from Gregorin and a momentary slackening of the fingers, but it was enough to wrest himself free, push Gregorin off balance, and flee down the exit passage again, bumping against walls with sickening jolts. With luck, however, Gregorin would assume he was going the other way.

As soon as he felt the corridor opening into an open space again, he stopped. Nothing. Then Gregorin's maniac shriek again. But in the *distance*, and too distorted to distinguish any words. He had fallen for it, and gone the other way, back towards the crypt.

Auguste tried to calm himself, to think more clearly. For a few minutes he remained still, fighting the instinct to put as much space as possible between himself and Gregorin. Gregorin might be behind, but ahead of him might be a locked door. Darkness could be a friend as well as enemy. Nevertheless the temptation to light the other candle was irresistible, and he did so.

Around him were the bones of the victims of the Revolution, and the massacre at the Tuileries, grim memorials of bloody death. He went cautiously round a corner – and froze. Ahead of him in the gloom was a man's figure. Entwhistle had remained after all. Entwhistle would not let him pass, but Auguste could not kill him in cold blood with his knife. It would be a desecration of an implement meant to produce glorious artistic creations, not death. No, better if it had to be used in self-defence to use it against Gregorin.

Horrified, he began to retrace his steps. He was the quail in a terrible sandwich between the two men. Perhaps there was still a chance that he could find himself in a cross passage and regain the entrance passageway. He had little hope though. Gregorin was after all a trained assassin, and Auguste Didier was a cook. At every step he expected Gregorin's mocking laugh to welcome him back. But none came, no scream in his ear of imminent death, no hyena laugh. He found himself back in the second crypt, and still all was silent. Should he take this cross passage and risk Gregorin waiting at the other end, or go forward to the crypt of Sacellum to see if there were any sign of him?

He needed to do neither, for his foot struck something soft, something that was not stone, or ancient bones. It was a body.

Auguste stepped back with a half cry, half retch of nausea, half expecting the body to leap up and kill him, as he held the candle down to see better. The body remained where it was, the blood spurting over the grey jacket, as red as the rose in the button-hole.

Gregorin was dead, and from his chest protruded something Auguste recognised only too well. It was a kitchen knife, remarkably similar to his own.

323

Auguste staggered into sunlight through the main entrance like a soufflé rising in the warmth of the oven. How could all these people be walking around in ignorance of the hell going on beneath? What should he do? Tell the *agent* he could see directing traffic? No. Telephone Inspector Chesnais at the Sûreté to tell him Gregorin was dead at the hand of his accomplice Thomas Entwhistle? Yes, but he could hardly ring from a public cafe. Chesnais would insist he should stay right where he was. There was, it seemed to Auguste, only one place to which he could and should go. To the apartment of the Comtesse Eleonore. She knew the truth about Entwhistle, and now that he had killed her lover would at least convince the Sûreté that Auguste had been right all along.

Eleonore's door was opened by a maid and from within came a sound Auguste knew well, the sound of satisfied diners after luncheon. The maid looked doubtfully at his attire, not looking its best since its tour of underground Paris, and he hastily demurred at her suggestion that he might wish to join the company.

'A few minutes of the comtesse's time on a matter of urgency, if you please. My name is Auguste Didier.'

Urgent or not, Eleonore took her time, before coming into the room, clad in a delightful pale-blue cotton that accentuated her dark hair and glowing cheeks wonderfully. It had clearly been a good luncheon, he thought, somewhat sourly.

'I am delighted to see you, Auguste.'

'You will perhaps not be, when I tell you Pyotr Gregorin is dead.'

'Dead?' she repeated blankly. She sat down heavily on a chair. 'Dead?' she said again.

'Yes, Eleonore,' Auguste said gently.

'You will excuse me for a moment, Auguste.'

'He told me you were lovers, and so this must be a shock to you. I am sorry.'

'Do you mean Thomas Entwhistle?' she asked in a flat voice.

'Let us not play games any longer, Eleonore. You know as I do that there were two men, and for you – as for me Pyotr Gregorin was the more important. Whether you were his mistress or not, I know you were his accomplice.'

She raised her head, regaining her usual mocking tone. 'You make me sound a criminal, Auguste. I am not. I am as devoted to my country and its interests as are you to yours. Our countries are different, that is all. Now tell me all that happened. *Everything* about how Pyotr died – I cannot believe it.'

Auguste hesitated. 'Very well, but we should telephone the Sûreté as soon as we can.'

'They can wait. Tell me.'

Auguste proceeded to explain exactly what had happened, and when he had finished she asked sharply 'Are you sure it was him and not Thomas?'

'Quite sure. Gregorin lured me to the catacombs to kill me, and Entwhistle would have no motive to kill me, but he might to kill Gregorin. He killed him and then fled past me.'

'Are you sure of that?'

He stared at her. 'Gregorin was *dead*.'

'That I realise. But was Entwhistle his murderer?' She got up and began to pace nervously round the room.

'Who else? There was no one else there.'

'There was you.'

He was in a nightmare. Could this be happening? She could not even face him, she was staring out of the window. *'Me?* But I would never have done it save in self-defence, and told you that I managed to get away from him.'

'The Sûreté may not believe that.'

'Of course they will.'

'I suggest you tell them then. I see through the window that they are at this very moment walking up the steps.'

'Quoi? How could they know I was here?'

She shrugged. 'I expect they followed you here. I imagine they have come to arrest you, Auguste, and I don't mind very much. I loved Pyotr Gregorin.' There were tears in the eyes that had once sparkled with the happiness of life.

Nine

'Might as well take down the thatch, Alf.'

Bert broke the heavy silence in the White Dragon bar. Out of its customers' respect for the landlord's grief, the bar tended to be empty during the evenings now, which piled yet more worries on Bert Wickman's bowed shoulders. He'd seized the opportunity of Wednesday's Empire Day celebrations (if that was the word for a lacklustre turnout to see the schoolchildren and the village band march down the street dressed in a motley array of red, white and blue) to call a meeting of the committee for the following evening. Its members had, without a word being spoken, disbanded themselves after the unfortunate events of May Day, without bothering to remove the visible signs of their toil.

'And them soggy paper tulips.' Adelaide sniffed.

'I haven't the heart somehow,' Bert muttered. Always spartan, the White Dragon was even to the least discerning eye in need of a woman's touch — as indeed was Bert himself. An unfaithful wife was considerably better than no wife at all in his bed.

'When's Bessie's hanging to be?' Aggie asked dolorously.

'She ain't been tried yet, you daft old besom,' Bert snarled.

'Don't speak to me like that. I'm an old woman.'

'You're an old witch, that I know. She's sent for trial at the next assizes. Don't you read the newspapers?'

'It'll buck up custom for the Dragon,' Alf pointed out with the kindest of intentions.

'It'll be doing without yours and that's a fact,' its goaded landlord informed his best customer.

When May is nigh out
Folks do shout.

Jacob suddenly woke up, and slurped angrily into his beer. 'There's no need for dat now, Jacob. All's over,' Aggie informed him. 'We done what squire asked.'

'He didn't ask for no murder,' Adelaide pointed out lugubriously. 'Reckon we'll still lose the pub, now Bessie done his lordship in.'

'Bessie didn't do it,' Bert howled. 'It was one of them up there.' He jerked a thumb in the joint direction of heaven and Farthing Court.

'Old Herne, it was,' intoned Aggie.

'Ghosts don't shoot bows and arrows and

well you know it, Aggie.' Stuart Tudor had come marching into the bar and, at this symbol of quasi-authority, Bert hauled himself behind the bar in a feeble effort to resemble mine host of a well-kept inn. 'Squire wants to see you, Bert. He's arriving next Tuesday.'

'What for?' Bert quickly waved aside a half-hearted attempt at payment for his pint.

'How should I know? Paid your rent, 'ave you?' Tudor guffawed in a way that would have astonished the walls of Farthing Court. 'Perhaps he wants you to lay on a buffet supper in the Dragon for the swells.'

'What swells?'

It was Tudor's big moment. 'Some of them are coming back for Whitsun. Lady Mont-foy, all them Pennyfathers, 'Er Grace the Dizzy Duchess, Buffalo Bill Bolland. Quite a party.'

'Returning to the scene of the crime,' Adelaide said knowingly.

Aggie cackled. 'The fairies are calling dem. What did I say? Old Herne's a-blowing his horn.'

'Shut up, Aggie,' Alf said quietly.

Four days in a cell at the Préfecture of Police had not been a pleasant experience. Quite apart from the terrifying feeling that he was about to be charged with murder, and the even more terrifying suspicion that

Inspector Chesnais did not believe a word he said, even the comfort that food could bring was denied to Auguste. True, he had been allowed the concession of sending out for his meals, but somehow even the finest *coq au vin* lost much of its appeal when surrounded at close quarters by four grey stone walls. It took on the quality of a last supper before the guillotine. Chesnais had done his best; he had been allowed the privilege of two books, but the ones supplied, Dickens's *A Tale of Two Cities* in English and Dumas's *The Count of Monte Christo* in French, failed to rouse his spirits. Eighteen years in the Bastille, and incarceration in the Château D'If made uncomfortable reading.

'Egbert!'

The clang of the cell door and the sight of his friend coming in did a great deal more than Mr Dickens could manage to cheer Auguste.

'This is a pretty how-do-yer-do,' Egbert remarked, removing his bowler, tossing it on the austere bed, looking round in vain for a second rickety chair, and sitting on the bed himself.

'Egbert, I didn't kill Gregorin. If I'd had to, I would have done, but I didn't.' Auguste did not bother to question how and why Egbert was here. There was hope, that was enough.

'Who did then?'

'Entwhistle, of course. He took a knife with him and waited in the passageway, listening to my conversation with Gregorin, then seized the first opportunity to creep back when he heard – or saw – us separate. Let me explain.' He did, graphically and carefully describing what had happened, even drawing Egbert a sketch plan to help, and reliving as he did so every terrible moment of his ordeal in the darkness. 'So that,' he concluded, 'is how I know Entwhistle killed Gregorin. I *saw* him.'

'Saw him kill Gregorin?'

'No – but–'

'Why should he want to kill him?'

'I don't know, Egbert, but that is the Sûreté's job to establish.'

Rose grimaced. 'The Sûreté say you had every reason to kill Gregorin and Entwhistle had none. There's no proof they even knew each other.'

'There is,' Auguste retorted eagerly. 'Ethelred Perkins and Stuart Tudor can testify to that. It was Tudor told me the two were meeting that morning.' Why was Egbert looking at him so pityingly?

'I asked them. They deny it. They've never heard of Gregorin.'

Auguste's head felt like Escoffier's mincing machine. How could he have forgotten? *Et in Arcadia ego.* These serpentlike inhabitants of his paradise had not only sent him to meet his death and been paid for it but, worse, were prepared now to see him hang for, they thought, the murder of their 'generous' employer.

'Then Jeanne Planchet, Lady Montfoy's maid, can tell you more. Her sister works at Gregorin's house, she says, but I suspect it was her. She most certainly knows him *and* presumably knows he masqueraded as Entwhistle.'

'I'll ask her.' Egbert did not sound hopeful.

'It was Gregorin, not Entwhistle, who was the host at the Place Vendôme.' Auguste stopped as a terrible thought came to him. 'Egbert, don't you believe me either? It was *Entwhistle* killed him, not me.'

'Auguste, it wasn't Entwhistle.' There was real pity now in Egbert's eyes and Auguste shivered at the horror that this was precisely what Egbert thought.

'How do you know?'

'Because at the time at which you were talking to Gregorin, according to what you told Chesnais, Entwhistle was escorting a party of respectable citizens round Notre Dame. He's a specialist in church history.'

'He bribed them, as Gregorin did the staff.'

'It was a party of nuns, Auguste.'

The mincing machine went berserk, unable to grip, as Auguste desperately

334

struggled to adjust the blades. 'Who told the police to follow me from the catacombs, if not Entwhistle?'

'No one did. The police had a telephone call to say where you were, and that they should go to the catacombs – where they'd find a dead body. And it wasn't Entwhistle. He speaks English, French and Russian. Not German. And this voice, according to the police, had a German accent.'

German? For a wild moment Auguste decided Cousin Bertie, who had had a heavy German accent all his life, was taking his revenge, but reluctantly dismissed the idea as on the whole unlikely. Then the blades of the mincer clicked home.

'Eleonore's husband,' he cried. 'He learned that Gregorin was Eleonore's lover, followed him to the catacombs, stole one of my knives, killed him, and then telephoned the police from a local café.'

Egbert sighed. 'Your powers of detection fail you when it's your own safety at stake, Auguste.'

Auguste noted his inadvertent pause before safety. The word Egbert had intended to use was life.

'If Eleonore's husband or anyone else, come to that, was bent on killing Gregorin, he'd have taken a weapon with him, and not had to pinch one of yours left lying around. Would you go in to tackle Gregorin with

335

your bare hands? No. You're getting lost in the maze, Auguste. Start at the beginning. So far only you claim to have seen Gregorin and Entwhistle together and that there is a connection between them.'

'Eleonore would confirm it.'

'She doesn't. She maintains that Entwhistle is Entwhistle, that she acted as she did to further the interests of her country and her husband as envoy to the Kaiser. She hints that she does have a lover, but that it is Entwhistle, not Gregorin.'

'Gregorin told me she was *his* mistress.'

'Only you, Auguste. No one else.'

Why should Eleonore lie? Even as Auguste asked himself the question, the answer came: because, firstly, she believes that I killed Gregorin, and therefore she has no reason to want to help me and, secondly, with Gregorin dead she wants to distance herself from the Okhrana. 'And Jeanne Planchet,' Auguste said once more.

'Round we go again,' Rose said sourly. 'I'm going to sort this out. That's why you're returning to England with me.'

Like St Peter's, Auguste's prison doors miraculously flew open. Oh, brave new world that awaited him yet. Freedom hovered, hope dawned.

'Under my eye all the time,' Egbert added warningly. 'My head's on the guillotine too over this.'

'You are very kind, Egbert.'

'No,' Rose answered shortly, embarrassed. 'The Sûreté are bearing in mind that you are a cousin by marriage to His Majesty. *If* you are innocent, the prime minister doesn't want to risk a diplomatic incident on his hands. It would be bad enough if you were guilty but that could be hushed up...'

'Thank you very much,' Auguste muttered savagely. To owe his liberty to Cousin Bertie was humiliation indeed. 'Are you going to lock me up at Scotland Yard?' He tried to keep bitterness from his voice.

'No. You can go home until Friday week, June the 9th. We're going to spend Whitsun in the country.'

'Not Farthing Court?' Auguste asked in dismay. 'But now Gregorin is dead...'

'Farthing Court belongs to Thomas Entwhistle, not Gregorin, and you'll be glad to know he's opening up the house again for Whitsun. You'll see a lot of familiar faces. His Majesty invited them all to the royal garden party at Windsor on the fourteenth, the day before the wedding, and Entwhistle thought up this idea.'

'I wonder *why?*' Auguste said bitterly.

'So do I.' Egbert relaxed his formality, and sounded almost human again. 'I came to the conclusion that there's a lot we don't know about Arthur Montfoy's murder.'

'Why should the real Thomas *Entwhistle* be

337

interested? He wasn't there at the time,' Auguste pointed out with a glimmer of interest now. He had assumed that with Gregorin's murder, Entwhistle would have melted away into the vast elusive army of Englishmen who roamed the world like Flying Dutchmen, belonging nowhere.

'So you *say*, Auguste. I still have to prove it. If there's no connection, then I've one murder on my hands, Montfoy's. If there is, I have two, though then Chesnais would be sharing one with me.'

'Gregorin's murder is tied up with Arthur Montfoy's, Egbert.'

'I hope you're not right.'

'Why?'

Egbert lost his patience. 'Because you'd still be suspect number one,' he shouted. 'Surely you can see that? I would have to testify that you were dotty on the subject of Gregorin at Farthing Court; lo and behold there's a murder in circumstances which make it only too likely you could have mistaken the victim's identity.'

'I didn't.' Auguste could see Egbert's point though, only too clearly.

Rose said quickly, 'That's why I want to clear it up before the fifteenth. I wouldn't want you to miss a royal wedding, Auguste.'

Auguste managed a laugh. 'How kind of you, Egbert. Where shall we be staying? Not at Farthing Court, I presume?'

338

'No. The rectory. It's hardly tactful to put up at the White Dragon.' Egbert paused. 'I'm afraid Twitch has to come too.'

'I will not try to escape,' Auguste said with dignity.

'No, but has it occurred to you that even though Entwhistle isn't a murderer, he might not be too pleased with you? *If* you're right, you've deprived him of a nice steady income by killing Gregorin – as he believes,' he added hastily. 'If you're wrong, then to say the least you've been spreading some highly unflattering allegations about him.'

'I am not wrong.' Auguste pondered this. 'You mean I shouldn't cook at Farthing Court in case Thomas Entwhistle tries to kill me?'

Egbert did laugh at this. 'I think it's highly unlikely the Pennyfathers would ask you to cook for them, don't you?'

'Why not?' Auguste was indignant. 'What is wrong with my cuisine?'

'They may be afraid you'll try to poison them.'

'You are jesting, Egbert,' Auguste said, aghast.

'I wish I were, but the fact is we all know there's possibly a murderer at large in Farthing Court, and my guess is everyone there thinks so too. They're just not sure who it is.'

Tatiana flew into his arms. Oh, the blessed familiarity of home. Even the painting over the Adam mantelpiece of Tatiana's first motor car acquired charm today. 'What has been happening, Auguste? Egbert would not tell me. I was so worried when I reached home yesterday.'

He held her close, aware that it was not the best of homecomings to have to inform your wife that her uncle has been murdered and her husband arrested for the crime.

She listened, aghast. 'You are *sure* he is dead, Auguste?'

'Yes.' He tried to keep his voice steady. 'Do you mind very much, Tatiana?'

'I don't choose my uncles, but I did choose my husband,' was her reply. 'He has wanted to kill you for years, so how can I be other than relieved and thankful you are with me now?'

'I am still under suspicion of the murder.' Would this understatement satisfy her?

'And did you do it?'

'No.'

'How could I blame you if you had? But I am glad you did not.'

'The Sûreté blames me. Even Egbert is not entirely convinced, and the only man who *could* have done it other than me has a splendid alibi.'

'Then there must be someone else. Gregorin had a thousand enemies.'

'But not a thousand who knew where to find him that day. Tatiana, tell me more about Gregorin. I only knew him as a killer, you as an uncle. It may help.'

'Very well.' She went to sit by the window overlooking Birdcage Walk, and he sat by her. The familiarity helped distance the memories of those dark passageways and the dead body he had found lying at his feet.

'Pyotr was my father's youngest brother,' she began. 'He came to live in Paris when I was six or seven, and he perhaps twenty-two or three. He was a wonderful uncle, and I saw much of him. He played endless games with me, he took me to places to which my father had forbidden me to go; theatres, puppet shows, the zoo, making everything exciting. It was he who whetted my appetite for life outside the walls of the Palace Maniovsky. Later, much later, when I knew what his role in Paris was, I realised I had been useful to him. Who would suspect an uncle escorting a niece of being the Tsar's chief assassin?'

'Did you like him?'

Tatiana considered this. 'I'm not sure. He was exciting but somehow I was always afraid of upsetting him. He only turned on me once in anger when I grew jealous of a lady who was taking his attention away from me. I read years later that she had died in strange circumstances and I often wondered

341

whether he was involved.'

'He never married?'

'It is not a profession that lends itself to marriage, but he was very attractive to women from all classes, even his own servants, so the gossip went. I don't think he knew or cared what love was, but he enjoyed pleasing women because he could manipulate them. He enjoyed the power as long as they pleased him. When he tired of them, he was ruthless. You think Cousin Bertie is – or was – flighty, but he is warm hearted whereas Gregorin was cold. The women could not strike back, either because of their reputations or for fear.'

'Did you ever hear of Thomas Entwhistle?'

'Only once or twice in Paris, and I never met him. Nor did I hear his name in connection with Gregorin's.'

'They would be careful not to move in the same society. Have you heard the name recently?'

'Yes. Apparently he has some lady of high rank as his mistress now, a comtesse.'

How lightly Tatiana said it. Auguste began to think he was in the mincing machine once more. Had Gregorin been lying to him about Eleonore being his mistress? Had it been Entwhistle at the reception all the time, and Eleonore his hostess? No, he couldn't believe it. Blindly, without thinking, Auguste decided he needed to seek the sure ground of the kitchens. Perhaps with the order and precision of laying out the ingredients, he could make some sense of this. He abruptly rose to his feet and was stopped only by Tatiana's puzzled voice.

'Where are you going, Auguste?'

'To cook. It is Mrs Jolly's day off.'

'My love, I am sure in that vast larder there must be something cold, or something that could be reheated, which would be perfectly acceptable. We have been apart some time–'

Guilt at his selfishness overcame him. 'You want to tell me about the Isle of Man trials.'

'Of course. If I bore you to sleep over our cold mutton, it will be no bad thing. And, Auguste, I shall come with you to Frimhurst.'

'No,' he said sharply. Suppose Entwhistle did take his revenge, but on Tatiana, not him? 'Aren't the Gordon Bennett trials being held in France around that time?'

'Motor cars are not everything, and nor is food.'

Almost, but not everything. He looked lovingly at his wife. What was a little cold mutton compared with her? Tomorrow would hold *coq au vin,* and tonight he would hold Tatiana.

'Hell's bells, what is it, Bert?'

Alf, enjoying his temporary job in control

of the White Dragon bar, looked up as Bert crashed the front door viciously behind him. Jacob, waking up abruptly, fell off his chair.

'It's all happening again, that's what!' Bert shouted.

'What is?'

'Squire says we've got to put on a show for Whitsun.'

'What sort of show?'

'Smocks, milkmaids, morris dances – all that old stuff again.'

'What the blazes for?'

'For the White Dragon, that's all I care about. Threatening me, he was. Not good for the village, he says, if anything *happens*. He means Bessie. He'll have me out sure as my name's Bert Wickman.'

Alf glanced at the seedy furnishings and fare of the White Dragon and privately thought this might be no bad thing, but loyalty prevailed. In any case, squire might close the place and that would be bad. 'He can't do that.'

'I tell you I'm not dancing round no more bloody maypoles. Look what happened last time.'

Aggie cackled in glee. 'Old Herne's a-blowing his horn again. I told you so.'

'You shut up, Aggie. Now, Bert, what's this about? For them swells, is it?'

'Mr blasted Tudor was right. Them

Americans are coming back.'

'You ain't thinking, Bert.' Alf tried to be fair. 'It would look a bit odd, wouldn't it, if they came back and saw the village looking different? No stocks, no flowers, no fairies, no thatch – bloody hell, I took the thatch down like you said,' he roared.

'Well, it'll have to go up again,' Bert said with gloomy relish.

'I've got a living to earn,' Alf said, aggrieved. 'Who's paying?'

'Squire said we'll have to foot the bill this time. I'll pay you, Alf. Somehow. Anyway, Mr Entwhistle said he'd try to help Bessie. He reckons he knows who really did it and can prove it.'

'Who?'

'The French chap, like I always said,' Bert belatedly recalled. 'That daft cook.'

'I remember him,' Alf exclaimed. 'Poking his nose in all the time. It'll be a pleasure to help, Bert. Right, we'll want rhymes and superstitions for Whitsun from you and Jacob, Aggie.'

'I wish it were midsummer,' Aggie replied regretfully. 'I could produce a good few for that.'

'They won't know the difference,' Bert said. 'You get Adelaide on to the morris dances, will you, Alf?'

'An 'orse.' Jacob woke up again.

'What about horses? You going to follow

345

behind with a dung-puller then?'

'A mummer's horse,' Jacob said hastily.

'That comes out for Christmas,' Aggie retorted. 'Anyone knows that. Even Americans.'

'I don't care a hang when it comes out if it helps Bessie,' her husband declared.

'That's a good idea, Aggie. I'll play the 'orse.' Harry Thatcher, coming in from the postman's round for a lunchtime drink, offered nobly. 'I'd like that. Frighten people.' His sweetheart Mary, for example. She'd just given him up in favour of the plumber's apprentice.

'You can scare that cook into confessing,' Adelaide suggested brightly.

'Is he going to be here?' asked Harry.

'Oh, yes.' Bert was only too happy to enlighten him. 'White Dragon's not good enough for him though. Scotland Yard is bringing him down in manacles to look for evidence. They're staying with the rector.'

'Sanctuary, that's what they call that,' Aggie said knowledgeably. 'So no one can do him in until the hangman gets the job.'

'Shut up talking about hangmen, Aggie.' Bert finally lost control.

'This one's your room, Didier. *Between* us.' Twitch pointed this out with great satisfaction. At long last providence had seen sense about the Frenchie. Twitch had never had much time for the French nation, but suddenly he could see much virtue in the *entente cordiale*. The Sûreté had turned up trumps and arrested the upstart Frenchie cook, putting him in his (and the chief's) custody. Twitch had a room on one side, the chief on the other. The disadvantage to this delightful arrangement was that every morning he would have to face the Frenchie across the rectory breakfast table, but this was a small price to pay in view of the power so unexpectedly placed in Twitch's eager hands. He had been most disappointed that this morning he and the chief were taking him up to Farthing Court without leg irons and manacles. Twitch had eyed those stocks wistfully, as a sure place for keeping the Frenchie out of mischief. He'd fancied throwing a mouldy tomato at him. Knowing the Frenchie though, and the funny things he ate, he'd probably think it was a present and eat it.

Next door Auguste was assessing his home for the next few days. It spoke of the dust of ages, since the rector's housekeeper was not much younger than he, and had long since given up the unequal task of keeping a strict eye on the general maid's performance. A print of Leonardo da Vinci's *Last Supper* hung over his bed, A Present From Margate in the form of an old china boot adorned the mantelpiece. The view from the window displayed a collection of outhouses dating from the sixteenth to the nineteenth centuries, giving the impression that rather than clear the litter from one storeroom a new one had been built. One of them, Auguste thought without enthusiasm, was undoubtedly a privy. Beyond them the branches of an apple tree could be seen waving enticingly and unattainably. Freedom was not for him.

The bed, with an ancient now non-white coverlet, was comfortable, the ewer on the washing table serviceable. The rector had in his youth enterprisingly installed a flush water closet in the rectory, and though Auguste had felt like His Majesty when he ascended this throne on his arrival, it was at least preferable to the daunting privy below him. A bathroom had followed the rector's rush of enthusiasm for modernity, but after this he had been content to remain firmly rooted in the mid to late nineteenth century. The oil lamps glowed as at Farthing Court, for the delights of gas had not yet reached Frimhurst, and candles were already lined up below for night-time duty on the upper floors.

Auguste had enquired cautiously what the housekeeper's idea of dinner would be, and had been dismayed to discover there was none. Dinner took place at noon, high tea followed at six, and something called supper at nine, consisting of biscuits, cheese and cocoa. On the whole the Préfecture did better, gastronomically, but gaolbirds on parole, he reminded himself forlornly, could not be choosers.

How could Farthing Court still look so mellow and peaceful with its grey stone glowing in the morning sun? As they walked up the driveway, exotic rhododendrons blazed on both sides, giving way nearer the house to June roses, and the catacombs and murder seemed far away. Auguste reminded himself that inside this peaceful house were, firstly, a kitchen seething with serpents, secondly, a host who might want to murder him and, thirdly, guests, all of whom were either oblivious of the woes of Auguste Didier or delighted that they themselves were thereby exonerated from suspicion of murder. Twitch's ill-concealed glee at his predicament was galling. Tables, he told himself, must be turned.

Somewhere here, he was sure, lay the answer to Gregorin's murder, and to Arthur Montfoy's. True, he could not suspect the real Thomas Entwhistle of the latter, since even he could not conceive that the real Entwhistle had been hiding in the attics of Farthing Court while Gregorin masqueraded here. Entwhistle's role must surely have been to remain in Paris. There were two keys to the Entwhistle-Gregorin puzzle: Eleonore and Jeanne. He would tackle both. And they, he reminded himself, were the only two suspects other than himself, if Egbert was right and the two crimes were linked. Or were they? Although he could (regretfully) see no motive for any other of Entwhistle's guests to slaughter Gregorin, there remained two other possibilities. One of these opened the door to them, ushering them in without a hint he had ever seen them before.

Auguste's tension grew as they waited in the morning room for Entwhistle to join them, not because he seriously thought Entwhistle had designs on his life – he was too useful as a scapegoat for that, but because this would be the first time he met the real Thomas Entwhistle face to face.

The door opened, and the owner of Farthing Court came in. Auguste's heart thudded painfully. Gradually he relaxed. There was no atmosphere of chill withdrawal, but the likeness was staggering: the way of walking: the height and build; the sharp features were such that he found it hard to believe Gregorin himself was not standing before him. Perhaps Entwhistle's cheeks had more colour than Gregorin's pale wraith-like face, the eyes perhaps lacked the feral stare of Gregorin. Certainly his manner was different. He showed an affability, even a warmth, which was alien to Gregorin. Auguste watched eagerly to see Egbert's reaction as to whether he thought this was the same person that he had met a month ago.

'My dear Mr Didier, I am delighted to meet you again. You made a deep impression on my Paris household.' Entwhistle paused. 'Also, so I'm told, on a gentleman in the catacombs, if you will forgive my turn of phrase. I understand from the police that he bore a certain resemblance to me, and I trust you were not under the impression you were attacking me?'

Before Auguste could answer, Egbert intervened. 'Funny you should mention that. We had a telegraph this morning from Paris.' Auguste looked up sharply, for Egbert had not mentioned this. 'The Sûreté have come up with a paper seller in the Place Denfert-Rochereau who saw two men going into the catacombs together who looked like twin brothers. He noticed particularly because they were both identically dressed. Have a look at this photograph. It's of Pyotr Gregorin, kindly provided by his niece, Mr Didier's wife.'

Tatiana? She hadn't mentioned it to Auguste. The thought that Tatiana and Egbert were consulting without his knowledge illogically increased his fear about his own situation.

'It's not a good photograph – he didn't like having his picture taken, so Mrs Didier says – but it's good enough for you to have to admit he looks much like you, Mr Entwhistle. Just for the sake of argument let's assume Mr Didier's thesis is correct that you doubled for Gregorin to provide him with an alibi on certain occasions. It doesn't mean you were a member of the Okhrana yourself, of course.'

'For the sake of argument,' the affability hardly wavered, 'let me remind you that I was nowhere near the catacombs that morning.'

'And I'm not doubting it. You could have gone in there with Gregorin, left quite quickly, and reached Nôtre Dame just as you said to conduct your party. But it might help us to find Gregorin's murderer if you confirmed it.'

'Top-hatted gentlemen with morning suits are all too likely to resemble each other.' Entwistle was unruffled. 'Besides, I had thought – forgive me, Mr Didier – that the Sûreté *had* found the murderer. And if your interest is in this Gregorin, why have you come to Frimhurst for your investigations? Farthing Court belongs to me, not to any putative Russian agent.'

'There was a murder here too. And since you were here, you'll know all about it.'

Of course. If only Egbert could find some

little detail about the May Day celebrations which Gregorin would have known about but which he had omitted to tell Entwhistle, he could break down his pretence.

'Again, you have the murderer under lock and key – ah, of course, you think Mr Didier may have carried out that murder too, under the impression it was me – or rather Mr Gregorin. You may well be right, Mr Rose. Somehow, I don't see Bessie Wickman as a murderess. She is far too fond of her own skin.'

To Auguste's disappointment, Egbert did not press Entwhistle further, and even more to his surprise, accepted his invitation to stay on for luncheon.

'What do you think of him, Stitch?' Rose turned to him, not Auguste, after Entwhistle left them, and Twitch swelled in the unaccustomed glory of being the first person the chief consulted.

'Looks the same fellow to me, sir.'

'Auguste?'

'Different. Very close, but it is not the same man.' He really did feel that, it was not just because he wanted to.

'I agree with you, Auguste.'

Auguste was overcome with relief. *Egbert agreed with him.* He was as good as free. It took him some time to realise this was not exactly correct.

Luncheon was a strange affair. Auguste was uncomfortably aware that he was the object of much attention, and worse, that the attention was decidedly unfavourable. His two neighbours, Gertrude and Belinda, leant pointedly away from him, and even the delightful cherry ice cream which Ethelbert produced hardly compensated for the chill which emanated towards him from the guests in general. Eleonore ignored him, Horace nodded, but talked to Richard Waites and Harvey talked to Gerald. Bluebell gave him an interested grin from time to time, but only Louisa and Entwhistle's continued affability relieved the atmosphere. Even this failed to induce any general thaw, and Auguste was glad to escape.

Egbert announced he was to see Jeanne Planchet, implying that he did not want Auguste's assistance. Twitch, hovering hopefully lest Auguste make a bid to escape to the high seas, was firmly summoned to attend Egbert. Auguste realised his friend was giving him a message and he must act on it. The rose gardens were the glory of Farthing Court and, seated on a bench in the midst of their blaze of colour, he at last found Eleonore.

'It's the first time,' she laid her book aside, 'I've been accosted by a murderer in a rose garden.' The words were harsh, but to his relief the coldness had vanished.

He too could be harsh. 'Murder doesn't upset you, Eleonore. It was Gregorin's trade after all, and it was he who told me you were his mistress.'

'How very ungentlemanly,' she observed.

'Why did you tell the police that you were Entwhistle's mistress, not Gregorin's?'

'Did I? How very remiss of me.'

'You don't seem very concerned about whether I live or die.'

Her face changed. Gone was the good humour and gentle mockery. 'I'm not, Auguste, and since we are alone here, I will tell you once again just why that is. Your life for his, Auguste. It was not for my husband, not for my country, that I took part in Pyotr's plans to discredit King Edward's reputation.'

'For money then.'

'I have already told you. Pyotr was the only man I have ever truly loved. We were well matched, he and I, in bed, in wit, in mind. And you killed him. Is it any wonder I asked my husband to telephone to the police after you came running to boast so proudly of what you had done?'

Put that way he supposed not. Then he realised her mistake, at the same moment as she did.

'*When* did you ask him, Eleonore?' He already knew the answer though. 'It could only have been during the time I was waiting for you to arrive, *before* I had told you of Gregorin's death. So that means–'

There was fear in her eyes now. 'Go on, Auguste.'

'That you knew Gregorin was planning to kill me that morning in the catacombs, so that when I turned up on your doorstep, you realised it could only be for one reason, that the situation had been reversed.'

'You murdered him,' she stated simply. 'That's all I cared about.'

'But how could you know that I was to be killed and do nothing?'

'Love blinds, Auguste. It is a powerful emotion. Besides, I believed you tried to kill him at Farthing Court, and killed poor Arthur instead.'

'But this is ridiculous!' The mincing machine was tearing the shreds smaller and smaller.

She looked at him. 'Is it? Then, Auguste, if you did not kill my Pyotr, and Entwhistle did not, who did?'

Tir Nan Og had to be faced. Now Auguste knew there were suspects within it was easier to do so, unless of course his own murder happened to be on their dinner menu. Appearances were beguilingly decep-tive. Ethelred was tasting the soup, Mrs Honey's skirt was whisking into the stillroom, and Jenny rushed to fling her arms around him in pleasure.

'Grannie said you'd been beheaded, Mr Didier,' she cried. 'I'm so glad you're not.'

'No doubt Mr Perkins would be only too happy to invent a recipe for my head,' Auguste jested bitterly.

Ethelred looked hurt. 'I'm sorry you're upset, Mr Didier, but I had to tell the police the truth. Maybe you misunderstood. Mr Tudor told you Mr Entwhistle was going to the catacombs to meet a Mr Gregorin, but I didn't know anything about it. Mr Tudor will bear me out.'

'I'm sure he will.'

Ethelred looked virtuous. 'And anyway, we only told the truth.'

'Especially if you are paid thirty pieces of silver.'

Ethelred grinned cheerfully. 'Not as much as that.'

'Then if I pay you, you might remember enough about your two masters to save my life.'

'*Two* masters, Mr Didier? We've only one.'

'You have now, I agree.'

Ethelred spoke very softly, so softly Auguste failed to hear him. 'Thanks to you, Mr Didier.'

Somewhere there had to be a way to fight his way into the sugar web of illusion that surrounded this house and all in it. Horace Pennyfather had always seemed to Auguste a reasonable, down to earth man, and at least if he had no words of comfort to offer, just to be with someone who possessed some common sense would be a change. He found him, peacefully contemplating the stone nymphs of the water fountain, with Gertrude sitting nearby. Their deep mourning made them a stark sight on the sunny June day.

'Ah, Didier. Any further forward on that catacombs affair?' Horace might have been talking about his latest deal on the New York exchange, so casual was his voice. At least he didn't flinch from his presence like the rest of the house party.

Auguste decided to accept the question as a gauntlet, rather than at face value. 'Does it strike you, Mr Pennyfather, that Mr Entwhistle has changed since May Day, and Paris?'

Gertrude looked up warily. 'Now, Pa—'

'Yes,' Horace answered simply. 'He plays a real awful hand of bridge now. He lost £10 last night.'

Auguste could have cried with gratitude. It was not much, but it was something.

'I hear you're in trouble, Mr Didier,' Gertrude said.

'Not for much longer,' Auguste tried to reply steadily to this kindly meant understatement. 'We shall find the true murderer of Pyotr Gregorin in Paris – and of your late husband here – very soon.'

Gertrude frowned. 'That's all over surely.'

'Not for Bessie.'

Gertrude said nothing, and Horace quickly intervened. 'What do you think of this house, Didier?'

'I think it will soon reveal a murderer.'

'As a *house*, Didier.'

Auguste was puzzled at this swift diversion of subject. '*Magnifique*, but...'

'Gertrude likes it.'

Even odder. 'Despite what's happened here, Lady Montfoy?' Auguste asked curiously.

'You may think this strange, but *because* of it.'

'Because your husband was murdered here?' He agreed with her. He did think it strange.

'I feel I owe a duty to the village, as his widow.'

'But Thomas Entwhistle is the squire. Surely–'

'Pa's thinking of buying the place for me. So I guess that makes me a squire's lady, Pa not having a wife now. That way I'd be able to carry out Arthur's duties to the village.'

So that was why Entwhistle was here. He was intent on selling the place, and then vanishing out of the limelight, as Auguste had assumed he would. As a murderer would.

Bluebell climbed down from the beech tree, appalled at what she had overheard, and rushed to the conservatory where she knew Harvey was enjoying a pipe with Richard Waites.

'Why do I get this feeling I'll never see the Rockies again?' Harvey was asking plaintively.

'Why don't you go back?'

'And leave the field to you? No, sirree.'

Bluebell interrupted this unwinnable battle of Tweedledum and Tweedledee. 'I've just heard something *terrible.*'

'What's that, honey?'

'Pa and Gertrude are thinking of buying this awful place.' The look of consternation on Harvey's face somewhat consoled her.

Richard, however, laughed aloud with pleasure, even as Harvey howled, 'What the heck for?'

'Gertrude wants to be the lady of the manor. But I've already thought of a plan to prevent it.' Bluebell glanced at Richard, but as he showed no sign of moving she went on. 'If Pa married again she wouldn't be lady of the manor, would she?'

'No,' Richard agreed.

'Well, suppose Pa did marry again.'

'Wizard.' Harvey suddenly got the idea.

'Would you really like Louisa as your stepmother?' Richard enquired politely, skipping several stages in the conversation.

'Don't you go and put the duchess off the idea, Richard, just to leave the coast clear for you,' Harvey scowled.

'If,' Bluebell remarked airily, 'Mr Waites is still here to take advantage of your absence.' She eyed Richard meaningfully. 'That policeman is still asking me questions about whom exactly I saw down near the maypole.'

Richard said nothing. There was, for once, nothing he could say, for he had seen from his window just who had been setting off in search of Arthur. It had been Gertrude.

'My dear Belinda.' Thomas Entwhistle came into the library where he knew he was sure to find her. 'It seems to me I have been neglecting you shamefully. Can't I tempt you away from Tutankhamun and into the gardens?'

Belinda quite agreed that he had been neglecting her shamefully, but all rancour suddenly vanished as she rapidly replaced her book on the shelves, clambered down the ladder backwards, tripped over the hem of her skirt in her haste, and fell into Thomas's arms. 'Why, certainly, Thomas,' she managed to say though without the calm deliberation she had planned.

'Should you mind if I sold this house,

361

Belinda?' he asked presently, as she was explaining the merits and demerits of half a torso of statuary in the Long Walk.

'Oh! To Gerald?' Discussion on the sale of a house had not been what she had been hoping for from this conversation, but as it might have the merit of dislodging Gerald from the Dower House, she was not altogether averse to it.

'I'm afraid he couldn't afford it. To the Pennyfathers, and of course Gertrude is Lady Montfoy.'

'Yes,' Belinda said doubtfully, then, 'What will you do?'

'I rather thought I'd travel,' Thomas Entwhistle said casually.

'Where to?' Belinda asked enviously.

'Egypt, Persia, Iraq–'

'*Egypt?*'

'If I had a companion of course.'

Belinda could hardly believe her ears, and her normal common sense deserted her.

The rectory high tea could not be compared with Farthing Court. Twitch and Auguste were locked in a silent but for once mutual disapprobation of Welsh rarebit when Egbert arrived.

'You look tired, Egbert.'

'I wouldn't say no to a cup of that tea.'

Auguste would, willingly, but Englishmen were different.

'I've seen Jeanne Planchet,' Rose grinned. 'Good news, Egbert?'

'For you, yes. She's admitted she knew both of them. Worked for Gregorin and that meant Entwhistle when he was away.'

'Why didn't she say earlier?' Auguste exclaimed.

'Because he'd paid her her passage money to America if she kept quiet.' Egbert took a gulp of stewed tea. 'My word, that tastes good.'

'Where does this leave us, sir?' Twitch asked gloomily, seeing the Frenchie slipping through his fingers.

'Coming up to the finishing post fast, wouldn't you say, Auguste?'

Auguste had been doing some rapid thinking. 'Yes, Egbert, I would.'

Ten

'Oh, don't deceive me; Oh, never leave me.' Annie, the fifteen-year-old general maid, was bawling outside Auguste's bedroom, either through a spontaneous inclination to burst into song or in an effort to impress on the rectory guests what a delightful place rural England was. 'How could you use a poor maiden so?' Annie finished with a triumphant yell. Perhaps later in the day Auguste might have appreciated this musical offering, but before seven o'clock he did not. It brought his present situation back in far too brutal a fashion and much aggrieved, he went to claim the jug of no doubt tepid water placed outside his door. Bathroom there might be, but old ways died hard in Frimhurst.

It occurred to him as he splashed water on his face in an attempt to brace himself for the day, that Frimhurst seemed to have a passion for old English folk songs far out of proportion to the talent available for rendering them. Indeed, Frimhurst seemed to be devoted to feudal times in all respects – such as thatching, which hitherto he had been under the impression was an alternative to tiling, not an addition, as it seemed to be in this village.

This last thought brought with it an interesting thesis. He had correctly deduced that the village was in a conspiracy to invent legends when it suited them. Was it involved in the same web of illusion that surrounded Farthing Court, and if so, was the same spider responsible for both? It would make sense, he argued. Gregorin would be anxious that Arthur Montfoy's wedding celebrations were a success, so that nothing should mar his own friendship with His Majesty at this fraught time of international relations, and Entwhistle would be equally anxious to ensure that the Pennyfathers were not dissuaded from a speedy purchase of Farthing Court. The legalities of who owned it, Gregorin or Entwhistle, might, Auguste conjectured, be somewhat complicated, but once sold to a prominent American the Tsar, whose secret service undoubtedly financed the purchase three years earlier, would be the last person to dispute ownership. President Roosevelt had just declared himself a player on the international stage, prepared to act as peacemaker between Russia and Japan to end the disastrous war. One Elizabethan manor house forfeited would seem a small price to pay for peace.

Pleased with the beneficial results of cold

water on his detective powers, Auguste decided on a pre-emptive raid upon the bathroom before Twitch was likely to have emerged. Twitch in nightshirt and dressing gown was an even more formidable experience than Twitch in all his inspector's glory. Just as Auguste turned away from the bowl of water, he glanced down into the garden. There, marching along the garden path, not in tribute to a beautiful English summer day, but with grim determination and clutching a suitcase, was Mrs Simpkins, the rector's housekeeper, and the set of her back made it clear she had no intention of returning. Had Auguste been her employer, he could have borne her departure with great pleasure, but he realised the rector might view it rather differently.

He shortly discovered that her musical efforts had not inspired Annie in the preparation of breakfast. The kidneys resembled gallstones in consistency, and the mushrooms winked up at Auguste from the plate like shrivelled evil black eyes. How he longed for the austerity of a French breakfast where the stomach could contemplate the day ahead in peace instead of being assaulted by the heavy ammunition deemed essential in this country.

'I regret,' the rector explained apologetically, meeting Auguste and Egbert in the entrance hall as he returned from Whit

Sunday matins, 'Mrs Simpkins did not quite see eye to eye with Inspector Stitch. I gather that last evening he compared her work unfavourably with that of Mrs Stitch.' For once Auguste felt fully united with Twitch. Egbert, used to such assaults upon his stomach, accepted unprotestingly what was placed in front of him.

'However,' the rector beamed comfortingly upon his lodgers, 'Annie has kindly said she will prepare luncheon.'

The kidneys and mushrooms united in protest inside Auguste. '*Non*, I will prepare the luncheon.'

'Oh.' The rector looked doubtful at this generous offer, and Egbert pinpointed the reason for his disquiet.

'You'll be safe, rector,' he explained kindly. 'Mr Didier is accused of murder, but not by poisoning.'

Any kitchen must be a haven, and this one, Auguste told himself, could have no serpents inside it. The drawback was, he soon discovered, that it didn't have much of anything inside it. He inspected the larder in dismay. The oven was waiting, but a large joint of beef sitting plumb in the middle of the larder was the only candidate for it, and its bright redness proclaimed it was intending to be very tough indeed. It would be a challenge. The larder also boasted an array of half-empty packets, glass jars with preserved remains of long-forgotten purchases of *lentilles,* and gravy powder, and some tins. The vegetable store possessed some busily sprouting old potatoes, two cabbages with yellowing leaves, and some bottled apples.

'Remember the vows that you made to your Mary.' Annie came into the kitchen still intent on music.

'Do you not sing hymns on a Sunday, Annie?'

'Not yet. I can't. Mus Wickman says keep it up just for a few more days.'

'Keep what up?' he enquired innocently, pleased at this apparent confirmation of his thesis.

Annie, realising she had spoken too freely, shut her mouth obstinately, then stomped out of the kitchen with the blacklead and the monkey soap.

It was a strange situation, Auguste reflected, that Bessie was in prison accused of murder and her husband was encouraging the village to sing old folk songs. Were they powerful prayers, born of the last vestiges of the old religions? He too was accused of murder; would singing help? Should he sing to the beef? He decided to try it out. There was nothing to lose.

N'est plus belle que ma Normandie,
C'est le pays qui m'a donné le jour.

'Ma Normandie...' It made no immediate difference to the beef, but it did depressingly bring Eleonore back into his mind. Eleonore who had loved not him, not even Cousin Bertie, but Gregorin, and was bent on vengeance for his murder. He carried out the beef, placed it on the ill-scrubbed table and sacrificed a little of the red wine he had been saving for Egbert and himself that evening (the rector and, rather reluctantly he felt, Twitch had declared themselves committed to Temperance) and poured some over in a libation to the old god of food, whoever he might have been. What else could he find in this vast rectory?

Then it came to him. *Le vrai Bon Seigneur* would provide. In the meadow and hedgerows and the rectory garden, He would undoubtedly have provided wild garlic, nettles and sorrel for soup, and dandelion leaves for salad, at the very least. The soup would have to be based on an ancient bouillon cube, but at least the meal would offer something in homage to a summer's day.

Perhaps after all there was something to be said for the old ways, the gathering of herbs and flavours for medicinal remedies, the singing of ancient folk songs, the interlocking of the affairs of the lord of the manor and the village however the latter were organised. True, in the case of Farthing Court the lord of the manor had only held the office for three years, but – Auguste stopped, his hand on the wicket gate, with a sudden feeling he had hit upon something important. What it was, however, unfortunately refused to reveal itself to him.

Preparations for luncheon at the White Dragon were somewhat simpler. Bread and cheese awaited Bert in his desolate parlour behind the bar door. Glasses of ale provided his hors d'oeuvre and that of the rest of his committee. Nevertheless Bert was happy.

'What's up, Bert?' Alf asked curiously.

'Nothing. Can't a man grin if he wants to?'

'It's not like you, Bert,' Adelaide pointed out.

Bert obliged her by reverting to the norm with a snarl. 'It is today, see?'

They hastily all decided to see, in the interests of a continued flow of ale.

'I done you a ballad, Bert,' Jacob said placatingly. ''Tis said Herne the Hunter stalks Frimhurst copses, Along with beetles, badgers and wopses. Beware the–'

'Not very tasteful, is it?' grunted Bert.

'It's tradition,' shrieked Jacob, indignant at this lack of appreciation for his best efforts.

'Only since May Day,' Alf pointed out. 'Never heard a word about Herne before then.'

'I think we done a Horn Dance years ago,' Jacob muttered defiantly. 'What for, if it weren't for old Herne?'

'All right.' Bert suddenly made up his mind. 'Let's give 'em old Herne.'

'Morris team is ready,' Alf said proudly. 'Smocks, flowery hats, the lot. We'll give 'em the Handkerchief, the Pipe and the Bean.'

'Don't forget the Horn,' Bert suddenly grinned again. 'We got to give 'em the Horn, ain't we? And the 'Orse.'

Sunday luncheon at Farthing Court was producing anxious moments in Pug's Parlour, as the upper servants gathered to parade to the lower servants' hall.

'It's true,' Tudor said gloomily. 'He's told me straight. They're signing the papers on Tuesday.'

Mrs Honey sighed. 'We can stay on, but it won't be the same.'

'You mean we won't get the same money?'

'We wouldn't anywhere. Besides, it's a roof over our heads.' Tudor was only too anxious to sink at least temporarily back into the straight and narrow.

'If I can cook American,' Ethelred pointed out doubtfully. 'That Miss Bluebell says it's easy. You just think big. Big steaks, big platefuls of grits–'

'What?'

'Grits. It's what they eat in the South out there.'

'I don't think Home Farm grows it.'

'They'll have to,' Ethelred snapped.

'Cheer up, Mr Perkins, the king is dead, long live the king,' said Tudor encouragingly.

Ethelred paled. 'It couldn't have been anything I cooked. Mr Didier did his meals.'

'Just a turn of phrase, Mr Perkins. One lord of the manor goes, another comes.'

'We've had a bit too much coming and going in that direction, it seems to me,' Mrs Honey observed. There was a pause while they considered this.

'Couldn't be helped,' Ethelred said at last. 'Just an accident, I expect. How could we know what was going to happen?'

The assembled gathering agreed only too eagerly that they couldn't.

'Your maid, Lady Montfoy, tells me she was only with you for a few moments the night your husband died. Then you sent her away. Is that true?' Egbert asked.

Gertrude for once showed discomposure. 'Yes, I guess it is.'

'Then why tell me she was with you all night?'

'I didn't. I merely said she was there when I returned.'

'Not your style to play with words, I'd have thought. Why did you? Because you were going to follow Lord Montfoy?'

'Yes. But I didn't.'

Egbert waited.

'I wanted to talk to him – I hadn't had a chance all the evening, and ask him how he could have treated me so badly. I couldn't find him when I left the dance, so I realised he must already have left. I dismissed Jeanne and then thought I'd go after him – but halfway there, I realised it was beneath my dignity to tackle him. Far better to do as Pa said and keep away. So I turned back.'

'What were you wearing, Lady Montfoy?'

'What an odd question. I still had my balldress on, and I put a coat over it.'

'A long one?'

'Short.'

'Thank you, Lady Montfoy.'

Gertrude seemed rather surprised to be let off so easily, but Egbert was well satisfied.

'A good piece of beef,' the rector said approvingly. 'Mrs Simpkins chose well. Such a loss.'

Auguste remained silent. Of such misconceptions, a chef's life is made.

'Good soup, Didier,' said Twitch approvingly. He hated it in fact, but was prepared to offer an olive branch in preference to accepting blame for the departure of a Queen of Chefs.

'Thank you,' Auguste murmured humbly.

'Tinned wasn't it?'

'Nettle soup. With almonds,' Auguste

374

replied, oblivious to any olive branch in view of this slur. 'Quite safe. The levels of cyanide are very low.'

Twitch, to Auguste's satisfaction, was silenced before he took revenge as soon as the rector left them. 'All set for tomorrow, Chief?'

'Yes,' Egbert replied shortly.

'Chief's come up with an idea, Didier,' Twitch said smugly. 'Can't tell you, I'm afraid.'

'Naturally not,' Auguste replied with dignity. 'Fortunately I have had an idea of my own.'

Twitch sniggered. 'To do with you not being guilty?'

'No. To do with who is.'

'Tell me, Auguste,' Egbert said quietly.

'It seems to me we have been thinking of the grand sirloin in this case too much, and not the humbler foods of life. We have thought too much of His Majesty and not of the baser, everyday emotions that turn the wheels of life.'

'Yes.' Egbert regarded him thoughtfully. 'Those are the lines I've been thinking along too. That's why,' he shot a glance at Twitch, 'my plan's to bring Bessie Wickman back tomorrow, for a prime seat at the festivities.'

Whit Monday kindly blessed the village of Frimhurst with a fine day, with the sun shining on small groups of villagers feverishly attaching flowers to hats and bells to legs, helping dress their co-conspirators in smocks, white stockings and dresses, and arranging hair to fall simply down milkmaids' backs.

'Bally flowers,' snorted Alf, struggling with decorating his hat with roses that persisted in having thorns to mar his efforts.

'Hell's bells,' Bert contributed, as a bell, incorrectly stitched on the coloured leather, fell off. Then he remembered Bessie would be back to watch him dance, and good humour was restored.

Adelaide, her fingers sore and bleeding from making her twenty garlands of flowers for village maidens to throw spontaneously over the swells' necks, summed up the general feeling, 'I'd like to strangle them with the bally bells.'

'No more murder, Adelaide,' Aggie giggled.

'They ain't solved the last one yet,' Bert said defiantly, looking at his team. 'Have they, Aggie?'

At twelve twenty-eight at Cranbrook station, the branch line train from Paddock Wood steamed in. Egbert was there to meet it, for Twitch had opted for the job of guarding the Frenchie. Rose, however, was not alone. Naseby had decided to attend to see justice done.

'I hope you know what you're doing. We'll have the French after us if Didier escapes.'

'We'll have the king on to us if the French hang him for murder,' Rose pointed out, glad that Auguste was not present. 'I'd say it was worth clearing his name.'

Naseby looked as though he disagreed, but at that moment the doors opened and Bessie, with a broad smile and handcuffed to an extremely good-looking constable, descended, swinging her hips like a latter-day Carmen.

Rose went to meet her. 'All ready, Mrs Wickman?'

She eyed him speculatively. 'For anything, inspector,' she drawled.

Lunch at Farthing Court had been disappointing, it was generally agreed, though not in Mr Entwhistle's hearing, chiefly because the *suprême de volaille* had been fried in batter and served with fried potatoes. How were the diners to know that Ethelred was doing his best to carry out Bluebell's instructions on how to please his pending American masters? Bluebell was making her desperate last-minute bid to forestall the sale. She was running neck and neck with Louisa in her bid to make the sale go through, in order that her loss of the title of duchess could at least be replaced by her position as lady of the manor.

The walk in the fresh air towards the Great Meadow where the festivities were to take place removed the faint feelings of nausea felt by most of the guests. Were it not for some unease at attending a Whit festival so soon after the terrible happenings of May Day, it seemed as though the afternoon ahead would be a pleasant one as the guests strolled towards the chairs, rugs and cushions placed ready for them by the footmen.

Some people were already seated when the party from Farthing Court arrived. One in particular seated between Egbert Rose and Stitch attracted attention.

'What's she doing here?' Gertrude demanded furiously of Rose as the guests realised who Bessie was. 'And, what are *you* doing, Jeanne?' Even in America maids were not honoured guests at entertainment laid on for their mistresses.

'I asked them both, Lady Montfoy. And all the upper and visiting servants,' Egbert said. 'I wanted to know where they all were, as they're helping us with our inquiries.'

'Into what?'

'Two murders, Lady Montfoy.'

'*Two?*'

'I imagine, Gertrude,' Thomas observed gravely, 'the second is that of Mr Didier's victim in Paris, a gentleman called Pyotr Gregorin.'

'What's that got to do with us?' Horace demanded angrily. 'And what,' he almost exploded, 'are all those antlers doing there?' He pointed to the table set up behind the dancing area, where the dancers' props were kept. 'And isn't that the deer's head again?'

'First, the two murders are connected,' Egbert replied. 'I believe they were committed by the same hand. The death of your husband, Lady Montfoy, was an accident. The murderer believed it was a Russian agent named Gregorin. And second, they are for the Horn Dance. It's not the same head, I gather.'

'This is quite ridiculous,' Gertrude declared. 'What can Bessie here know of a Russian agent?'

'Nothing, Lady Montfoy. That is the point. Now, I believe Mr Wickman is anxious to begin the afternoon's dancing.'

Reluctantly Gertrude, a sombre figure in her unrelieved black, took her place next to her father and Richard Waites and Bert, a fatuously pleased smile on his face, as he beheld his beloved wife once more, began.

Auguste began to feel a reluctant admiration for Englishmen who could dance in bells, wearing flowery hats. He tried to imagine the same scene in France and failed completely. French fêtes and fairs were solemn affairs devoted to the passionate appraisal of who had grown the best garlic in the year, or the sweetest violets. Now if murder occurred at a French fête, he would be less surprised, but here, following a wedding on an afternoon on a summer lawn, was still to his mind extraordinary.

The fiddler struck up, and Jacob took his place as his hour of importance arrived. Six dancers, staves in their hands, began mysterious movements with clashes of staves on high and twisting down low. Jacob coughed, and declaimed:

O mother elder, bless our seed
Keep it free from bird and weed.

The standard of verse was going down and Bert hit Alf's stave viciously.

Next came the Handkerchief Dance and the Pipe Dance. What did Egbert have in mind? There was no sign of any plan yet, and Auguste shifted uneasily in his seat. On the other side of Egbert, Bessie, maintaining a bland smile, seemed to be doing her best to seduce Twitch, so far as Auguste could judge. Now that *was* a plan, and as the dances continued without much variation so far as Auguste could tell, it took his mind off his own worries wonderfully. Finally Bert, aware the dénouement must be near, glanced at Egbert. 'The Horn Dance,' he announced.

Seeing all the deer's heads and antlers

advance, Horace stood up angrily. 'I won't have it. Haven't you any sense of tact in this country?'

'We've a sense of murder,' Egbert pointed out.

'It's all right, Pa,' Gertrude said bravely. 'If it's the tradition, I'll stay with it.'

'Dat it is,' Jacob replied, doffing his ancient top hat, dusted off and bedecked with flowers for this grand occasion.

The six men donned their antlers, and Bert, their leader, the deer's head. The slow dance began, a weird but stately twining and intertwining of the six without the vigorous shouting and noise of the previous dances. Periodically they would unite, present themselves to their leader, and retreat again into dance formation.

'Old Herne do walk by night, To give our maidens a fair fright,' Jacob began, and Aggie, selected as a maiden fair, quavered to Bert, 'Oh sir, who are you with those horns … I must know before day dawns.'

Horace began to show signs of renewed impatience. 'I guess our native Indians do better than that,' he snarled. Gertrude laid her hand comfortingly – or warningly? Auguste wondered – on his arm.

'Where's Clown?' called Bessie.

'No Clown, my lady. Not today,' her husband's muffled voice announced. 'We're having a Hoodening.'

The Hooden horse leapt out onto the lawn, his head covered in a cloth in which nose-holes had been made, and large wooden jaws attached which opened and snapped shut to great effect, mainly to terrify several small children who had been dragooned into coming to signify 'village life'. On his feet were Harry's best postman's boots, and corduroy trousers. Behind this elegant horse came 'Mollie' wielding a broom. Bert, against the rules, removed the deer's head to watch.

'Ain't Christian, is it?' Jacob muttered, foxed by this departure from the script.

'That's a man,' Bluebell yelled, unnecessarily since the trousers and hobnail boots would have denoted Mollie's true sex.

'Now, Mrs Wickman.' Egbert Rose stood up. 'Suppose you tell us what you saw the night Lord Montfoy died.'

Bessie stood up, leaning slightly backwards so that the splendid bosom could be seen to best advantage, and staring insolently at Lady Montfoy.

'I arranged to meet Arthur at the maypole. He wanted to give me a present to make up for the fact he was getting married – he always admired me, though me being a married woman, he had to admire in vain,' she explained hastily. 'I wanted to make him look silly – wasn't fair him creeping off to see me on his wedding night.'

Gertrude half rose from her seat in outrage, but Richard abruptly pulled her down again.

'So I tied him up. I pretended it was part of the old ritual. And I'd told Miss Bluebell what I was planning to do, so anyone who wanted to see him looking so mazed could come down. Miss Bluebell came, but I saw no one else, and Arthur was beginning to shout rude things, so I told Miss Bluebell to go home and I went off myself. Then I saw someone else, just like Miss Bluebell did, a man, in the trees.

'Well me being a simple village woman and Miss Bluebell a young foreign lady, we were scared. We thought it was Old Herne the Hunter come to get us, so we ran. And that's all. I reckon,' she said anticlimactically, 'that man was the murderer.'

'And just what have we learned from Bessie's so simple story?' Gertrude asked coldly.

'Not much from Bessie's story, but a lot from the Horn Dance,' Rose said. 'Harry, Mary – here.'

The Hoodener and Mollie came forward, and Mollie removed her heavy wig plaited of hay to reveal Harry Thatcher.

'Then who's that?' asked Alf, bewildered, pointing to the Hoodener boots and trousers. He, like the rest of the village, thought Harry was the Hoodener.

The cloth was thrown off to reveal a grinning Mary Smith, elegantly clad in Harry's corduroy and boots.

'Egbert!' Auguste exclaimed. At once he realised.

'Yes,' said Rose with satisfaction, 'a little melodramatic, more your style really, to prove that appearances are deceptive. Miss Bluebell – Mrs Wickman, this figure in black – how did you know it was a man?'

'By the boots,' Bessie said smugly, glancing at Gertrude.

'I suppose I did too,' Bluebell agreed reluctantly. 'And the trousers, of course.'

'You mean Bessie did it after all?' Bert got muddled in his fear.

'No. The murderer came from Farthing Court, convinced she was to murder Pyotr Gregorin, having borrowed his trousers and footwear previously.'

Belinda, Gertrude and Louisa sat very still. Jeanne Planchet screamed.

Egbert looked at Auguste complacently at breakfast the next day. A breakfast, needless to say, prepared by the master chef and not Annie. 'Good news. I'll be in touch with Chesnais and my guess is you'll be able to go the royal wedding next week without a stain on your reputation. You can even cook for it, if you want to.'

'Inspector Chesnais has dropped the

charges against me?'

'Yes. I told him we had our man. Or rather woman. Another French citizen, Jeanne Planchet.' Egbert waited for comment – perhaps even thanks – but none was forthcoming to his surprise, which was unlike Auguste.

'She has an alibi,' Auguste began slowly.

'So she told me. She was, she now claims, not with Lady Montfoy but with Gerald Montfoy.'

'He confirms it.'

'Of course. He had asked her to provide him with an alibi in case he were suspected of killing Arthur. He likes to have a trick up his sleeve in case of dangerous situations. So when her conveniently provided alibi from Lady Montfoy failed, what better than to fall back on the second one conveniently supplied?'

'But–'

'So–' Egbert accorded his friend the kind of look with which Auguste might have honoured a three-day-old herring – *'Jeanne* carried out both murders. She ran down to the maypole to attend to Gregorin – as she thought – and she followed Gregorin in Paris until an opportunity occurred to make sure of it the second time.' He paused. 'What's wrong with that, Auguste?'

'I don't think she murdered them.' The words jerked miserably out of him. Oh, the bliss if he had been able to say: Egbert, that is undoubtedly right. But he couldn't. Instead he said, 'It's a question of hats.'

'Your hats, Your Grace.'

'Ah.' Louisa smiled beneficently at Auguste and Egbert. 'They came back, thank you. I shan't be making an official complaint.'

'Especially since the thief is now dead,' said Auguste.

'Dead?' The blue eyes opened in astonishment. 'Poor Mr Entwhistle. I only saw him half an hour ago. What a tragedy.'

'Mr Entwhistle's double. As I suspect you knew, Your Grace, from the interest you have taken in my affairs and those of His Majesty.'

'I have just informed dear Mr Pennyfather that I have decided not to marry him, eager though he is,' Louisa remarked apparently inconsequentially. 'The demands of a career cannot be easily combined with marriage and I daresay Mr Roosevelt would object if I practised mine in the United States.'

'Career?' The only career Auguste associated with Louisa was mistress to the king, but Louisa did not seem to be referring to that. Egbert Rose grinned, however, having had the benefit of a talk with Special Branch.

'I had a most interesting life with my late

386

husband – an army man. This gave him a taste for odd corners of the world, which was frequently of use to the War Office. When he died, they were kind enough to suggest I carried on his most interesting work, because I led – um – such an interesting life myself through my friendship with His Majesty. Otherwise I fear the War Office would not look kindly on ladies in their masculine world. I have greatly enjoyed my career – and have just had a special commendation from the War Office for my work in Paris. For which I have to thank, I understand, dear Mr Didier.'

Auguste reeled at this last revelation of how the fairies at Farthing Court had been mocking him. 'I'm not clear–'

'I'm an intelligence agent. For the British, of course. Not like Pyotr Gregorin.'

'It gives the duchess a motive for killing Gregorin.' There was a note of hope in Auguste's voice.

Egbert sighed. 'Forget her, Auguste. We both know who it is we're looking for.'

They found her sitting in the conservatory. An apt place for such an exotic bloom as Eleonore. The late afternoon sun streamed in through the windows. A Sèvres china teacup remained full in front of her, untasted. She sat docilely, like a child, hands folded in the lap of her peach muslin dress.

'Oh, don't deceive me; Oh, never leave me...' ran through his mind, as Auguste said to her gently, 'Gregorin rejected you, Eleonore, and you could not bear it. If you could not have him, no one should. So you killed him, and by mistake killed Arthur too.'

'Did I?' She raised her dark eyes at last to his. 'What do you think, Chief Inspector?'

'Oh, I know you did, too. I can't prove it – yet – but I shall.'

She shrugged. 'A political crime. My mother was Russian, one of the millions ground into dust by the Tsar's autocracy.'

'No, Eleonore. Simple hatred of the man who didn't want you any longer drove you on. You pretended not to mind, so that you could remain near him. You obediently remained his loyal servant in his political plans for His Majesty's downfall, and he never suspected you at all; even when it occurred to him Arthur might have been mistaken for him, he assumed it was me who had designs on his life.'

'And how did you reach this interesting conclusion, Auguste?'

'Jacob Meadows' rhymes.'

'Whose rhymes?'

'The villager who entertained us on the Saturday before the wedding.' Auguste quoted:

'"Oh Herne,' must Farthings' lord cry, 'pray spare/Your horn to hear my prayer..."'

'Most people there believed the lord of the manor to be Arthur, Lord Montfoy. Some like the Duchess of Wessex, the Penny-fathers, Mr Waites, Gerald and Belinda Montfoy knew the lord of the manor was now Entwhistle. But they would assume that Jacob was intending the rhymes to apply to the Montfoys. Certainly it would never occur to them that Jacob might be intending to summon Entwhistle to the maypole. Only you, as the mistress of Gregorin, who had doubtless been at his side while he planned the whole purchase of Farthing Court, would not only know he was lord of the manor of Frimhurst but be so used to thinking of him so that the alternative would not occur to you.'

'As ingenious as your *timbale de crabe*, Auguste. However, your twelve good men and true are likely to regard that as rather flimsy evidence. They would prefer me to have been found with the bow still quivering in my hands. Was that all that made you suspect me?'

'There was the matter of the hats.'

'*Hats?*'

'Louisa's on the day of the wedding. You, it seemed, were guiltless of the theft and yet you were the only one to benefit from the result. When I knew that this was not the case, and that Gregorin had benefited too, because it enabled your seduction of the king to begin, I began to think further. If I were a woman whose lover was prepared to sacrifice her honour, if I may use the word in this context, to further his own ends, how would I feel? Especially a lover who had recently rejected her. I know from my wife what a reputation for ruthlessness Gregorin had in his dealings with women.

'If you had not stolen the hats, then only Gregorin had a motive for doing so. Perhaps you asked him after the wedding whether he had taken them when he knew Louisa, not you, was to be the king's escort for the day, and his sheer determination to make use of your body incensed you beyond endurance. When Bluebell reminded you in my presence of the lord of the manor's impending visit to the maypole, the way to revenge was clear. Did Gregorin ever find out you had shot Arthur in mistake for him?'

For a moment it seemed to Auguste that Eleonore's face looked as feral as Gregorin's own, but then she laughed. 'Oh yes. He found out. In the catacombs. As soon as he saw me in the trousers I had worn to go down to the maypole, he realised. He had boasted to me of his plan to trap you there. What easier than to make a fourth at the party? You should be grateful to me,

Auguste. I saved your life. I had a candle, you see, and oh, the pleasure when he realised this gentleman who faced him was not you or Entwhistle but me. I should have made an excellent career on the music halls with a Vesta Tilley turn, should I not? I had taken my own knife, but I felt you would like to be included in my vengeance. Was that not thoughtful of me? You are quite right. I'd seen his ruthlessness used on others. Not on me. It was not to be endured.'

'You would have let me hang, even though once you invited me to your bed?'

That made her laugh. 'I knew you would not come. And incidentally you still will hang,' she pointed out. 'It is your word, Inspector Rose, against mine. You said yourselves you had no proof, and I shall deny, on the word of the wife of an international diplomat, that this conversation took place.'

'Bessie Wickman will walk free, and so will Auguste, even if you do as well, comtesse.'

'No, there you are wrong, Mr Rose. I shall not walk free. I shall walk shackled in heart and mind to Gregorin for the rest of my life.' She rose to her feet, bowed slightly, and the folds of the peach muslin swayed as she walked out of the conservatory.

'I guess I won't be marrying Louisa, honey.' Horace stood near his daughter by the terrace balustrade looking out over the domain that was shortly to be theirs. 'Shall you like living here? I won't be with you all that much. Not fair on Bluebell.'

'I think after a suitable time I'll have good company.'

'Richard Waites? I'll second that choice. What will he think about living here?'

'I think he'd like it, from my tentative enquiries.'

'Fairies and all?'

'He had one stipulation, at Mr Didier's suggestion. He said I should wash the glamour from my eyes about Frimhurst.'

'What's that supposed to mean?'

'That Frimhurst is not so deeply buried in tradition as it seems. That Frimhurst at our host's persuasion has been putting on a show for us.'

'But honey, that's what you said the first day you arrived. We've known it all this time.'

'Yes. Apart from poor Arthur, it was fun spurring them on, wasn't it?' She caught her father's eye, and to Bluebell's great surprise as she came out to join them, the widow burst out laughing.

'She's right. We've no proof. We have to let her go.' Egbert steamed in anger. 'I'll see Bessie released of course. I suppose I should feel sorry for the comtesse, but I don't.'

'Why not?' Auguste asked. He was still torn, thinking of the vital, laughing woman he had known.

'Well, it's a funny thing, Auguste, but I often ask myself a question if I'm in doubt about someone: would Edith like her?'

'And what was the answer this time?'

'No, Egbert. Not very much. Incidentally, what about His Majesty?'

What indeed? Auguste thought as Egbert went in search of Twitch before they left.

'Mr Didier.' Thomas Entwhistle stepped out before him, startling him as usual by his resemblance to Gregorin. 'I trust we shall meet again on Tuesday, at the garden party.'

Amid the six thousand guests invited to Windsor? Auguste had every hope that they would not, but he bowed politely.

'Thereafter,' Entwhistle continued, 'we may not meet for some time.'

Auguste could not find it in him to be polite this time, for he felt uneasy in Thomas's company. For all his serious face, he could not help thinking he found this all highly amusing.

'Tomorrow I sell Farthing Court – and its title as lord of the manor, to Mr Penny-father. A new age, Mr Didier, in which English manors are handed to our American cousins.'

'And what of you? To Paris?'

'No. I intend to travel. To the east. Perhaps even to marry.'

Visions of some exotic Eastern beauty flitted before Auguste's eyes. 'I trust you will be happy.'

'Oh, yes. I shall marry Belinda Montfoy, if she will have me.' He laughed as he saw Auguste's face. 'After all, I am the soul of English respectability.'

As Auguste walked on, he called after him. 'I have a message for you from Eleonore.'

Auguste stopped still. 'She has left?'

'She asked me to tell you the carriage is taking her to Cranbrook station.'

What could he do? Tell Egbert? What was the point? They had agreed there was no proof. And even if they had sufficient, think of the international furore if a very public – if short-lived – mistress of His Majesty were on trial for murder. Cousin Bertie would blame one person, Auguste Didier, for being *innocent*. It was an unjust world.

'You know?' he asked Thomas quietly.

'Of course. It is – was – my job to *know*, as you put it, if not to act. My dear Mr Didier, if I might advise you, do pray remain in the kitchen in future. That is where your forte lies.'

Auguste ignored this. 'So what will Eleonore do now?'

'She will catch the 8.19 train from Cranbrook to Paddock Wood.'

'And after?'

'After?' Thomas's face was sombre. 'Her lover is dead, her husband now estranged. Like Anna Karenina, what way out other than to catch the railway train? Who knows, Mr Didier, save *le Bon Dieu*, what lies after?'

Epilogue

The royal garden party at Windsor on the eve of the wedding of Princess Margaret of Connaught and the heir to the Crown Prince of Sweden, Gustavus Adolphus, was a glorious affair. With Tatiana on his arm, for once not in baggy bloomered overalls and smeared in oil, but in lemon voile and lace from parasol to the hem of the elegantly draped skirt, Frimhurst and the fairies seemed to Auguste far away. The royal sandwiches were excellent, and the dazzling array of European royalty and American diplomats to whom Tatiana introduced him flitted before his eyes like pictures in a magic lantern. The excellent claret cup made the world a wonderful place, even if it did have Cousin Bertie ruling over a major part of it.

Somewhere deep inside Auguste, however, was a niggle, He put it down to the fact that he had not yet seen Cousin Bertie, who was slowly making his way round his guests. This was quickly remedied, as the royal party approached, Tatiana sank towards the grass in a flurry of lemon voile, and he bowed deeply. As the queen engaged Tatiana in conversation Auguste found himself eye to eye with Cousin Bertie. For once royal etiquette worked in his favour. His Majesty must speak first. He did, and nobly – for Bertie.

'Glad to hear all's well.'

'Thank you, Your Majesty.'

'I hear–' Bertie said offhandedly – 'the Comtesse Eleonore died in a tragic accident.'

'Yes. Tragic indeed.'

His Majesty drew closer, a great honour. 'Looking back, it might have been just a little unwise of me to go to Paris that week-end.'

Auguste bowed, since he could think of nothing to say that would not be incorrect or damn him further. By the time he rose again, the usual jaundiced eye was back.

'But don't go committing any more murders, eh, Didier?'

'No, Your Majesty.' Was he expected to agree he was lucky to be reprieved? Apparently not, for this confidentiality had exhausted Bertie and he moved on. He and Tatiana were free to enjoy the delights of the garden party.

'My dear Mr Didier.'

Tatiana stopped aghast, and Auguste, seeing her shock, hastily intervened. 'Tatiana, may I introduce Mr Thomas Entwhistle?'

Very pale, Tatiana managed to regain her composure. 'Auguste has told me much about you, the likeness–' She faltered and stopped.

'Is but a likeness.' Thomas smiled. 'I leave tomorrow, Mr Didier.'

Auguste could not speak. His eye had fallen on the rose in Entwhistle's button-hole. The fairies had not done with him. They had reminded him that one of the two men to come to the café had bought a rose in the crowded Place Denfert-Rocherau. Which man?

He remembered the dead body at his feet in the chill and dark of the catacombs. He remembered the blood, as red as the rose in its buttonhole.

This Large Print Book for the partially sighted, who cannot read normal print, is published under the auspices of

THE ULVERSCROFT FOUNDATION